ESCAPING THE DASHIA

THE PARAXOUS STAR CLUSTER
BOOK ONE

REBECCA INCH-PARTRIDGE

Published by Water Dragon Publishing
San Jose, California
waterdragonpublishing.com

ISBN 978-1-969655-38-8 (Trade Paperback)

10 9 8 7 6 5 4 3 2 1

*In loving memory of my mom, Caroyl Inch,
who taught me a love of literature and enthusiastically listened
to my tales from the Paraxous Star Cluster for hours on end.
I miss you every day.*

ESCAPING THE DASHIA

Chapter 1

EIGHT YEARS AFTER COMING TO EARTH, I sat at the kitchen table in our apartment pretending to do my schoolwork while actually sneaking in some video game time. My only worry was how to beat my new *Zombies V Vampires* game without my mom catching me. If she caught me playing instead of researching my history essay, I'd lose video game privileges for a week.

Every time she glanced over, I clicked my laptop screen back to my essay. As she bustled about the kitchen making dinner, Mom hummed her favorite eighties tunes. Though a bit past middle-age, she was beautiful. She had huge, soft brown eyes, long raven-black hair, high cheekbones and a brick-red tan. Laugh-lines made up her only wrinkles.

Dad came in and took a whiff of the roast cooking in the crock-pot. "That smells delicious." He gave Mom a hug and turned to me. I'd switched to a site on the United Nations for research. "How's your schoolwork going?" he asked with enough humor in his voice to make me think I'd been caught.

The doorbell rang and Dad went to answer it, giving me a wink on his way out. I bowed my head. No more games for me today.

I heard the front door open. The voice of my real father, Colonel Ebon Milett, came from the living room. "I've come for my daughter."

Shock and disbelief gave way to fear. I hadn't heard that voice since being sent into hiding on Earth. Since then, Tina and Bill Splendor had adopted me and given me a home—something I'd never really had before. While I was glad to know my father was alive, the fact his return might mean losing the life I had here with the Splendors wasn't lost on me. And the thought of returning to the hell my life had been scared the crap out of me.

I twisted in my chair to look at my mom, Tina, hoping for some reassurance. She stood frozen, mixing bowl in hand. Her expression showed every bit as much fear as I felt. She and Bill had become my parents when Colonel Milett failed to come reclaim me. I'd arrived on this remote planet with some serious issues, and it had taken them years to win me over. Now my nice, comfortable life with a mom and dad who loved me, and that I could love in return, might be over.

"Where is she?" Colonel Milett's demand resounded from the living room.

Mom's tan face paled to sheet-white. She glanced at the kitchen door and then back at me in panic. "Twyla, stay here," she ordered in a hushed tone. She dropped the bowl on the counter with a clatter. Sauce splattered the "happy yellow" wall. Ignoring the mess, she rushed into the living room.

"I have no idea what you're talking about." Dad sounded pretty harsh for him. "Who are you?" Somehow, I could sense he knew exactly who this guy was, and it terrified him.

"I know Twyla is here," Ebon said.

Despite Mom's effort to hold me back, I entered the living room. Ebon stood at the front door of our apartment with Dad blocking his entrance. I moved toward them with faltering steps. "Father?"

He'd changed. His black hair was now almost completely gray. Dark bags hung under his eyes.

"You ... you came," I stammered. "You finally came."

"Of course, I did," he replied with a mix of anger and defensiveness.

"I thought you were dead." I was about to run to him, but he took a step back.

A horrified expression contorted his once handsome face as he looked me over. A wave of revulsion hit me. It wasn't my emotion I was feeling; it was his. My empathic powers had returned.

Suddenly, I knew that he'd come for his little girl. But at fifteen, I now resembled my real mother so much that he recoiled at the sight of me.

Memories of my life before coming to the Splendors flooded my mind, knocking me back to the day my parents split up.

My father had been a brave and decorated officer in the Zartous Regime's military, yet he'd crumbled under my mother's telepathic onslaught. As she ripped through his mind, I'd felt it. At seven, my own mental shields weren't strong enough to block the sensation of the stabbing penetration of her attack or my father's anguish.

Once she'd finished, I'd gone to comfort him. My mother, Cassie, wrenched me from his arms and hauled me out the door. I'd kicked and screamed, begging my father not to let her take me away. But he had done nothing.

My body trembled at the memory as Tina pulled me into her arms, breaking me free from the flashback. She rocked me side to side and whispered in my ear. My adopted mom's soft, sweet voice anchored me back in the present.

I'm not sure which hurt worse: feeling how much my own father hated me, or realizing I was my mother's daughter after all. With my empathic abilities back, was I destined to become a monster like her?

Dad stepped aside to let my father come in. "I'll deal with our guest," he said, giving Ebon a wary glare. Mom started to usher me toward my room.

"I am Colonel Ebon Milett and *that* is my daughter. Hand her over," he demanded, pointing at me. For a second, he became the man he used to be. His sharp steel-grey eyes narrowed. He might not have been wearing his uniform, but his posture and bearing shouted military command.

Revulsion still emanated from him. It wasn't just that I have the same dark auburn hair and pine-green eyes as Cassie, I could have been her clone.

"Why should they give me back to you?" I shouted. "You don't want me!" Mom tried to get me out of the living room, but I refused to go. I broke from her grip and charged at Ebon. "I can feel it, you son-of-a-bitch! I can feel everything now."

"Twyla!" my parents said at the same time and in the same tone. I wasn't allowed to cuss.

I could sense their panic. Their emotions felt completely different than Ebon's. Their love for me squelched my temper's fire. I gave in to Mom's embrace. "Make it stop," I sobbed. "I don't want to be a mutelouge."

She stiffened. Apparently, she knew "mutelouge" was a profane term used for hybrids in the Paraxous Star Cluster, where I was from. A strangled cry escaped her, but it was Dad who spoke. "You are not a mutelouge. You are a Kobbi. It's going to be okay, Twyla. We knew this day would come."

"We just didn't think it'd be so soon, or that your powers would come back so suddenly," Mom said. Then she glared accusingly at Ebon. "You should have warned us you were coming."

His expression changed from disgust to confusion. "What the hell? I don't understand. Are you telling me she'd lost her abilities?"

As Mom led me away, Dad explained in his deep, rich voice, "She was sent to us with all her empathic powers blocked. Seeing you must have somehow released them."

"You mean she could have been normal?" I heard Ebon say before Mom closed my bedroom door.

She sat me on the edge of my bed and knelt in front of me. She was talking, but I was too lost in her emotions to listen. I tried blocking the empathic whirlwind, but it was already inside me, and I had no clue how to get it out.

Mom called to me. I followed her pleading voice like a lifeline. She saw she had my attention again and gave me an encouraging smile. "That's my girl. You can control it. You just have to learn where your mind ends and where the empathic energy of others begins."

I understood the concept and tried to separate what was me from what was her. It didn't work. Her love and fear overpowered me, engulfed me, drowned me. I couldn't breathe.

"Just go away," I gasped. "I need to be alone."

Shouts came from the living room. She glanced at the door and back at me as they intensified. Reluctantly, she told me to stay in my room and left.

Little Miss, my cat, crawled out from under my bed and jumped up beside me. She rubbed against me, purring. We'd gotten her as a kitten, not long after my arrival. Now the tuxedo cat weighed over twenty-two pounds, making her name rather ironic.

My cell rang. I ignored it. A moment later it beeped, letting me know I had a text. Out of habit I glanced at it. My best friend, Vance, was asking my ETA. We were supposed to watch a movie tonight.

If there was anyone I could have talked to about my father's sudden appearance, it was Vance. Like many of the residents in our apartment complex, we were both refugees from the Paraxous Star Cluster living in hiding here on Earth. He was also the only one of my friends who knew the truth about me being half Kobbi.

At the moment, I was sure my empathic powers would go berserk if I talked to anyone, so I replied that something had come up and I couldn't make it. Then I curled up with my back against the wall forcing myself to just breathe. Little Miss crawled onto my lap as I stared out the window.

Pixar Studios, where my mom worked, was visible; so was the bay beyond. But my mind's eye pictured the view from my brother's bedroom back on the planet Oweena. I could see the four moons in the sky, the enormous buildings with people of different avian races flying between them, and the hover-cars zipping by above.

My mind slipped from memory to a flashback replaying the last conversation I'd had with my brother, Terrel.

He'd opened his eyes and grimaced. Over the last several weeks, I'd watched Terrel go from a strong fourteen-year-old boy to a living skeleton. He'd run away, and before our mother's people found him, he'd caught a wasting disease.

"Twyla," he said with a pitifully weak voice, "I need to talk to you."

He patted the bed. I climbed up and sat beside him with my feet dangling over the side. He was the one seriously ill, yet he looked at me with concern. "I'm going to tell you something very important. Something you might not understand right now, but you need to remember. Promise?"

I just nodded, so he could continue.

"You know how there are Humans, Katians—"

"Flagoans and Sians. Yeah, yeah. I know my races," I huffed impatiently. "I might be five, but I'm not stupid."

"I know you're not stupid." He smiled indulgently. "In fact, you're extremely smart. But there are things you haven't learned yet. Do you know what a Kobbi is?"

I huffed and rolled my eyes again. "Of course. Everyone knows that. They're mixed breeds."

"There's more to it than that, but it'll do for now." He reached his knobby-knuckled hand out to take mine. My big brother hesitated before asking, "Did you know you're one?"

I jerked back, but didn't let go of his hand. "Nuh-uh! No way. We're Human. We don't look like cat, or bird, or tree people. We're not mixed."

He licked his chapped lips and tried to swallow, but couldn't. I grabbed a cup of water from the bedside stand and gave it to him. He took a small sip, then handed it back.

"Thanks. Now let's see if I can get through this. There are two kinds of Kobbies. It's the Drey-Kobbi that look like mixed breeds. The Crean-Kobbi look like pure-breeds. You can't tell by looking at them that they're hybrids. There are Crean-Kobbi Flagoans and Crean-Kobbi Katians ..." He paused to take a deep breath. " ... and Crean-Kobbi Humans, like you."

"Me? What about you? If I got bad blood, you got it, too."

He rubbed his forehead, obviously in a lot of pain. "Okay. Sorry. Crean-Kobbi Humans, like us."

I gasped and pulled my hand away. "You're lying. I can tell. You know I can!"

He stared at the holo-screen on the wall rotating through pictures from the last time our father had been home on leave. "You can tell because you're an empath. That means you can pick up on people's feelings. It's a Kobbi ability. One you shouldn't have at your age."

"But you lied to me. You promised you'd never lie to me. Lying's bad. Mommy lies. Mommy's bad."

"Yes, Mommy's bad. Sorry I lied, but it's complicated. I can't say 'we're Kobbies' because I'm not. We have the same father but different mothers. Our dad is Human and my real mom was Human. But she died before Dad met Cassie—"

"You're not supposed to call her that. It's Cassiopeia, Mother or ma'am. She gets mad when you call her Cassie."

"That's why I do it." For the first time in days, he grinned. A twinkle sparked in his eyes then died. "You're right, Twyla. She is bad. She's very bad. She's a Dashia."

"No!" I jumped off the bed with a shout. I crossed my arms over my chest and stomped my feet. "She can't be! Daddy's not broken, so she's not Dashia!"

Even as I denied it, I knew it was true. It all made sense now. The way she would invade my mind to punish me. Only a Kobbi could do that. The way she controlled our father. Only the group of Kobbies called Dashias abused their telepathic powers like that.

I crawled back into bed and snuggled up with Terrel. "Sorry I yelled at you. Sometimes I get mad and can't help it."

He hugged me with what little strength he had left. "It's okay. I like your red-hot temper. It matches your red hair. You keep that temper. It will help you fight Mom when I'm gone."

I sat up, wailing, "Gone! Gone where? Terrel, where are you going?"

Tears leaked from the corner of his eyes.

"Die? You're going to die?" I sobbed. "No! No! No! You can't! I won't let you. I'll take care of you until Dad gets here. He'll be here soon."

We both knew it wasn't true. Our father was stationed on some planet in another quadrant. Even if he'd noticed our weekly messages had stopped and found out something was wrong, it would take him several days to get to us.

"I love you, Twyla." Terrel reached out his hand to me again. [[Henshe?]] he said in Ruslo.

I took his hand. [[Henshe,]] I agreed. It was one of the few words in Ruslo I could pronounce correctly. It stood for the love and bond between siblings and had no equal in Standard.

He kissed my forehead. "Don't ever let Cassie change you." He didn't add, "like your sister," but I'd heard him fight with Daylight enough that he didn't have to.

"I won't," I promised.

He smiled, then drifted off to sleep and never woke up. I was left alone to deal with Cassie and Daylight until my father returned home months later. Even then, it was two more years of hell before a Dashia Hunter rescued me from my Dashia mother and sent me to this remote halo-world.

Since I'd woken from cryo-sleep to find myself on Earth, my previous life in the Paraxous Cluster had grown vague and distant. Over the years, I'd almost been able to forget the pain of Cassie's abuse. Of course, years of therapy with some dweeb from the Cluster had probably helped.

But all the therapy in the universe couldn't change the fact that my mother belonged to an illegal, genetically engineered race. Worse yet, she was a mind-raping Dashia. That sect of Kobbies had nearly destroyed the Paraxous Cluster. The Dashia were the reason the entire Kobbi race had to be banned.

•　　•　　•

Mom and Dad came into my room to find me crying, a rare thing for me. Our empathic connection immediately reestablished itself. Their fear of losing me invaded my own thoughts and feelings. Through it, I sensed their desire to undo the damage that had been done and stop my pain.

"Twyla, it's going to be okay," Mom said.

"Stop saying that!" I snapped, "It's never going to be okay!"

"It's just going to take time—"

"Time!" I shrieked. "Time isn't going to change the fact that I'm a vreking mutelouge."

"Twyla," Dad said in that firm parental tone he reserved for when I really got out of hand. "We understand you're upset. You have every right to be. But that's no reason to yell at your mother—who loves you very much—or to use that word."

I felt him calculating the best way to cut through my hysteria. He continued with a speech he'd obviously prepared for the day my empathic abilities resurfaced. "You are a Crean-Kobbi. And don't you ever use the term mutelouge again. The Kobbi race proudly served the Paraxous Star Cluster for centuries. It's not something to be ashamed of. It's something to be proud of."

"You want me to be proud of being a monster?" I cried in disbelief.

They obviously didn't know the real story of the Kobbi race. We were a genetic experiment gone wrong. All this time, I'd hoped my empathic powers would never return. I'd hoped being only half Kobbi would save me from their curse.

"You are not a monster," they answered in unison.

"You're not from the Paraxous Cluster. You don't understand!" I knocked the knickknacks off my bedside stand. Little Miss gave an irritated hiss and jumped off my lap. After giving me a disapproving meow, she scampered under the bed.

Caught in the storm of my temper, I continued, "I should just go with my *real* father. That way you won't have to deal with me!"

Mom started crying, and I immediately regretted what I'd said. My anger deserted me. "I'm sorry," I said. "I guess I just can't understand why you'd want to keep a mutelouge around."

Dad bristled at the term, but his tone was more exasperated than angry. "Twyla, stop using that word. We may be Earthlings, but we do know something about the Cluster's history. The Kobbi were heroes—Guardians, leaders, who bridged the gap between the races. It was, and still is, the Dashia who abused their power."

"And my mother is one of them," I shot back. The memory of her mental invasions hit me so hard my gut twisted. I threw up without warning.

Dad grabbed a trash can and shoved it in front of my face, catching most of it. He helped me to the bathroom and brushed my hair back as I knelt at the toilet.

Mom appeared a moment later with a syringe in hand. "This will help your body recover from the shock." She rolled up the sleeve of my tee shirt, pinched my forearm and jabbed me with the needle.

After a minute, I stopped throwing up. After another minute, I sat back on my heels, feeling a bit more normal. "Will it stop my empathic powers?" I asked.

"No. The medicine slows their return and makes it easier for you to control," Dad said.

"Can you just keep giving it to me?" I begged, looking desperately at Mom. She was usually the softer touch.

Mom looked to Dad. Finally he said, "For a while. Just until you have a chance to adjust." He saw that I was about to argue and raised a hand to stop me. "We can talk about this later. Right now, I need to know what to tell ... what to tell Colonel Milett."

Anger reignited like a fire within me. "Wait. My father's still here?"

I got up and charged toward the living room, ready to tell my father what I thought of him. When my parents held me back, I yelled loud enough to make sure the man who'd deserted me to the mercies of a Dashia could hear. "You can tell him that I hate him, and I never want to see him again!"

"No! Twyla. Stop." Dad took me by the shoulders and knelt in front of me. "A Dashia Hunter was after your mother. Ebon convinced the Hunter to rescue you instead of killing one of the most notorious Dashias in the Paraxous. Your father had his mind wiped so Cassiopeia DeConnett wouldn't know what he'd done. It's because of his sacrifice that we have you."

Mom continued the story. "He was fully aware she'd know he was hiding something. But with the memory itself gone, she couldn't find out what he'd done no matter how deeply she dug. He was in a near vegetative state at a mental reconstruction center when the Dashia Hunter sent you to us. He wasn't expected to recover."

All my rage turned to guilt. Part of me had hated my father for deserting me. I hadn't understood just how much he'd sacrificed to save me from Cassie. My shoulders sagged; tears filled my eyes. I rushed to the living room to apologize only to find that my father was gone. I ran to the front door, opened it, and looked both ways down the hallway. I was about to call out for him, but Dad yanked me back inside.

He closed the door. "We can't draw any attention to ourselves. I know how to contact him. So if you wish to reconcile with your father, we can arrange it."

My earlier words about Ebon Milett being my real father bit at my conscience, but there was no bitterness in his voice. There was a universe of fear in his next statement, though. "The real question is: how did he find us? And since he did, how long before Cassiopeia DeConnett does?"

Mom took Dad's hand and gazed up at him; her laugh lines became creases of worry. "Does this mean what I think it means?"

He gazed back at her with a peaceful smile. His hazel eyes held a depth of wisdom few could match. I'd always thought my adopted dad looked a lot like Abraham Lincoln, only without the top hat and beard. "Yeah. We'll do just what we've always planned to do if this day ever came."

Mom blanched, and I felt a wave of grief for the life we'd have to leave behind. Then her expression and her emotions became almost as serene and determined as Dad's.

"Do you think we should cancel tomorrow?" I asked. They both winced. I added, "Sorry, but you guys aren't that good at being sneaky. It's been kind of obvious you're planning a surprise birthday party for me."

Tomorrow wasn't actually my birthday. It was the anniversary of the day Bill and Tina took custody of me when I was seven. They'd chosen that month and day for my fake birth certificate and put the year as 1993. So as far as everyone else knew, I turned sixteen tomorrow.

Dad considered for a minute, then answered, "No. We can't let on that anything's wrong. It'll take us a couple days to make arrangements. Until then, it's business as usual." With a reassuring smile he added, "Besides, the nearest Paraxous planet is over a week away. Even if Cassiopeia gets word that your father found you, it'll take her a while to get anyone here. We'll be long gone by then."

"You mean we're leaving Earth?" I asked in dismay.

He forced his expression to brighten. "I've always dreamed of seeing the Paraxous Cluster. I guess now's our chance."

Chapter 2

SOMEONE KNOCKED at the front door, and we all stiffened. Dad checked the peephole then relaxed. He opened the door to reveal Vance standing in the hallway, shuffling his feet awkwardly with his head ducked and shoulders hunched. "Uh, is Twigh home?" He spotted me and asked, "Can I talk to her?"

I rolled my eyes. Vance was nothing if not persistent.

Dad stepped aside with a nod. He put an arm around Mom, and they went into the kitchen. As he passed me, he gave me a slight shake of his head, indicating that I wasn't to tell Vance anything.

I opened my mouth to argue. After all, his family had been helping refugees from the Paraxous Cluster settle on Earth for nearly a decade. Dad mouthed, "Later." I assumed he wanted to talk things over with Vance's father first.

As soon as the kitchen door closed behind them, Vance asked, "Everything okay? I thought I heard shouting."

His family lived in the apartment directly above ours, and I wondered just how much he'd heard. "I'm fine. Just have too much homework to do a movie tonight."

My friend cocked his head, eyeing me in a way that said he could tell I wasn't fine. "Homework? Really? That's what all the shouting was about?" He knew the Splendors well enough to know they never yelled.

"Shouting? Nah, must have been the TV."

Outwardly, Vance looked like a stereotypical teenage boy: lanky and awkward. His black hair, though washed and combed, always looked a bit oily and unkempt. He had tannish skin that could have marked him as any number of ethnic groups. When asked, he'd tell people he was a genuine American Heinz 57 mix.

In truth, Vance was an alien using the combination of a cloned body and an android's cyber-brain as an avatar. Like all the non-humans who lived in our building, his real body was kept in a medically induced coma and hidden in a vault somewhere. Vance and his family happened to be Sians, one of the avian races from the Paraxous. I sometimes tried to picture my friend with golden wings and glacial-blue skin.

One time, Vance had tried to take me to his family's vault, so I could meet the real him. We got caught. Dang, did we get in trouble. We even had to go before the building's council and promise never to do anything that might jeopardize our sanctuary again.

Avatar or not, I was especially fond of his big, brown puppy-dog eyes which were soft with concern as he asked, "Twigh, what's going on?"

"Nothing." I crossed my arms and looked away, glancing at the large oil painting over the fireplace. Mom had bought *San*

Francisco at Sunset from a local artist and framed it with ivy that grew from containers on each side of the mantel. It was one of Mom's many touches that made our apartment a real home. One of many things I'd miss.

"Everything's just fine," I said with more of a growl than intended.

"Yeah, right. Whatever. Can I help?"

I was glad no creepy empathic stuff happened. I wouldn't have been able to contain myself if I'd sensed his concern. Dad didn't want me to tell him anything yet, so I said, "Nah. Not right now. It's a long story. I'll tell you later. Okay?"

He shrugged and donned his ridiculously huge grin complete with dimples. "Okay. If you say so."

I'd miss his grin even more than our home. I'd miss all my friends, but Vance was practically family. We hung out together nearly all the time. He even lived with us a couple of months every year when his parents were "away on business."

It wasn't just that, though. He had the easygoing, friendly nature that I lacked. If it weren't for him, I might not have had any friends. He'd introduced me to Cameron and Nina. And he was the one who'd put together our band.

He shoved his hands into his pockets. "Well, make sure your 'homework' doesn't keep you from practice tomorrow."

Dad came through the door before I could bail on our plans. "Oh, hey," he said. "You guys are going to the movies after band practice, right? How about I give you a ride? You can get lunch at that place you guys like. My treat."

Vance's expression brightened. Mine darkened. I gave Dad a subtle shake of my head. "I think I'd better stay home and work on my school stuff."

"I'm sure you'll get it done," Dad said with a smile. To Vance he said, "You'd better let her get to it. See you in the morning."

Vance took the hint and left. The moment the door closed, I protested, "I get you not wanting to cancel the party, but I don't think I can handle being around people *all* day tomorrow. What if I go all … empathic?"

Dad came over and took me by the shoulders. "You'll be fine. The medication should last for a day or two. Besides, when this is over, you'll be glad you got to spend time with your friends before we had to leave."

Though that medication kept me from being drowned in waves of mental contact, it didn't prevent me from sensing that he wanted to keep up appearances. If Cassie had people watching us, he didn't want to give them any reason to suspect we were about to run. However, he no longer felt safe letting us take rapid transit to The Plaza like we usually did. Actually, he didn't want to let me out of his sight, but he'd arranged an important meeting right down the street from the theater.

I withdrew, disgusted with myself for accidentally trespassing on his thoughts.

•　　　•　　　•

The next morning, I wanted to cancel band practice and just hide in my room. My newly wakened empathic powers scared me. The idea Cassie might be coming for me scared me even more. It took all my parents' gentle powers of persuasion to get me out the door. They argued that the med was controlling my powers, and our garage was just as secure as the apartment. Mom and Dad had given up the garage that came with our apartment so my friends and I could use it for practice. Both mine and Vance's parents had spent a weekend soundproofing our "studio" in order to prevent complaints from the neighbors.

Somehow, I made it through practice without a meltdown, but I just couldn't get into it. I kept thinking this might be the last time I ever sang with Vance, Cameron and Nina. Heck, once we left Earth, I'd probably never see any of them again.

I glanced at Cameron as we wrapped up. Dang, he looked fine. He always did. He was just wearing jeans and a white tee shirt, but he sure made them look good. With his bright blue eyes, blond hair and beautiful complexion, he could have been a teen star.

Okay, stop that, I told myself. *I'm going away, and he belongs to Nina.*

Nina pulled her guitar strap off over her shoulder and set the instrument down. While she may have appeared Human, we all knew she was actually a Katian. Or rather half Katian, since her father was Human. She and her family had fled the Cluster because of how half-breeds were treated since they were often mistaken for Drey-Kobbi.

Nina sauntered over to Cameron and draped herself on him. Having a crush on my best-friend's boyfriend sucked. Not that I would ever betray our friendship by making a play for him. Besides, I could hardly compete with someone whose avatar looked like a damn Barbie-doll come to life.

"Helllooo … Twyla." Apparently, I'd missed something she'd said. As with most Katians, patience wasn't her strong suit. "What is with you today? Sam would have kicked your butt back to the Paraxous if he'd heard how off key you were."

I'd been disappointed that Sam, the fourth member of our band, hadn't made it to practice. But I was sure he'd be at my party tonight. The garage door opened, saving me from having to explain why I'd sucked.

Dad waved to us from the Tesla. We piled into the car excited to see the latest *Star Trek* movie. Instead of just dropping us off at the Emeryville Plaza like he usually did, Dad parked and walked us to the theater. He insisted on paying for everyone's ticket.

Maybe he felt guilty at not letting me say good-bye to my friends, or maybe it was just an excuse to make sure we got safely inside.

Vance, Nina, and Cameron spent the movie cheering and tossing popcorn at each other. We loved *Star Trek* in all its incarnations, and were super excited about this reboot. But all I could think about was how to safely stay in contact with them. Even people in witness protection had methods of sending and receiving letters. And if there wasn't an approved method, Vance was a master hacker and I wasn't half-bad myself. Somehow, we'd figure out something.

Still, life would get pretty lonely with only Little Miss to keep me company. Then a realization struck my heart. What if I wouldn't be allowed to take my cat with me? *No,* I told myself, *Mom and Dad will find a way.* They'd know with all my friends gone Little Miss would be my only companion.

When the movie ended, Vance leaned over and asked, "You okay?"

For the lack of a better lie, I said, "I just remembered today's my birthday."

Vance and Nina fell all over themselves wishing me a happy birthday. If I hadn't already known about the surprise party, their reactions would have given it away. But I couldn't keep from messing with them. "Hey, did you guys get me anything?"

"Yeah," Cameron said, not missing a beat. "The privilege of our wonderful company this afternoon." He looked me right in the eyes and asked, "You and your parents doing anything special tonight?"

Nina looked at Cameron in alarm. Vance went into a coughing fit and "accidentally" elbowed Cam in the ribs. "Anyone else hungry? Let's go eat."

As we headed up the aisle, a whirlwind of excitement washed over me. The emotions were coming from Vance. He couldn't wait to see my expression when he gave me the complete DVD collection of *Babylon 5.*

The contact faded, but left me shaken. Not only had I sensed his feelings, I'd relived his memory of us as little kids watching the show with our parents.

My head ached like a brain freeze from sucking down a Slurpee too fast. I staggered a few steps, rubbing my temples furiously. Vance was instantly at my side asking if I was all right. But I knew if I tried to answer him, I'd throw up. I made a dash for the bathroom.

Nina followed me and waited outside the stall. When I'd finished puking up all the popcorn and soda, she said, "Vance has your dad on the phone. He's on his way."

"Tell him I'm fine."

Nothing could have been farther from the truth. The emotions of everyone around crowded my senses. Nina worried that my party would have to be canceled, Vance was trying to figure out what was going on with me, and Cameron—well, he was being Cameron. At that moment, he was distracted by twins walking by. They wore matching shorts and tank tops despite the chilly spring weather. The girls were pretty and flirtatious.

I bit the side of my cheek to bring myself out of Cameron's fantasy. Vance was still on the phone with Bill when I walked out of the bathroom. My dad was saying something about an ear infection causing vertigo. I heard him as clearly as if he were talking to me instead of Vance. Apparently reading minds wasn't the only Kobbi ability that had been released. I now had super hearing.

Vance handed me his phone. I knew the errands Dad was running were critical to our escape. At the same time, though, I figured he needed to know what was going on. So I told him, "I think the medicine's worn off, but I'm okay if you need to finish your meeting."

"Actually, I'm almost there."

We signed off with our usual, "Luv ya, bye" and I gave Vance his phone back. We left the theater and walked over to the drop off and pick up area.

As soon as Cameron and Nina were in their own little cute couple's world and oblivious to everything else, Vance asked, "So are you going to tell me what's going on?"

Part of me wanted to tell him everything. For a second, I considered seeing if he wanted to run away with us. But how selfish was that? He had his own family to consider.

I decided that somehow I was going to convince my parents to let me tell Vance we were leaving for good and not just going on vacation. I couldn't see what harm it could do to say goodbye.

"Later," I said in the conspiratorial tone he liked so much. "Let's wait until no one else is around. Okay?"

Suddenly, my new spidey senses went all tingly. Someone was watching us. No, not us. Whoever it was, was watching me specifically.

I stretched, trying to look around without being obvious. This big guy in a hoodie, standing alone a few yards from us, turned away. Something about him seemed familiar, but I couldn't get a good look at him through the crowd without being too obvious. I wasn't sure, but I thought I remembered seeing him at the theater.

I didn't know what to do. If this was one of Cassie's spies or henchmen, we were in serious trouble. I reached for my phone, but realized it might be monitored. Part of what Dad was doing today was getting us burner phones.

Maybe I was overreacting. Without meaning to, my mind instinctively reached out to see if this guy was a threat. He knew who I was and not just my alias. He knew my true identity. He knew my mother was a Dashia and that I was half Kobbi.

I pulled away from his mind and focused my thoughts to reach out for Bill. *Dad, Dad. Hurry. Danger!*

Somehow Vance picked up on the message as well. He swung around panicked. He kept jerking his head side-to-side, looking for the danger.

Cam noticed Vance's confused and frightened expression. "What's your problem?"

It took Vance a second to answer. "I think I forgot my cell phone at the theater." He patted down his pockets and pulled out his phone with exaggerated relief.

"Dufus!" Cam said, giving him a smirk and shake of his head.

Poor Vance probably had no idea what had scared him so. He threw me a quizzical glance. I met his gaze then looked away, feeling my cheeks redden. He released a long, whistling sigh, and our eyes met again. He knew it had been an empathic thing but was smart enough not to say anything in front of Cam and Nina.

Dad pulled up just then. The tires screeched to a stop, he jumped out of the car, and ran over to me. He puffed like an asthmatic. "Are you okay?"

"Damn, I wish my Dad got that worried when I got sick," Cam teased.

I said I was fine, but nodded toward the guy watching us.

Dad was so relieved he nearly had a meltdown. He gave me a big old bear hug, still breathing hard. In my ear he whispered, "Don't you recognize Gerry? I asked him to keep an eye on you."

Now that he mentioned it, of course I did. Gerry was one of the building's security guys. I'd just never paid much attention to him, and I'd never seen him out of his rent-a-cop uniform. "Sorry," I whispered back. "I was just too freaked out to think straight."

"It's all right. But try not to send any more empathic messages until we're safely relocated."

With our secret conversation done, he said loud enough for everyone to hear, "Let's get you guys home."

We piled into the car. Vance was stuck in the back with Cam and Nina as they cuddled and giggled. He caught my disgusted expression as I looked at them in the rear view mirror. He couldn't understand my crush on Cam and was often annoyed by it. But to give him credit, he'd never betrayed my confidence, and he never used my feelings against me.

I wondered what he'd say if he found out the whole truth of what was going on. Here the most dangerous criminal family in the Paraxous Cluster was probably coming after us, and I was caught up in the drama of a teen crush. I started to laugh at my own foolishness, then stopped.

The DeConnetts weren't after us, they were coming after me. Most likely, they couldn't care less about the Splendors. Unless they got in the way, that is. If I ran away, my mom and dad would be safe.

In order to save the parents who'd loved and cared for me, I'd have to desert them.

Chapter 3

T HAT EVENING, WHEN I FOLLOWED my parents into
our apartment complex's rec-room, all thought of running
away vanished. At least a hundred people yelled "Surprise!" —
somewhat in unison. After my new super-ears quit ringing, my
jaw dropped. It seemed like everyone we knew was there.

There were relatives from both Mom's and Dad's side of the
family, including my favorite aunt all the way from Iowa. Nearly
all of the kids from our home-school group were there with their
families. Even Vance's brother who'd supposedly been away to
college, but was actually attending vocational training in the
Paraxous, was there. So were lots of coworkers from both Mom's
and Dad's jobs.

This must have taken months to plan. They'd obviously
decided to throw me a big sweet-sixteen party long before our
cover had been blown. Now this had become their goodbye

party as well. They were giving up their home, their families, careers, and friends to protect me.

Tears blurred my vision. I put my hand over my mouth and swallowed back a sob. Everyone stared at me, waiting for me to say something, but I was too choked up. I wanted to turn and flee, but Mom and Dad stood on each side of me with an arm around my shoulder.

Finally I stammered lamely, "I don't know what to say. Everything's so nice. Oh my god. I can't believe you all went to so much trouble."

A gigantic "HAPPY BIRTHDAY, TWYLA" banner was spread across the back wall. Helium balloons, all midnight blue or hunter green, which happened to be my favorite colors, covered the ceiling. White Christmas lights twinkled everywhere like the fireflies I'd been fascinated with when we visited Mom's relatives in Iowa.

My favorite Adele song began to play. Through the crowd, I could make out the big-screen TV rotating through pictures that told the story of my life with the Splendors. The day we moved into this apartment complex in the Bay Area; the group photo from each year's home-school club; hiking and other trips. There were pictures of me with my friends, including one from when our band had played at the open-mic night at the local under twenty-one club. It was the first and only time we ever performed in public.

Now I understood why my parents had forbidden me from pursuing a singing career: I'd almost split my voice into a cantor that night, something only Katians and Kobbies could do. Since few Earthlings even knew Katians existed and had no idea what cantoring was, hypnotizing an entire audience by singing with dual voices would have definitely attracted a lot of unwanted attention.

Sam hustled from the kitchen carrying a tray of hors d'oeuvres. "Come on, Twyla, try some of the food. We have all your favorites."

The caterers Mom had hired were friends of hers from Pixar. They followed Sam in a procession around the room showing off the sumptuous menu: sautéed mushrooms, crab cakes, ribs smothered in barbecue sauce, and corn on the cob drenched in butter. And chocolate. Lots and lots of chocolate. Some of the crew went around offering hors d'oeuvres and drinks while others set their trays down at the buffet.

Sam presented his tray to me. Now I knew why he'd missed band practice and the movie. Since I had no siblings—at least none that they knew about—he was filling in as junior host. Like Nina and Vance, he looked completely Human, but was in fact an alien using an avatar body. He happened to be a Flagoan, also known as Elm-men because they look like tree people. Also like Nina and Vance, I had never seen his real body. It seemed so unfair that I didn't even know what my friends really looked like.

Sam had shared enough about Flagoan culture with us for me to guess he was treating this as a Commemoration Ceremony. The ceremony was a long-standing and highly valued custom of his people that celebrated the anniversary of life-altering relationships.

I managed to get my emotions under control and even enjoyed the party until it came time to open the gifts. It just felt so awkward having everyone watch me unwrap presents. It was especially awkward when I got to Vance's gift. Since I'd accidentally read his mind and already knew what it was, I'd have to fake being surprised. Trouble was, I was a horrible actress.

I opened the shoebox to find a palm-sized black box with a switch. When I flipped the switch, a stunning holographic image leaped to life. Large birds flew silhouetted against a twilight sky. A waterfall shimmered in the lavender and gold rays. A rainbow framed the top of the image every bit as magical and ethereal as the real thing.

I gaped in shock. A collective gasp rippled through the crowd. Those who were in the know believed the thing had to be contraband Paraxous tech. Those who didn't know the truth about us were just amazed and dazzled by the hologram.

Vance ducked his head into his hunched shoulders. "Do you like it?" he asked nervously.

"Like it? Vance, it's freaking fantastic!" I couldn't say anything more in front of everyone, but I knew he was in big trouble.

He straightened and puffed his chest. "I built the holographic projector myself," he bragged, then added to the amazement of some and the relief of others, "using directions I found on the internet." Then he cocked his head and gave me an almost challenging look. "Were you expecting something else? Maybe a *Babylon 5* DVD collection?"

He knew. He knew our minds had touched, and he didn't hate me for it. He also knew we were leaving. This was his goodbye present. I wished everyone would just go away and leave us this moment. I couldn't say half of what I wanted to with them around. "What could possibly be better than this? Vance, you're the best friend anyone could ever have. I'll treasure it forever."

"Hey, helllooooo ..." Nina protested, "Don't forget your BFF over here. Open my present next."

That was it. I just couldn't take any more. I looked to my parents for help, but Mom had her hand over her mouth and was crying for me. Not only did she understand how difficult this was for me, it broke her heart that there was nothing she could do about it. She put an arm around me as I brusquely wiped the corners of my eyes before opening Nina's gift.

It was a trendy pair of jeans and a cute top. "Clothes. What a surprise," I said with playful sarcasm. Nina thought my lack of the "shopping gene" was shameful. So every birthday and Christmas, she made sure I got at least one cool outfit.

Mom handed me their gift last. "We wanted you to know how much we both love you. And how glad we are to have you." My mom's voice was so raw. Had she guessed I was considering running away?

Would it be a betrayal if I left them for their own good? Or would it be selfish of me to stay with them, knowing their lives would be in danger?

The little box sat in my shaking hand. "Open it," Dad prompted. Under the wrapping was a jewelry gift box. I opened it, and a lung full of air caught in my throat. Inside sat a pendant in the shape of three linked hearts outlined in diamonds. It glittered like nothing I'd ever seen before.

Dad pulled the necklace from the box and read the inscription aloud. "To our daughter, with all our love. Always remember, you are our sunshine." His emphasis on the word daughter said it all. I was theirs, and they would never let me go. It didn't matter they weren't my birthparents. They were my real mom and dad.

Then, to my horror, the entire crowd started singing, "You Are My Sunshine." It was the song my parents had sung to me every night during my first year with them to banish my nightmares and help me sleep. It meant so much more to me than the traditional "Happy Birthday" song would have.

When they finished, my dad knelt in front of me and reached around to fasten the necklace in place. I held up the pendant to read the words to myself. I looked back and forth between them. "Thanks ..." I started but choked, "Mom, Dad, I love you."

Amid all the "ooohs" and "ahhs," I launched myself from my chair and hugged my dad with all my fifteen-year-old might. Mom came over and joined our embrace. For a moment, I felt like a baby bird safely tucked into a nest so high up that no predator could ever reach us.

•   •   •

After the party, I crawled into bed too exhausted to worry about anything. We'd be leaving tomorrow supposedly due to a family emergency Mom had arranged with her sister. As far as anyone knew, we'd leave directly from there for our vacation in Australia. Vance's dad had even made it so fake Facebook posts would automatically be added on Mom's account, leaving a false trail. In reality, we'd be going to our prearranged extraction site and waiting for word from the Dashia Hunter.

The sound of multiple cell phones and the home phone ringing woke me in the middle of the night. My parents were speaking in low, hushed whispers as they shuffled and thumped about in haste.

Suddenly, Mom burst in to my room. "It's going to be okay. But we need to hide you right now." She took me by the shoulders and hustled me into their bedroom.

Dad had already unlocked the door to our hidden safe room. He opened it and motioned me inside. "Twyla, it's very important that you listen to me carefully. I'm going to give you a sedative and more of the empathic blocker. That way your mother won't be able to detect you. Hopefully, after they leave, we'll be able to make our escape as planned. If not—"

"No. No. Let's just leave now."

He looked so sad in that moment. "It's too late. They're already here."

He jabbed my arm with one shot right after another. Instantly, all my muscles went limp. At first, I couldn't even breathe. But soon my breathing returned in a slow rhythm I had no conscious control over.

My dad held me and looked into my panicked eyes. "I know you're scared, Sunshine. But you're going to be okay. If they take us away, use the hatch to get to Vance's." He pressed a thumb drive into my hand and folded my fingers around it. "This has the location of our backup extraction point and contact information for the Dashia Hunter."

Someone banged on the door. "Police! Open up!"

Mom and Dad each gave my paralyzed body a hug before leaving me lying on the floor of the safe room and closing the door. My eyes were locked open. In one corner I could make out the monitor that displayed the front door and living room.

Soldiers in body armor rammed the door open before my parents could reach it. They stormed in and surrounded my embracing parents. Two men wearing police uniforms told Mom and Dad to put their hands up. The other four wore New Federation uniforms. That seemed rather reckless since the general public on Earth wasn't supposed to know about the Paraxous Cluster and the factions fighting to control it.

Cassiopeia DeConnett entered behind them. I'd forgotten just how evil she could look. That evilness warped her flawlessly-beautiful, genetically-engineered features to the point she resembled an over-the-top, demented movie villain. Despite having the same auburn hair and green eyes, I didn't think we looked anything alike.

"Where is she?" Cassie demanded.

"Where's who? Who are you? What do you want?" Dad asked.

Cassie sighed. She gave one of the soldiers a nod. He opened fire. An energy pulse ripped a hole through my mom's torso. Dad cried out in disbelief. He clung to her even as life left her body.

Holy Makers, this can't be happening. Not because of me, I pleaded with deities I'd quit believing in when my brother had died.

A New Fed soldier ripped Mom from Dad's arms and dropped her to the floor with a sickening thud. Her brown eyes stared up as if pleading for life.

Dad knelt over her. He pressed his hands against the wound trying to stem the flow of blood that gushed from her abdomen. But blood bubbled out between his fingers and pooled on the floor around her.

Cassie signaled for a couple of the soldiers to search the apartment. Then she focused her attention on my dad. "Let's try this again. Where is she?"

"Where's who? I don't know what you're talking about!" he choked. His tears fell to the floor mixing with Mom's blood. He looked up from her limp form to meet Cassie's stare. His face was beet red from a combination of grief and rage.

I'm here! my mind screamed. It wasn't that I wanted to return to Cassie's abuse, but maybe, just maybe, she'd let Dad live.

"You do know who I am, don't you?" Cassie asked.

"I have no idea who the hell you are, or why you just killed my wife." His lie wouldn't have convinced her even if she wasn't empathic.

Cassie smiled hungrily. "Allow me to introduce myself."

I knew she was about to bore her way into his mind to get what she wanted. Without any empathic powers of his own, my Dad's mind would be turned to mush. Once again, I tried to send her a mental message, but either she couldn't receive it or I still couldn't transmit empathically.

"I am Twyla's mother, and I know she is here somewhere."

Dad looked down at Mom's body, the body of his high school sweetheart and the love of his life. Then covered in her blood, he stood to face Cassie. "I don't know what you're talking about." Though he managed to sound brave and strong, he couldn't stop the tears that streamed down his face.

Cassie stepped forward. Her eyes narrowed with the concentration it took to breach someone's mind. Dad reacted to the invasion by lunging at her. My pacifist, peace-loving daddy grabbed her by the throat.

One of the New Fed soldiers fired. Dad collapsed to the floor. He didn't die immediately like Mom had. Instead, he dragged himself an inch at a time back to his wife. Cassie hovered over him, fixated on his dying thoughts. He reached out and took Mom's hand before going limp.

Cassie's peach complexion turned blazing red. She rounded on the soldier who'd fired. "You idiot! He died too fast for me to read. If we don't find my daughter, you're paying the price. Is that clear?"

The soldier bowed submissively. "Forgive me, Madam DeConnett. It appeared he was going to harm you."

"Shut up before you make even more of an idiot of yourself. They were pacifists. He wanted to die to keep me from finding out where they hid Twyla."

My stomach heaved. Bile came to my throat. I couldn't force myself to swallow it back. I couldn't make my head turn to the side to spit it out. I was going to choke to death, and I didn't care.

The sedative finally had its intended effect. Instead of just being paralyzed, I became drowsy. I couldn't tell if I was suffocating or falling asleep. I was just grateful for the blackness when it finally took me.

Chapter 4

M Y MIND RETURNED from the darkness to hear the voice of Vance's father saying, "I told you to stay home."

"Please tell me she's not dead!" Vance begged.

"Hold her on her side, while I clear her airway."

I felt my body being jostled. A finger poked around in my mouth. I just wanted to go back into the nothingness and the peace it offered.

"Twyla, Bill and Tina would want you to live," Mr. Volkner said firmly into my ear. "Don't let their sacrifice be for nothing."

"Twigh. Twigh!" Vance cried. "Please, don't die."

My eyes flew open. I gagged up the last chunks of vomit. Vance pushed past his father and gathered me in his arms. He cradled me against his chest, weeping. "You're okay. You're going to be okay, Twigh."

"Mom? Dad?" I asked, hanging onto hope beyond reason.

"I'm so sorry." Mr. Volkner cleared his throat and worked on controlling his own emotions. "They're dead."

I twisted to look at the monitor. Bill and Tina's bodies were gone. "Where are they? Where's my mom and dad?"

Mr. Volkner looked me in the eyes, a hint of guilt in his expression. "They took their bodies away. The police just finished processing the scene." He glanced away. "I couldn't risk coming until they'd left."

"Mom! Dad! Oh god, she killed them," I forced myself to explain. "My real mother showed up with a bunch of f'ederationers, and they killed them." I purposely used the insulting slur for the New Federation, a group of terrorists bent on overthrowing the Zartous Regime.

Vance and his father exchanged doubtful expressions. They had always been a bit too sympathetic toward the f'ederationers in my opinion. I pointed at the monitor and rasped in fury. "I saw them!"

Mr. Volkner held up a hand. "All right. We can talk about what happened later. Right now we need to get you out of here." He motioned toward where part of the back wall had retracted, revealing the alcove with a ladder and hatches above and below. "Do you think you can make it?"

I nodded, though I could barely stand even with their help. As we started toward the ladder, I glanced around for anything to take with me. Besides the sparse furnishings, the only things in the room were a couple of food cabinets and our three emergency backpacks. "Little Miss." I swung back around to the door that led into the apartment. "I need to find Little Miss."

"They turned her over to animal control," Mr. Volkner said, swinging me back around toward the ladder. "We'll figure out how to get her back later. Right now, let's get you to our place."

We couldn't leave Little Miss caged and scared in the pound. I couldn't save my parents, but I had to at least save my kitty. Before I could say anything, Vance spoke up. "Don't worry. We'll have someone get her as soon as they open." Then to his dad he said, "Aren't you going to be late for work?"

Mr. Volkner entered the alcove, unlocked and opened the hatch above. "I'll call and let them know I won't be in."

"Won't that be a little obvious? We're not supposed to know that anything's happened yet."

"I guess we could hide Twyla in our safe room until we officially get word and I come home. Then I'll—"

"Mr. Volkner," I cut in, "thank you. But there's no way I'm going to your place. It's too dangerous. I can't risk getting your family killed, too. I'll just go out the passage and get to the safe house we were assigned to."

He cocked his head and put a hand on my shoulder. "You're a very brave young lady. But I'm not about to let you go all alone. I promised your parents that if anything ever happened, I'd look after you until your aunt or uncle could come get you."

"Besides," Vance chimed in, "you can hardly even walk on your own."

It suddenly occurred to me that my hands were empty. I whirled around looking for the thumb drive my dad had given me with the Dashia Hunter's info. When I didn't see it lying on the ground, I patted my pajamas, but they didn't have any pockets.

"If you're looking for the USB, my dad has it," Vance said.

"It has information I need." I put out my hand in an unspoken request for him to give it back.

Mr. Volkner leaned down so he'd be eye level with me. "I'm pretty sure I know what's on it, Twyla. And I'm going to need it in order to figure out what to do next. Okay?"

Reluctantly, I nodded. "Okay. But you can't risk taking me to your apartment."

"I can take her to our safe house," Vance volunteered.

"No," Mr. Volkner and I both said.

"Why not? I know the way and they might be watching you," Vance pointed out. "As far as anyone will be able to tell, I never left our apartment. I'll take her and sneak back using the passages. They'll never know I was gone."

Mr. Volkner checked his watch. "You can take her to Gerry. He'll take her to one of the safe houses. Now I'd better get going. You're right. It might look suspicious if I'm late for work, but I'll be back soon."

"Um, I should probably get dressed before going anywhere," I said, a bit embarrassed at worrying about something so mundane under the circumstances. "I have clothes in my pack."

Vance went back up to their apartment with his dad to borrow a pair of shoes from his mom for me. I threw on jeans and a tee-shirt from my backpack. Once I was dressed, Vance came back down to find me eyeing Mom's and Dad's packs.

"Let's just take them with us, so you can go through them later."

I nodded. Besides wanting something of my parents to hang onto, taking them was the practical thing to do. They might have stuff I could use. And if the room was ever discovered, it wouldn't be so obvious that I'd gotten away, taking my pack with me. We each put on a pack and took turns passing the third one to each other as we climbed down the ladders to the building's basement.

Vance opened yet another hidden door. From past evacuation drills, I knew it led to a tunnel that would take us to an old house near the rapid transit station. Gerry, the security guy, lived there. After walking a mile through the dimly lit passageway, we entered the sublevel of his house. We roamed around the musty and rather dingy little house looking for Gerry. No one was home.

We both agreed it wasn't safe for Vance to turn on his cell and call his dad for instructions. "You should just go back," I said. "I can make it to the safe house on my own."

He set his jaw and furrowed his brow. "You know there's no way I'm leaving you. Come on, I know a safe place to take you. It's not that far on BART, and there's no way they'll find you."

We were old pros at the Bay Area's rapid transit system; the problem was all the security cameras. We put on windbreakers, ball caps, and sunglasses that were kept by the door in case of an evacuation. I tucked my red hair up into the cap. Still no Gerry.

Vance went to open the front door. I stepped in the way, blocking him. "Vance, I don't think you get it. The people who killed my mom and dad are after *me*. And my," the next word nearly gagged me, "my real mother, my biological mother from the Paraxous Cluster, will hurt anyone who gets in her way. She's a Dashia. I don't want you involved in this."

Vance didn't even bat an eye. "Too late. Now let's get going before the medication wears off, and she senses you and tracks us down."

A sudden realization struck me like an uppercut to the chin. "You knew? You knew about the medication? You knew about my mother?"

"Yeah."

"And you realize who and what she is?"

"Yeah, I know exactly what she is and how dangerous the DeConnetts are. So can we please go?"

He was right. We couldn't wait around for Gerry. With a frustrated groan, I stepped aside and let him open the door, then followed him down the front steps. He bought us tickets, and we hopped on a BART train, then got off at the next stop. We switched trains so many times, I quit trying to keep track of where we were or where we were going. I just let Vance lead me around.

Vance had the sense not to try to comfort me during the trip. He just stayed next to me, a calming presence. If it hadn't been for him, I might have completely fallen apart. Adding to my grief was the fear that any second Cassie and her henchmen would pop out of nowhere and catch us.

"This is it," he said as we came to the exit where Vance's family sometimes hiked. We gathered our backpacks, and I followed him in silence. Eventually, the two of us came to Point Edith Wildlife Area. It was swampy grasslands with lots of birds and only a few trails. Once we were out of sight from the road, we came to a small storage shack that had fallen into disrepair. Its door had been boarded shut, and there were signs all around saying "KEEP OUT."

Vance ignored the signs. After retrieving a key from under a rock and unlocking the door, he crawled under the boards and into the closet-sized room. I scrambled in after him, glad to be out of the open and under cover. Vance opened a hatch in the floor and flipped on a light. I looked down the hole into a small room with a cot, a couple of chairs and a table. There were a few crates and boxes stacked against the cinderblock walls. Stale air wafted up from below.

"This sure isn't like either of the safe houses my family was assigned." I waved a hand in front of my nose. "Who'd you guys piss off to get stuck with this as your safe house?"

Vance didn't answer. He started down the ladder. "Wait here," he ordered.

A minute later, there were noises I couldn't identify and then silence. I waited for what I thought was a reasonable amount of time and then called down in a hoarse whisper. Nothing.

I climbed down and looked around the dimly lit room. A Sian stood in the corner hidden in shadow. He flipped on a light nearly blinding me. "I told you to wait until I called you down," he said.

"Vance? Is that really you? I mean is it the real you?"

"Yeah, Twigh, it's me." His real voice was a bit reedier than his Human avatar's. His black crown feathers were a sharp contrast to his stubby, white-feathered wings, which marked him as a prepubescent Sian. His glacial-blue skin and large golden-brown eyes were beautiful. Even though my friend's beak was fairly small, it still seemed too big for his face.

"I wanted you to see the real me before the Dashia Hunter takes you away."

"Vance, that's sweet. And don't take this the wrong way: But are you freaking nuts?! You brought me to your family's vault! How could you be so stupid?"

He placed his talon-like hands on his hips and puffed his chest. "This is only one of the ways into our vault. Me and my family will be moved tonight because of what happened, but they'll use a different access, so we'll be perfectly safe. And I promise you: no one's going to find you here."

Vance mistook my dubious expression as distaste for the accommodations. He hurriedly pointed out the amenities, which included a bathroom with only a toilet and sink, a cot that could be folded up against the wall, and several boxes of MREs—Meals Ready to Eat. He showed me how to activate the heat packets and started an omelet despite my protests of not being hungry.

He sat me down on the cot and reached into a pocket. "Oh, and I figured you might want this." He held out a little black cube. "It's a duplicate of the one I gave you."

I took it from him and ignited the picture. Was it just last night everyone I cared about had gathered around me to sing, "You Are My Sunshine"? It seemed so long ago. I stared at the sunset hologram. "Thanks," I said, my voice flat. It was a nice gesture, but hardly helpful.

"Oh yeah, here." He took it back and changed the settings. Instead of a picture, a table of contents appeared. "It's got all sorts of information on the Paraxous Cluster. I figured you could use a cheat sheet when you guys left."

Even the vague reference to the Splendors stabbed my heart. Vance bowed his head and muttered, "Sorry." He offered me the steaming hot MRE containing what was supposed to pass as an omelet.

I shoved it away. His attempt to comfort me only upset me more. I didn't want to feel better. I deserved to suffer. My mom and dad were dead because of me.

I tugged the necklace out from under the collar of my tee-shirt, glad I hadn't taken it off when I'd gone to bed. I pressed the three-heart pendant to my lips. There should have been some solace in the fact that I'd told them I loved them. Only there wasn't. If their show of affection and devotion hadn't convinced me not to run away, they might still be alive. I'd been selfish and weak; they had paid the price.

"It's my fault. It's all my fault." I threw my head into my hands.

Vance sat down beside me. He leaned over to look up and into my eyes. "Twigh, there was nothing you could have done." Once again, he offered me the packet of disgusting smelling food.

My temper exploded. I slapped the packet from his hand. It flew across the room and smacked into the wall, splattering its contents. "Don't you get it? I knew I was putting them in danger. I should have left a long time ago. At the very least I should have left when my birthfather showed up."

"You think that would have made a difference?" Vance's stubby wings fluffed and fidgeted while he figured out how to put his logic into words. "Let's say you'd left yesterday or even weeks ago. By the Fates, Twigh, it wouldn't have mattered. Your mother would still—"

"She's not my mother," I shouted. "She may have given birth to me, but she is not my mother. My mother, my mom, is dead. That ..." There wasn't a word in English strong enough, but there was a Paraxous term that almost fit. "That bemfornte killed her." To me, even the term for a pregnant memform on a rampage wasn't bad enough.

"How the hell did you know about Cassie, anyway?" I asked.

He twitched his wings in a shrug, shifting nervously as he chose his words carefully. "It's how my parents met Bill and Tina. They recruit parents to take in Paraxous refugees, especially mixed breed orphans. They got involved with the group that helped my aunt and her two boys escape the internment camps. They're ..." he hesitated, then finished, "mixed breeds."

"Mixed-breeds, really. Wow, I mean cross breeding is so rare." Even half-breeds like Nina were fairly uncommon and nearly always sterile. If they could breed, it was almost exclusively with a member of one their parents' races. The term mixed-breed specifically referred to someone of more than two races. "I mean, isn't that why the Kobbi had to be genetically engineered? Besides, you're definitely no mixed-breed. I mean, both your parents are pure Sian, right?" I asked.

Vance's face paled and then flushed. For a second I expected him to tell me he was part Kobbi like me. That's what would have happened in the movies. But this wasn't a movie.

"Yeah, we're Sians," he answered. "But my mom's brother met and married my aunt, who is a mixed-breed and already had two mixed heritage sons. They're very involved in the fight for mixed-breed rights."

That was all very interesting, but I found myself distracted by my best friend's new appearance. It fit him so much better than his Human avatar. The way he shrugged his wings instead of shoulders. How he ducked and cocked his head. So many of his gestures had always seemed slightly birdlike, even with the Humanizing algorithms programmed into his avatar.

I was glad he'd let me see him as he really was. "Sorry I snapped at you. And thanks for this," I said gesturing to his Sian form.

He gave me a smile that looked really odd with his beak. "Ah, I was due for a download anyways."

Those utilizing avatars only had to live in their real bodies for a couple of days every few months. However, they had to update their real minds every few weeks so there wouldn't be any integration issues.

I gaped at Vance in sudden realization. Cassie's invasion and the murder of the Splendors constituted a breach of our haven's security. According to protocol, the residents would have to be dispersed. They'd be relocated with no means of contacting each other. Avatars would begin initiating emergency downloads, and all those in stasis would be awakened but remain in hiding until their avatars underwent reconstructive surgery and new identities were issued. Then all the safe houses and vaults would be scrapped. I wasn't sure of the details, but the goal was to make it seem like we'd never existed.

"Vance, you need to get home. Your mom's going to be worried sick. By now, the resident council is going to be reacting to what's happened." I thought for a second, realizing the truth even as I said it. "And Vance, you've got to convince your father not to tell any of them you guys found me. Cassie will be monitoring the building. You have to pretend to believe I'm missing or even dead. You can't even tell Cam, Nina and Sam. You could get yourself and them killed."

Vance didn't argue; he understood what was at stake. To keep our friends safe, he was willing to let them think I was dead. He'd have to watch them grieve and pretend to grieve with them. Then he'd have to say good-bye to them when everyone was forced to relocate.

With a steadying breath, I added, "And tell your dad not to contact any of my parents' relatives. I don't want anyone else involved. Just have him tell me when the Dashia Hunter gives the date and time for my extraction. I'll meet the Hunter by myself."

He gave a shake that fluffed his feathers. "That's insane. You're going to need help and you know it."

"No one else is going to die because of me. That includes my aunts and uncles. And that includes you. You are getting out of this mess while you still can. Understood?" I snapped the last part in military fashion, sounding like Colonel Ebon Milett.

Vance wasn't fazed a bit. He came right back at me with a scolding talon-like finger in my face. "Don't worry about me. My dad knows what he's doing." Then with a knowing cock of his head, he continued, "And don't you go taking off either. I'm guessing the USB my dad found has the extraction site?"

When I nodded confirmation, he said, "So you don't even know the location, do you?" More hesitantly, I shook my head. "So you need us. We'll figure out how to get you out of here safely, but you're going to have to trust us."

My mild-mannered friend had never stood up to me like this before. Since his dad had the thumb drive, I really had no choice but to leave things up to him. "Fine," I growled. "We'll play it your way. Just promise me to be careful." Then, subdued and very sad, I asked, "And do me a favor: make sure someone gets Little Miss out of the animal shelter as soon as possible, okay?"

"I promise. She'll be taken care of, Twigh. Don't worry."

He tried to hug me, but I sprang from the bed, still unwilling to be consoled. My voice nearly broke as I said, "Okay. You'd better get going before someone does notice you're gone and puts one and one together."

Vance just looked up at me with an expression that said he wasn't going anywhere, so I added, "Please. I really need to be alone."

He bowed his head and slowly got to his feet. "Twigh," he choked. "I don't want this to be the last time I ever see you."

It occurred to me if his family stayed on Earth, his new avatar body would bear no resemblance to the Vance I knew, so seeing his real body wouldn't do me any good. The thought of losing my best friend made me want to throw myself into his arms and share a good cry with him.

Instead I laughed ruefully, "Oh don't worry. There's no way this is the last time we see each other. I promise. You're not that lucky."

Chapter 5

THREE DAYS WENT BY and nobody came for me. With no computer or cell phone, there was nothing to do but wait and worry. Had Cassie discovered that the Volkners had helped me? Had she gone after Bill's and Tina's relatives? Were my friends in danger?

At night, the soft whistle of the ventilation system sounded like ghostly whispers. I imagined it was Mom and Dad calling to me. Unable to sleep, I went through the supplies in the dungeon-like room again. Except for emergency provisions, there wasn't much: data-pads from the Paraxous that had their power-cores removed, and bags of what seemed like the personal items of those who'd come to Earth. I considered trying to jury-rig a power supply for the data-pads but feared activating them might make it possible for Cassie to track me down.

Finally, I resorted to reading the files Vance had on that holo-imager. The basic encyclopedia of races didn't take me long to get through. I remembered most of the information from my early childhood in the Cluster. The medical texts, however, proved interesting. They covered the basic anatomy and physiology of all sixteen races as well as emergency treatment protocols. They kept me distracted for a while, but eventually I had to get up and move. I was just too restless to sit still for long.

The only pack I hadn't gone through was one that had apparently belonged to a child. It was full of toys. I imagined how the kid must have cried at having to leave all his or her most prized possessions behind as part of transitioning to life here on Earth. Sorting through the pack felt nearly as morbid as when I'd gone through Mom's and Dad's backpacks.

It turned out the toy gun was actually an ancient ricochet gun. I recognized it from the old historical holo-vids Terrel and I used to watch. Ricochet gun and shield contests used to be a popular Kobbi sport before the race had fallen from grace. I searched through the rest of the contents and found the handle to a Guardian's shield. The energy shields had been used by the Kobbi Guardians during the old Federation, when they served as the peace-keepers of the Paraxous.

Holding the handle out at arm's length, I ignited the shield. A three-foot circle of energy glowed pale gold. The fact that it was visible at all confirmed it was a training shield and therefore not lethal. I touched a cautious finger to the shimmer. The energy field tingled but didn't really hurt.

I wondered about the kid who'd once owned the shield. Had he or she dreamed of becoming a Guardian someday? *Probably dead by now,* I realized with a twinge of sorrow. After all, only Kobbies could use the shields, and their race had been nearly exterminated. *My race,* I corrected myself. I might have only been half-Kobbi, but that was enough to make me an outlaw.

Setting the thought aside, I pulled the trigger of the ricochet gun. The bolt of energy hit the wall and bounced back, smacking me in the shoulder before I could react. I looked around frantically, afraid of getting hit again. The bolt was gone. It had been absorbed by my flesh, leaving a localized tingling sensation.

I pushed the foldout cot back up into the wall recess and cleared as much space as possible before firing the gun again. I tried, but failed to bring the shield into position in time. The bolt struck my leg. "Son of a memform!" I cursed, hopping around on one leg.

For the first time since the death of my parents, I felt something other than icy numbness. It may have only been pain-induced anger, but it was something. For the next two days, I slept and ate little. Every time I fired the gun or smacked the energy bolt with that shield, I fantasized about killing Cassie.

•   •   •

On my fifth day in hiding, the door above opened while I was in the middle of a ricochet round. I glanced up at the hatch only to have the energy bolt smack me in the face. The shock knocked me on my butt. The shield fell from my hand and automatically shut off. I aimed the gun at the hatch.

Vance poked his head down, let out a squawk and jerked his head back up. "Don't shoot!"

I dropped the gun and put my hands over my throbbing nose, rocking back and forth, not bothering to get up.

"Twigh, you okay?" he asked, squatting down beside me and checking me over.

I nodded with a groan. Once he'd assured himself that nothing was injured except my pride, he glanced from me to the ricochet gun then to the handle of the Guardian shield. He actually had the nerve to laugh at me. "What the heck were you doing messing around with Guardian stuff?"

"Forget about that," I snapped. "What the hell are you doing here? I told you to stay away."

The humor in Vance's expression vanished. Nina appeared at the hatch and made her way down the ladder. I grabbed Vance by his shirt and yanked him closer to me. "What's she doing here? Vance, you promised not to get anyone else involved!"

"You bemfornte!" Nina screamed at me. Her eyes were red, and her cheeks were streaked with tears. "You let us think you were dead! How could you?"

Cameron wasn't with them, and Nina hardly ever went anywhere without him. Nina's anger gave way to sobbing wails of despair. Vance pulled a cell phone I didn't recognize from his pocket. "You'd better see this for yourself. Cassie's got Cam."

He started the message. Cassie's face filled the little screen. "Mr. Donner, allow me to introduce myself. I am Cassiopeia DeConnett. I am Twyla's real mother. Needless to say, I'm quite concerned about her disappearance. I understand that your son, Cameron, has also gone missing. Please contact me as soon as possible."

She leaned in to the screen and her eyes narrowed. "Perhaps we can be of assistance to one another. The police are often useless in these matters. In fact, they often make matters worse." She leaned back and added, "I do hope to hear from you by noon tomorrow."

"Shit. Shit. Shit," was all I could say. She had Cameron, and her message was a not-so-subtle threat. Then I noticed the message contained contact information and was dated yesterday at seven P.M. "Have they arranged the trade?" I asked.

"What?" Vance started. "Trade? No! We aren't about to just hand you over to her. My dad's playing it as if you were already gone when we got to the safe room."

Another thought occurred to me. "Oh god, are you sure you two weren't followed?"

Vance looked insulted. "I'm sure. Of course, I was careful. Dang, why do you think I didn't come rushing out here to you last night when Cameron's dad told my dad about the message? I figured Cassie's people would be watching us. As far as anyone knows, Nina and I are at Sam's doing our school work. We're both logged in, and Sam is doing all three assignments. Good thing he's so smart."

"Good thing we're all home schooled," I commented absently. My mind was on Cameron and what would happen to him.

Vance shrugged. "Yeah, I guess so. I never thought I'd be grateful for not being allowed to go to regular school."

"None of this helps us get Cameron back," Nina snapped impatiently. "We need to figure out what to do."

Three hours wasn't nearly enough time to devise a rescue plan. And if Cassie didn't get what she wanted before noon, there was no doubt in my mind that she'd do something terrible to Cameron. Most likely she'd either kill him or use him for Dashia target practice. The thought made me wonder about my sister, Daylight. She'd be eighteen by now, and unless she'd drastically changed, she could be a practicing Dashia in her own right. She always tried so hard to make Mother proud.

That meant, while we sat around trying to figure what to do, my very own sister might be bonding Cameron. "There's only one thing to do," I announced.

Before I could continue, Vance said, "You aren't handing yourself over to her."

"It's not like I have a choice," I said, getting to my feet. "You two get back home before anyone realizes you're gone. I'll call Cassie and arrange the trade."

Nina shook her head. "Don't be an idiot." Her lip curled into a snarl that made it easy to imagine her as a Katian, but her voice was raw with emotion. Her life revolved around Cam. Even so, she argued, "That woman is a Dashia, right? She killed Bill and Tina, right? So you really expect her to just let Cameron go if you give yourself up?"

I turned to Vance. "You told her my mother's a Dashia?"

Before he could answer, Nina got in my face. "Yes, he was finally honest with me. And yes, he told me about your lineage. Something you should have done a long time ago."

"It's not like being Kobbi is something you go around telling everybody," I said defensively.

She raised a hand, and I knew if she'd been in her Katian body, she'd have bared her claws. "I am not everybody," she growled with slow deliberation. "I am your vreking best friend. Or at least I thought I was. The truth is you never even trusted me."

"It wasn't that I didn't trust you. We weren't allowed to tell *anyone* what I really am for their own protection."

"Yeah, that worked out really well for Cam, didn't it?"

"Can we fight about this later?" Vance interjected. "Nina's right, we need to figure out what to do."

"Well, what are the grown-ups doing?" I asked.

After a few hems and haws, Vance said, "Cameron's dad is understandably upset. He's mad that the Resident Council hid the daughter of a Dashia in the complex without warning everyone."

"So he wants to hand me over in exchange for his son," I said simply. Nina and Vance both started to defend the guy. I put up my hands to silence them. "It's okay. I totally get it. If I were him, I'd feel the same way." I looked to Vance knowing he would have found a way to eavesdrop on the meeting. "So what does the Council propose to do? Do they know you guys found me?"

Vance shook his head. "No. My dad's playing this one close to his vest. He sent a message to the Dashia Hunter and plans to keep you hidden until the Hunter comes for you. As for the Council ..." He took a deep breath then released it with a huff. "They're making arrangements to relocate everyone. They're hoping once Cassie figures out that Cameron's dad doesn't know where you are, she'll let him go."

"In other words," Nina said with a snarl, "they aren't going to do a damn thing."

"So we're back to me making the trade," I sighed in frustration. "Unless either of you have a better idea."

"As a matter of fact," Vance said confidently, "I do." His eyes tracked back and forth as if reading lines of computer code. "It might even work."

Chapter 6

A N HOUR AND A HALF LATER, Vance, Nina, and I
rendezvoused at the San Francisco Public Library. It was the
safest place we could think of near where Cassie was staying.
Vance's father had uncovered her location not long after Cameron
went missing. It hadn't been hard. The pretentious bemfornte had
rented the entire top floor of the Ritz-Carlton.

Now we had to hope Cameron was with her in order for
Vance's plan to work. Me, I had serious concerns about his plan.
The entire time I laid a false trail for Cassie to follow, I tried
coming up with an alternative that had a reasonable chance of
success, yet wouldn't put Vance and Nina at risk. I'd failed.

So I sat at a table in the back corner of the library in my
disguise—a cheap black wig and fake tan—listening to Vance and
Nina talk in hushed voices. Vance had injected each of us with a
dose of the medication that blocks telepathic contact. Bill had

given some to Vance's father just in case. So, I wasn't too worried about Cassie sensing us.

Vance had taken a couple of 0-grav belts from one of the safe houses, giving us a way to get Cameron out if we could get to him. Nina had managed to steal three housekeeping uniform tops from the Ritz along with a keycard. She didn't say how, and I didn't ask.

"Just let me go in disguised as a maid and deliver a belt to him," I said for the third time, interrupting their plotting.

"You're the last person that should be going in," Vance insisted. "They're bound to be watching for you. Besides, I've got it set so Nina and I can do emergency disconnects if we need to. Cassie will have two dead bodies on her hands and no way to trace our real ones."

That was the only reason I'd even considered letting them come. But their avatar bodies weren't something to be sacrificed lightly. It'd take months to grow replacements. In the meantime, they'd be trapped in their real bodies—their very alien bodies. That meant they'd be forced to stay in hiding and just hope Cassie's people didn't find them or their families.

Another problem occurred to me. "But you guys would lose your memories of what happened?"

Vance and Nina gave me the, "Are you stupid?" expressions. And I realized, "Oh yeah, of course you guys downloaded before coming here, huh?"

"No duh?" Nina said, using Cam's favorite expression. Then she let out a growl. "We have a plan. You set off the fire alarm and get out in the rush. And we," she said pointing to herself and Vance, "plant the belt and make sure Cameron gets out."

I raised my hands in surrender. "Fine. Where are we with the Hunter?" I asked Vance, who'd been tapping away at his laptop. "Can we check for messages without giving ourselves away?"

Vance gave his dimple-to-dimple grin. "We can now." He turned his laptop so I could see all the hacking he'd done to make it possible. It was impressive work, but more importantly, there was a message. We crowded around the screen as he dumped it into his program so we could safely access it.

It read: "Both messages received. ETA five days. Meeting location site C. If unable to meet, second option is site E in 7 days. If capture imminent, subject must be eliminated due to extreme threat level. No other options. Compliance mandatory. No further communication permitted."

Icicles ran through my veins. I gulped, trying to force myself to say something. Nina beat me to it. "Did the Hunter just order your dad to kill T—" she cut herself off, remembering we were trying not to use our names. "—to kill her?" she finished with a gasp.

"If it's the only way to keep Cassie from getting me," I said, trying not to sound upset. "It makes sense. No way a Hunter can risk another Dashia being set loose in the Paraxous. And if she gets her hands on me ..."

"All the more reason for you to stay here," Vance pointed out. "It'll only take one of us to deliver the belt."

We started arguing again. Nina quickly lost patience. "Both of you, shut up." Her eyes glittered with a predatory glare. "We've wasted enough time. We stick to the plan. Now let's go."

We went into the bathroom to change into our uniforms. As soon as we were alone, Nina brandished a pair of scissors. "You still look too much like you," she explained. "Trust me. I know what I'm doing."

A few minutes later I had a shaggy bob with bangs, or at least my wig did. Nina brushed the sides forward covering a fair portion of my face. We stuck our caps and sunglasses on before stepping outside and walking the mile or so to the Ritz.

Once there, I hung back while Nina went in the employee entrance and secured a cleaning cart. Vance joined her after a couple minutes. I waited five more minutes before sneaking in and making my way to the nearest bathroom.

Once Vance and Nina figured out which room Cameron was in and planted the 0-grav belt where he could get to it, Vance would call me. I'd set off the fire alarm. He and Nina would then bang on doors calling for an evacuation of all guests, distracting any guards while Cameron dove out a window. Yes, using Paraxous technology was against all the rules, but it's not like we cared at this point.

I hid in a stall waiting for the call, wondering what was happening. Had they been able to figure out which room Cameron was in? Had something gone wrong?

Suddenly, a strange wave of emotion hit me. It wasn't Cassie. The brief contact tasted like panic and anger mixed together. It took me a second to realize it was Nina. I'd tried to prepare her and Vance for what Cassie's people might have done to Cameron. We'd feared every form of torture, but we'd never imagined this.

She'd walked in to find two skimpily dressed, big-chested women hanging all over Cameron, who reclined on a chaise lounge with a foolish grin covering his face. The woman with neon blue hair massaged his shoulders while twirling some melody in his ears. Nina recognized the words as Felniez and figured that female was actually a Katian. This was just her Human avatar.

The second woman had an exaggeratedly feminine figure and reminded Nina of a green Orion slave girl from *Star Trek*. She was a Sentagil with her maroon skin simply died dark brown in order to pass as African-American. Her gaudy Sentagil body art showed through the dye job but just looked like elaborate tattoos.

A distinctly Katian growl emanated from the back of Nina's throat. Luckily, the two women were too busy doting on Cam to notice, and there weren't any guards in the room. There were some by the elevator and in front of the presidential suite, but they were too far away to hear.

Still, no one had to hear a thing for this to all go to hell. No Katian could tolerate such attentions being slathered on her intended. Worse, Nina guessed these women were Dashias in training. Terror sent her emotions off the chart. Sooner or later Cassie was bound to pick up on it. Obviously, the medication had worn off. Both Nina and I were exposed.

I tried to break the contact as Vance came up behind Nina and placed a calming hand on her shoulder. "We're not supposed to clean this room yet."

To Cameron he said, "Excuse me, sir. Your host requested we deliver a change of clothes, so you can freshen up. Would you like me to put them in the bathroom for you?"

Cameron had frozen in place when Vance and Nina had entered. He forced himself to nod, still too stunned to speak. The Sentagil waggled her brows. "Oooh, bath time. How lovely."

•　　　•　　　•

The contact faded. By some miracle it didn't seem like Cassie had picked up on Nina or Cameron's reaction. However, the medication had worn off enough that she was aware of my presence. I could sense her scanning empathically, trying to find me. It wouldn't take her long to get a fix on my location.

Chapter 7

I DASHED FROM THE BATHROOM and pulled the nearest fire alarm. Cassie increased the force of her scan. I focused my thoughts so it would seem to her that I expected Cameron to be evacuated by her henchmen. Once out in public, I'd make the trade.

I got ready to blend in with the fleeing masses before her people spotted me. Trouble was there were no fleeing masses. People just milled around, confused. The hotel manager had to order the staff to usher the guests outside.

I broke the link with Cassie before helping herd guests out the door. Two big men in suits eyed the guests as they poured out, but paid no to attention to me. I guess it's true what they say about people not seeing past a uniform.

Once clear of the building, I used a disposable phone Vance had given me to call Cassie. "Let him go," I demanded.

"As soon as you're here with me where you belong." Cassie's voice was carefully neutral, but I could feel her trying to reestablish our telepathic link.

"Let him leave first. Then I'll give myself up."

I sensed her disgust at what she considered to be my juvenile attempt to outwit her. "Now come, dear. That's not how this works. I've already called the front desk and apologized for my daughter's unfortunate little prank. They've canceled the alarm. So you can come to me in the presidential suite, and we'll talk."

"Talk? There's nothing to talk about. Let Cameron go."

"Oh, I will. I just need to make sure you're going to behave yourself first."

A shudder ran through my spine. She was lying. I could tell but didn't let on. "Fine!" I snapped before hanging up the phone and ditching it. Once again, I severed our empathic link.

After finding a good hiding place across the street from the hotel, I injected myself with the last dose of the medicine we had. I waited, watching the window that should have been Cameron's room. No one came flying out. Something had gone wrong.

We didn't have a backup plan. I could only come up with one way to save my friends, and it sucked. It involved something I thought I'd never do: becoming my sister. Glancing down a side street, I spotted a young woman with a big purse and stiletto heels. "Excuse me," I said, stepping out onto the sidewalk. "I'll give you a hundred dollars for those shoes and any makeup you have in your bag."

She scoffed. "My shoes are worth twice that."

"Fine."

She scowled in disbelief, openly appraising me and my housekeeper's uniform. I reached into my pocket and pulled out a wad of cash. Vance had given me some of the cash he'd appropriated from the emergency funds kept at the safe house. "Two hundred and fifty bucks. But it has to be right now."

She shrugged and started unstrapping her high heels. We exchanged shoes. She fished a cosmetic bag from her purse, took the cash and departed without even a farewell.

I ran to the crosswalk, wobbling every few steps. I'd rarely ever worn heels and never three-inch stilettos. I managed to make it to the back of the hotel and in the employee entrance without falling down or getting caught.

I hurried into the women's restroom, this time placing a "closed for cleaning" sign outside the door. I stripped off the Ritz-Carlton uniform shirt leaving me in a black tank top, black slacks, and heels.

After removing the wig, I stared at myself in the mirror. My sister and I weren't twins, but since Kobbi genes are so dominant, we both looked a lot like 'dear ol' Mom' with the same auburn hair and pine green eyes. However, my blood-shot eyes with dark circles under them made me look more like something the cat had dragged in.

Daylight was a damn Dashia, sex personified. I had no idea how to pull that off. My parents hadn't even allowed me to wear makeup until recently, and I sucked at applying it. Nina usually had to doll me up for special occasions. I found a bottle of eye drops in the cosmetic bag and used some to clear up the red from my eyes, then did my best with the makeup. With foundation to cover the dark shadows, and my cheeks and lips painted, my face would just have to do.

I checked my waistband to make sure the ricochet gun and training shield were secure and accessible yet discreet. I took a moment to get into character before leaving the room. My memories of Daylight were vague at best, but I figured she was our mother's daughter. So I'd just play up the bitch factor.

I marched to the elevator and took it to the top floor. When the door opened, a man who was obviously one of Cassie's henchmen turned to confront me. With a rush of rage, I realized he was one of the guys who'd been with Cassie when she attacked our home.

With a superior and obviously dismissive glare, I tried to bluff my way passed him. "Excuse me, ma'am," he called after me.

I swung around to face him with my hands on my hips. "What?"

Now he hesitated. "Um, ma'am."

My jaw dropped. "Yes. What is it? Hurry up. My mother wants me to check on our 'guest'."

He wasn't completely convinced but wasn't sure what to do. He didn't dare risk pissing off a DeConnett. At my mention of the guest, the guard glanced toward a door that wasn't the presidential suite. With a huff, I turned from him and headed to the room. I saw the cleaning cart, but no Vance or Nina.

The door was locked, and of course I didn't have a key. With a growl of haughty frustration, I called, "Open the door. It's me, Daylight."

The door swung open. The black woman with the tattoos did a double-take. Her eyes narrowed with suspicion. I pretended not to notice. Another woman, the one Nina had pegged as a Katian, stood triumphantly with a 0-grav belt dangling from her index finger.

Nina clung to Cameron. Vance seemed to be trying to work his way toward the woman with the belt but had frozen at the sight of me.

Sounding like a total snot, I told the Sentagil at the door, "Go tell my mother, she was right. His friends are here."

She didn't move.

"You heard me. Go." I had to make her believe before she dared call my bluff. "Get moving unless you want to go from Dashia in training to Dashia target practice."

She cast me one more suspicious glance but then left the room. As soon as she spoke to Cassie, my cover would be blown. But I had to force myself not to act rushed. I sauntered up to the woman holding the 0-grav belt. "So they were stupid enough to think they could just fly away. Makers, how dumb can you get?"

She nodded with a smirk, but didn't take her attention off my three friends.

I pulled out the ricochet gun and shot her twice in the face before she realized what was happening. It didn't knock her out, but I knew firsthand how much the energy bolt hurt. So I got ready to follow it up with a punch.

What I'd failed to take into account was that even though she was in a Human avatar, she was actually a Katian. And pain doesn't stun Katians; it just pisses them off. She eyed me with a predatory glare only someone descended from feline ancestors could manage and then tackled me.

We ended up in a brawl. Cameron and Nina dog-piled her. Vance grabbed the nearest lamp and smashed her over the head. She went limp but was still breathing. We looked at each other in disbelief.

"What the vrek?" Cameron asked, looking at me and taking in my disguise.

But there wasn't time to explain about my sister. "Cassie or her guards will be here in a second. Where are the other 0-grav belts?"

"They're still out there in the cart," Vance admitted with a bowed head. He jerked his shoulders and groaned. I knew he was wishing he had his wings.

I hurried to the door. I peeked out only to see Cassie and Daylight coming out of the presidential suite with the Sentagil and two guards. *Shit. So much for us all just flying out.* I shut the door and flipped the deadbolt. It wouldn't buy us much time, but hopefully it'd be enough.

Knowing what I had to do, I steeled my resolve and turned to face Vance. "You and Nina are going to have to cut your connection."

Even as he and Nina began to protest, I scooped up the belt that had been dropped during the scuffle and tossed it to Cameron. "You fly out as planned."

"But what about you?" Vance asked. "We can't leave you here."

Hoping they wouldn't catch on that I was lying, I said, "I'm Kobbi. Remember? I can just climb down the side of the building."

"Really?" Cameron asked, astonished.

In truth, I had no idea how I was going to get out of this mess. Someone slid the keycard into the lock and tried turning the knob. Cassie's voice came through strong and commanding even though she didn't yell. "Twyla, open the door. It's over. I'll let your friends go. Just open the door."

"All right. All right. Just hang on for a second," I replied, while shaking my head to my friends. I mouthed, "She's lying." They all nodded in understanding. I pointed for Cameron to get the 0-grav belt on. As he did so, I picked up the ricochet gun and pulled the shield from my waistband.

Vance opened the window and popped the screen. He gestured excitedly. There was a compartment hidden in the window ledge's thick architecture. Inside was a rope fire ladder.

"Well, don't just stand there. Go! Go!" I urged him.

He threw the dropdown ladder over the ledge. It almost reached all the way to the patio of the 4th floor restaurant. He and Cameron made Nina go first. Vance motioned for Cameron to go next, but Cameron said, "I've got the belt. I can just fly away."

Vance nodded grimly, then followed Nina out the window. Cameron waved me over. "Your turn."

The door burst open. Two guards stepped in. I fired the ricochet gun and then brought my shield to bear. "Go!" I yelled back to Cameron.

"Not without you," he called and came toward me instead of going out the window.

I backed up to meet him by the window. One of the guards fired. To my surprise the training shield turned out to be strong enough to block the energy bolt. Of course, his weapon was set for stun. "Go!" I ordered.

"The grav belt can support us both," Cameron argued.

It was just the kind of unrealistic thinking that both endeared Cameron to me and drove me nuts. There was no way the 0-grav belt could take the weight of both of us. The other guard fired. This time the shield winked out for a millisecond. The two guards exchanged glances with a knowing smile. They'd coordinate the next shot so one brought down the shield and the other stunned me.

I shouted to the empty doorway where Cassie had yet to appear. "Okay. Okay. I give up. Just let him go."

"Twyla, what are you doing?" Cameron asked in dismay.

I only half turned to glance at him. "Saving your hide, you idiot." In the movies, I'd confess my love for him, and we'd fly off into the sunset together. Instead, Cassie stepped into the doorway.

Chapter 8

I SLAMMED MY FIST that held the ricochet gun into the 0-grav belt's controls, activating it. Cameron floated up off his toes. Keeping the shield raised protectively with the other hand, I shoved Cam out the window.

The guards shot. My shield winked out. The second stun bolt struck me, sending me to my knees. I raised the ricochet gun at Cassie. She rolled her eyes. "Really, Twyla?"

In answer, I pulled the trigger. Cassie shifted slightly, avoiding the bolt. She reached out telepathically and clamped my airway shut.

I struggled to force air in and out of my lungs, but to no avail. Over my shoulder, I watched Cameron gain control of the 0-grav unit and fly off. He was safe for now.

However, I had no idea how far Vance and Nina had made it down the ladder. Cassie picked up on my concern for them and reached out to grab their minds. She instantly knew they were avatars. It wouldn't take her long to discover the location of their true bodies.

I fired again, but missed. The guards rushed forward to disarm me. The distraction was enough to loosen Cassie's vice-like grip on my throat. I shouted to Vance and Nina. "CUT YOUR CONNECTION! NOW!"

She closed off my airway again. I crumpled to the floor. My vision tunneled into a black and white hazy orb. I felt the gun and shield being yanked from my grip. Cassie stepped into my narrowed field of vision, leaning over me. Her empathic voice resonated in my head. *So you fancy yourself a Guardian, do you? You foolish, foolish girl.*

Despite my dulled senses, I heard the sounds of screaming coming from the window. A guard peered out and immediately jerked his head back in. "There are two bodies splattered all over the patio."

I smiled defiantly at Cassie. She might have me, but my friends had gotten away. Her scowl warped her delicate feminine features. *Do not imagine for one second this means they're safe.* As she thought this, she said as if truly mystified, "Now young lady, please tell me why you're acting so insane. I'm your mother. We're your family." She motioned to where Daylight now stood in the doorway. "You belong with us."

Cassie released her hold just enough to allow me to breathe again. "You killed my parents," I rasped bitterly. "Then you threatened my friends."

"Those Humans were not your parents. I am your mother. Don't ever forget that. You belong to me."

Even to my inexperienced empathic senses, it was clear she regarded me as her property. I was like an expensive piece of jewelry to her. Bill and Tina had simply paid the price for stealing something that belonged to her.

The thought of my parents lying dead on the living room floor tripped my temper. I swiped at Cassie, intent on digging my fingernails into her flawless, genetically-engineered face.

She grabbed me by the wrists and reached out mentally to clamp my throat shut once more. With an annoyed sigh, she asked Daylight, "What do you think it will take to make your sister see reason?" Then she added in a telepathic flash, *Her friends mean so much to her. Maybe I should have them hunted down.*

I looked over at Daylight standing passively at the doorway. Dang, did we look a lot alike. We were both younger incarnations of Cassie. Besides the same auburn hair and green eyes, we both had her soft, oval jaw line, delicate nose, and full lips. The only difference between us was Daylight's large chest—something I'd failed to consider when trying to impersonate her.

I stared at my sister in desperation. She stared right back at me with an expression that said, "What are you looking at me for?" She took her sweet time before answering our mother with a well-rehearsed yawn of boredom. "Who cares if she sees reason right now? As long as she does what she's told, it doesn't really matter." She folded her arms across her oversized chest and flashed, *Can we go home now? I hate this backwards Halo-world.*

Cassie gave an indulgent chuckle. *Of course, dear. I just need to make sure Twyla isn't going to cause us any more trouble.*

Daylight glared at me. "I'm sure she'll behave herself. She knows if we're still here when this planet's version of security shows up, her friends will end up involved."

I could kill one of her friends before we go to prove how serious I am, Cassie taunted. *Which one should it be? Cameron, Nina, or Vance?*

I bowed my head in defeat. "Fine. I'll behave. You don't have to hurt anyone else. But let's go before the cops get here."

•   •   •

I spent the twenty-day flight in the ship's brig on minimal food and water rations with nothing to do but worry about what awaited me once we arrived at Cassie's home on the planet Oweena. My only consolation was that Cameron, Nina and Vance were safe for the moment. But my life, at least as I'd known it, was over. And while I wasn't sure exactly what to expect from this new life, it couldn't be good.

Terrel and I had lived with Cassie in her fetshous—a city contained in a single building—for about a year while our father was on an extended mission. Her private residence took up the top two stories of the building that spanned several square blocks. There, she no longer had to keep up the pretense of being a loving mother. She demanded total obedience, and she tortured Terrel and me empathically whenever we didn't comply. Often she'd demand to know why we couldn't behave like Daylight as she did.

Most of what I knew about Oweena I'd learned from reading the material Vance had encrypted into that holographic imager. It was a Sian home-world and one of only two planets within the Paraxous Cluster where Kobbies were permitted to live. They were supposed to be restricted to the relocation camps and subjected to mandatory sterilization. However, since Oweena still hosted a large population of half-breeds, it was possible for some Kobbies to escape the camps and blend in.

That was probably why Oweena served as a DeConnett stronghold. Still, the DeConnetts had to have some pretty powerful officials in their pockets to avoid the relocation or elimination order. Hell, Cassie owned an entire fetshous. Someone had to know what she was; yet, no one did anything about it. And when Terrel had run away, he'd been returned by local security. I had to assume they were on the DeConnett payroll.

I couldn't help wondering how things might have turned out if I'd had the courage to go with him that night. To escape, we'd have to climb down several stories to the balcony gardens beneath his room. I'd panicked and refused to follow him out the window. He'd told me it was okay. He'd go and come back with help. Only there was no help to be found. Even after ten years, guilt over my cowardice still ate at me.

Once the ship reached orbit around Oweena, Cassie came to see me. There were two females with her: one Katian, one Sentagil. Since the Sentagil bore the same body art as the woman at the hotel, I assumed these were the same two wannabe Dashias. The Katian snarled at me. Her lion-like mane stood on end and her tail slashed the air. The Sentagil tossed the bundle of clothes she'd been carrying into my cell.

"We'll be taking a shuttle down in a few minutes," Cassie said. "Wash up and make yourself presentable."

I didn't give a damn about making myself presentable. I wanted to rip her throat out. Before I could lunge, the buzzing in my head started. Cassie smiled as I shrank back in pain. "Of course, HelaShia and Serenade would be happy to help you."

The two wannabe Dashias stepped forward. The threat of such humiliation was enough. I grabbed the bundle of clothes and marched to the bathroom. I showered, dressed, and even brushed my hair to avoid giving them an excuse to "help me."

I came out of the bathroom to find Cassie waiting for me. She smiled with fake warmth. "You look lovely, Twyla."

Before I could throw the compliment back in her face, she sent out an empathic wave of approval and joy that overwhelmed me. It made me feel good. Scarily good. Addictively good. I consciously pulled away, ending the contact. Cassie shrugged and motioned for me to come with her.

Chapter 9

ONCE THE SHUTTLE LANDED, Cassie took me by one hand and Daylight by the other as she led us down the ramp. I tried to pull free, but Cassie dug her perfectly manicured nails into the thin skin on the back of my hand. *Don't even think of doing anything to embarrass me,* she flashed with a quick mental slap.

A handsome Zartous captain separated himself from the rest of the crowd and strode up the ramp, his eyes locked on Cassie. I guessed this was her latest victim and wondered if he'd already been bonded.

Must have a thing for captains. It seemed bitterly ironic that he was the same rank as my father had been when she'd destroyed him.

This captain had the typical soft facial features, long lashes and muscular build of a Sentagil. However, his skin was an unusually light shade of maroon, making me guess he was part Human.

When they embraced, Cassie looked up into his eyes like some character in a sappy Hollywood romance. It made me want to puke. On the other hand, he seemed genuinely worried. "Oh, Mirra, I'm so glad to see you. You gave me quite a scare taking off like that."

The fact that she used an alias didn't surprise me. She couldn't exactly go around introducing herself to her targets as Cassiopeia DeConnett, the notorious Dashia. But if he still knew her by that name, it meant he hadn't been bonded yet. That did surprise me. For Sentagils, sex is pretty much just another way of saying, "Hey there, how ya doing?" And as far as I knew, sex with a Dashia automatically meant being bonded.

"I take it everything went well?" he said, finally releasing her. She smiled, nodded and wiped a pretend tear of joy from her eye. He greeted Daylight, then turned to me. His broad smile exposed deep dimples that reminded me of Vance. "You must be Twyla. Your mother has told me so much about you."

I opened my mouth to warn him just who it was he was romancing. My airway swelled shut again. Only a raspy croak came out. I glared up at Cassie with a hateful frown.

He looked to her in concern. "Is she all right? Do we need to take her to a med-unit?"

Cassie patted me on the head. "You'll have to excuse the poor dear. The people who took her abused her terribly. Of course, I had her examined during the flight. They say there's nothing wrong ... physically. She's just been traumatized. We've started therapy, but it'll take time to undo the damage. Time and a lot of motherly love ..."

To me she said in a sickeningly sweet voice, "Do you think you can manage to say hello to Captain Constantien?"

I had no intentions of bothering with hello. Dashia was the only word I wanted to say.

Cassie tightened her telepathic grip. I found myself paralyzed and in eye-watering pain. *You will stop right now, or I will keep your trachea shut until you pass out.*

•　　　•　　　•

I woke up in my brother's old room. It had been completely redecorated, but I was sure it was the same room. The view from the huge bay window overlooking Cassie's cherished rooftop garden hadn't changed. Leave it to my sadistic mother to stick me in the room where I'd watched Terrel die.

Three of Oweena's moons shined through the window. I pressed the release, but the thing had been permanently sealed. There wasn't even an emergency override. I looked around for something to smash the window with, but everything began spinning. Bile soured my throat.

Now you pay for your defiance this afternoon. As Cassie intensified the link, her meaning became clear. She was enjoying a romantic evening alone with Captain Constantien.

She locked the contact on, so I'd experience every moment of the seduction. I ran to the bathroom and vomited at the disgusting images and sensations forced upon my mind. I'd never even so much as kissed a guy yet. Now I was experiencing every gory detail of my mother having sex. I threw myself into the sonic shower with my clothes on, but it did nothing to weaken the link.

I felt his love for her through the increasingly deep scan she performed. She gripped those emotions and intensified them. His desire, love, devotion, and dependence multiplied until it consumed him. He became aware of the mental contact between them. I hoped by some miracle he might be able to escape. But he thought he was feeling her love for him, so he didn't mind the fact that his intended was Kobbi.

As a mixed breed, he'd suffered prejudice and discrimination all his life. It even turned out that his own great-grandmother was a Crean-Kobbi Human. The poor fool was happy to have found someone who'd be accepting of what he was. He thought the warm, loving feelings he sensed were from her. He had no idea they were his own feelings for her reflected back at him. He reveled in the intensity of the emotions, unaware that she searched his neural-network for his willpower. For a dozen or so breaths, she coaxed him into cooperating by sending him waves of pleasure and joy.

Captain Constantien seemed like a genuinely nice guy, and Cassie was about to destroy him. I had to do something. If I could pick up on his thoughts through the link, then perhaps he could pick up on mine if I projected them strongly enough. *Get away. Dashia. She's a Dashia.*

Cassie laughed at me. Nothing got through she didn't want him to receive. She ensnared his will and started to force the bond. The pressure became too intense for him. When he tried to pull away, she held him firm.

Mirra, easy. You're hurting me. Shock and fear shot through him when he discovered that he couldn't move or speak.

The churning in my stomach erupted again. I had to bail out of the shower and knelt over the toilet, vomiting repeatedly. The truth became undeniable to him now. He'd fallen prey to a Dashia. That struck him as rather ironic since he worked for the Kobbi containment unit.

He fought to hold on to his will, to not surrender all that he was. He managed to call out for help, but the effort cost him the last of his strength. And even if anyone heard, no one in the fetshous would care. No one but me.

Cassie ripped at the very core of his personality. I staggered to the door and pounded on it, yelling for someone to let me out. No one answered. Soon it no longer mattered. Constantien had surrendered.

Chapter 10

CASSIE CAME TO MY ROOM early the next morning. I charged her like an angry bull. She sidestepped my attack and hit me with a telepathic jab that left me sprawled on the floor. "Well, you obviously didn't adopt the Splendors' pacifist ways, did you? Now if you're done making a fool of yourself, you need to get dressed. You meet your instructors today."

"Like hell," I snarled. "I'm not going to cooperate with a damn thing you want."

"Did last night teach you nothing?"

"Sure it did. It taught me you're nothing but a psychic vampire. I'll never let you turn me into a Dashia like you!"

"My dear Twyla, you are a DeConnett. Of course, you'll take your proper place within the family. Stop trying to make 'Dashia' sound like a dirty word. It's a term for Kobbies with extraordinary telepathic gifts."

Ignoring my string of profanities, Cassie walked into my dressing chamber and returned with several outfits draped over her arm. "You think what I did to Constantien was wrong?" At my derisive snort, she continued. "Have you considered what he would have done to us once he discovered we were Kobbi? He's the head of the local Kobbi containment unit. What I did, I did to keep our family—including you and your sister—safe."

She held up one of the outfits, decided against it and held up another. "Besides, he's quite happy now. You can see for yourself at dinner tonight."

"You totally gutted his will. He doesn't have enough sense left to realize you've ruined him. Bet he'll figure it out real quick when you leave him, just like you left my father a complete mess."

"Your father?" she asked, seemingly taken aback. "What does this have to do with Ebon?"

I couldn't believe she couldn't make the connection between what she'd made me experience last night and what she'd done to my father. Then again, she seemed more concerned with picking out my clothes than with our conversation. I banged my fist on the wall to get her attention. "You destroyed him! You bemfornte, you tortured him. And I felt it. Every vreking time you messed with his mind, I FELT IT!"

"Stop using such language." She held up another outfit. "Now, I promise you that Ebon Milett was insane and was so long before we met. I tried to help him—"

"No! I know what I felt, and you definitely weren't trying to help."

"Perhaps your memories were twisted by the block. That is how the Dashia Hunter smuggled you away from me, isn't it?" She pretended not to care about the conversation as she approached with a Sian-blue blouse and floral skirt. "Just how much do you remember from when they took you?"

She hoped to gain some information about the Dashia Hunter who'd helped my father rescue me from her. At least I could honestly tell her I knew nothing about what had happened. A flash of disappointment crossed her face before she shrugged it off and handed me the outfit. "You'll look lovely in this."

She headed to the door but then turned back. "At some point you'll realize I'm not the holo-vid villain you make me out to be."

I let out a scream. "You killed Bill and Tina!"

"They kidnapped you! You're my daughter, and they took you from me." She set her hands on her hips. "If they'd just opened the door and handed you over, they'd both be alive ... Or if you'd come forward, of course. Where, exactly, were you?"

I sank back onto my bed, pierced through the heart. I threw my head into my hands and rocked in misery. In a gentle voice that I hardly recognized as Cassie's, she said, "I am sorry, Twyla. I hadn't realized they meant so much to you. I'd always assumed whoever had you treated you badly." She sat down beside me. "But let me ask you this: if they really did care about you, wouldn't they want you to have a decent education?"

I sprang from the bed. "Don't you dare use them to manipulate me. They wouldn't want me to have anything to do with becoming a Dashia!"

She put her hands out, palms up in a gesture of peace. "This has nothing to do with becoming a Dashia. We're talking about your general education requirements. After all, you're only 15 Standard years old, so by both planetary and Zartous law—"

"Just leave me alone." I wasn't about to agree to anything. "I can't think straight after what you did to me last night. Go away, and I'll think about it."

Her expression brightened. "Fine. You think about it. In fact, I'll tell you what: after meeting your instructors, if you find any of them or their curriculum objectionable, you can select something else to take."

I bowed my head and looked away. It was probably the best deal I was going to get. "Fine. I'll meet with them. But if there's anything Dashia about them or their lessons, I won't cooperate." I dumped the outfit she'd given me at her feet. "And I won't wear this crap."

"I don't care what you wear. What's important is you're being reasonable." She walked out the door sending me a wave of pleasure that dissipated before I could reject it.

•　　　•　　　•

A couple of the instructors were obviously loyal DeConnett minions. I told them to go to Hell. Since they didn't get that reference, I told them to take the first flight to Montara. Montara was home to the most notorious penal colonies in the Cluster. With average temperatures well over a hundred degrees and mines full of toxic gasses, it was literally Hell.

The rest of the instructors were just unlucky enough to have been hired by Cassie DeConnett. In fact, the last guy to come to my room was rather young and obviously in over his head. My rather rude, "What do you want?" completely flustered the poor Sian.

His feathers fluffed and he ducked his head. "I—I'm sorry, DeConnett daughter. I was told that you had some objection to your Standard Language instructor, so I was sent as an alternative."

I stepped forward fists clenched. "It's Twyla or Splendor daughter. Never call me a DeConnett."

He tucked his head into his shoulders like a baby bird afraid of having it bit off by a vicious predator. "Sorry. Sorry," he squawked. "I meant no offense ..." His voice trailed off as he stared at me.

The intensity of his gaze made me feel like a freak. "What are you staring at?"

He blinked his big avian eyes and bowed his head. "Pardon again. It's just that you look so much like your sister—"

That did it. "Get out! I don't care who you are or why you're here. Get the Hell out!"

His glacial blue complexion paled to a glossy white. He rushed forward. "Oh no, please. Don't send me away. Forgive my lack of manners. By the Fates, I've forgotten to even introduce myself." He bent his avian knees in the formal Sian greeting bow. "I am Dovain DeNorial. Of course, you may simply call me Dovain. No one ever uses my formal name. And you'd have to drop the 'De' anyway out of respect for—for the DeConnetts."

I cut him off with a loud snort.

He had blue-black crown feathers like Vance. However, his wings were golden instead of white. His big brown eyes reminded me of the Caldaxian mooring pup my father, Ebon, had given me when I was only four. They're kind of like large rabbits with the head of a harbor-seal.

Dovain's beautiful brown eyes darted about while he searched for something to say. He began rattling on nervously about how important language skills are and how he'd be honored to assist me. As he went on and on and on, he reminded me more and more of Vance. Dovain was taller and leaner, and his beak was more proportional to his face. Still, he made me think of a grownup version of Vance. The thought made me realize how much I missed my best friend.

The poor guy was so nervous I had to bite my lip to keep from laughing at him. Then again, he had every reason to be scared of me. To him, I was just another DeConnett. When he finally took a breath, I said, "I'll warn you. I hadn't spoken Standard for years until ... Well, until a few weeks ago."

He looked at me with a shy smile. "But you are willing to give me a chance?"

"Sure. Why not?"

His wings sagged with relief. "Thank the Fates. I really need this job. And your mother threatened to have my credentials revoked if I failed to convince you to let me teach you."

"I wouldn't thank your Sian gods just yet if I were you. I'm going to be way behind on the proficiency exam."

"Well, together, we should be able to have you caught up by the end of the term." He extended his hand and we grasped forearms. He gave me a real smile then, wide, open-beak, and silly, a Sian version of Vance's lopsided grin. Instinctively, I knew there was nothing false about the guy and couldn't help but feel sorry for this poor shmuck who'd gotten himself tangled up with the DeConnetts.

Cassie arrived and Dovain nearly tripped over his own feet in his rush to excuse himself. She ignored him and took in my baggy black pants and matching shirt with only a quirk of her brow. "Did you forget that we have dinner plans with Captain Constantien tonight?"

"I don't want anything to do with your target. I met with the damn tutors. Isn't that enough?"

"May I remind you that you're the one who made a big deal about what I'd done to him. Don't you want to see for yourself that he's perfectly all right?"

I bowed my head and motioned for her to lead the way. She gave my clothes another quick glance. I waited for her to suggest that I change. Instead, she just smiled and led me to the nearest lift. We went up and up and up. It turned out the restaurant where we were meeting Constantien, The Diamond Sky, was located at the junction of where Cassie's fetshous had a private link to one of the space elevators.

The Diamond Sky was one of the most beautiful places I'd ever seen. The panoramic vista from the massive windows was breathtaking. Dramatic space-scapes covered the interior walls climaxing in a ceiling that depicted the Paraxous Cluster itself. Every chair and table was a unique piece of art. I'd never eaten anywhere so fancy.

Although the clothing style varied according to race, all the other customers were dressed quite formally. Cassie fit right in with the little black number she wore. My black baggy clothes, not so much. We joined Daylight and Captain Constantien at a window-side table.

My sister looked me over and grimaced. *You let her come here dressed like that?* she asked our mother while getting up and giving me a hug of pretend affection.

Now Daylight, you must remember that she spent the last eight years on a Human Halo-world. You can't expect her to have any fashion sense.

I ignored their telepathic conversation. Instead, I stared out the window. The view was high enough that some wisps of clouds floated by, breaking up the landscape below. But not so high that the lights from the many fetshouses below weren't dazzling. Sunset painted the metallic, vertical cities in soft pinks and lavenders. Sians were silhouetted against a magnificent sky as they flew between the massive structures. Sure, there were a lot of big buildings on Earth, but nothing even close to this scale.

In the awe of the moment I wished Bill and Tina could see it. The spectacle instantly lost its appeal. Now all I saw was how different everything looked from Earth. Here everything was steel grey towers or white creostone, or brown dirt. There was nothing of nature left in the area. At least on Earth, even very urban areas like San Francisco had some green: trees lining the streets, parks and little front yards with flowerbeds.

Through my thoughts, I vaguely heard Captain Constantien as he kept up a pleasant flow of conversation with Cassie and

Daylight. Several times he tried to include me, but I didn't feel like talking. Then again, I finally decided, there was no reason to be rude to the guy. After all, he was a victim here same as me. He just didn't know it yet.

So when he asked what I did today, I told him I'd met with my tutors. He smiled, pleased to have finally hit upon a subject that drew more than a one-syllable answer from me. "Oh, to be young and have a universe of options before you! When I was your age, I studied to be a pilot. Thought it sounded so romantic to fly all over the Cluster. What classes are you taking?"

Making it clear I was talking to him and not Cassie or Daylight, I said, "Just the mandatory general ed. stuff. Primary language, which is Standard for me, though it's more of a second language for me now."

He smiled encouragingly, "Oh really? You're doing just fine." I had to work not to smile back at him. The last thing I needed was to befriend Cassie's target. It was too late to save him, so best to keep my distance. "What else?" he prompted.

"Secondary language, which will be introductory Ruslo."

"Of course," he said. Ruslo was the other main language of the Paraxous and was considered the language of trade, diplomacy, and culture by many races.

"Then math, Paraxous Cluster History, and Government." I finished the list quickly to end the subject. I took my first bite of the food and fought to hide my pleasure. I had no clue what it was, but damn, it was amazing. While nothing was better than one of Tina's home-cooked meals, this was culinary art. Of course, I refused to let my pleasure show and worked to make sure Cassie didn't pick it up empathically.

Continuing to ignore her, I confided to Constantien. "I was a bit disappointed that there weren't any computer classes."

Daylight swallowed a chuckle. *Oh, you've got to be kidding. Like you're going to be allowed anywhere near a computer.*

I glanced at my bare wrist. I was the only one at the table—probably in the entire restaurant—not wearing a computer interface band. Cassie pretended interest. "Perhaps next quarter." *If you behave.*

"Are you interested in computers as a potential career?" Captain Constantien inquired.

"Maybe." I shrugged.

"Personally, I hate computers. Having all that stuff floating around in cyberspace can come back to bite you." He sat back with his drink in hand. Like most Sentagils, he was gifted in the art of storytelling and had entertained Cassie and Daylight with several whoppers already this evening. At least the bond hadn't destroyed that part of him.

"This one time," he began, "when I was in officer training, I'd been up all night working on a report. A fellow candidate sent me a copy of a recent policy change along with his rather scathing remarks. I wrote up my own thoughts on the subject, bashing the mid-level bureaucrats responsible, and sent it back. Only I had so many applications open, somehow I managed to send my friend the report … and my reply with the critique to my instructor."

"Oh no," I gasped.

Seeing he'd gotten my interest, he went on with a wink. "Of course, I try to recall the message. That doesn't work. So I call the instructor and tell him to disregard the first message and that the assignment is in the second message. But stupid me, I sound so panicked, now he's curious. He reads my first message while keeping me on the line. I must have gone white, the way he smirked at me. Then he proceeds to tell me that me and my friend have to rewrite our assessment of the new policy and give a presentation to our class that afternoon. Now I have to tell my friend … my Katian friend, that I'd broken one of the most important rules of surviving military life."

"Don't get noticed," I finished the old military axiom that was apparently just as true in the Paraxous as on Earth.

Constantien lifted his cup in a silent toast and continued, "She chased me all over the dorms, trying to beat the tracky dung out of me, while the other candidates cheered her on."

I laughed despite myself.

•   •   •

That night I drifted off to sleep thinking that maybe I had a bit of a reprieve. Cassie would be busy with Constantien for a while, and it seemed he'd be fine until she dumped him. In the meantime, maybe I could find a way out of this mess.

Then I dreamed of Terrel. He was teaching me to play rochi, which became my favorite card game. I'd bug him to play constantly, and he'd take the time for at least one game every day. The happy memories, however, were soon overshadowed by his prolonged death. I relived lying there next to him waiting for him to wake up, only to realize he was dead.

[[Henshe,]] I woke myself by whispering the Ruslo word for the love and bond between siblings. Only, of course, Terrel wasn't there to hear it.

Cassie had waited too long to have him treated. Then a memory stirred. That wasn't exactly how it had happened. She had offered him treatment. He'd refused. He said the price was too high. Fates only knew what she had demanded. Whatever it was, my brother died instead of paying it.

Terrel's voice now played in my head, telling me not to trust any truce Cassie offered. It told me to get out of there. I bolted from bed. No plan. No idea where I'd go. I just had to get away.

The door and windows were locked. The room's control panel and computer interface had been disabled, so I had no way to override the locks. The configuration of the room's built-in furniture left me with nothing I could use to pry or smash.

I spent a half an hour clawing at the door's control panel but only succeeded in tearing my fingernails off at the quick. The datapad I'd been given for school stuff was nothing but a basic reader/writer with no networking capabilities. As far as escaping went, it was only good for one thing. Gripping it with both hands, I swung it with all my strength at the door's control panel. It smashed through the cover with a sprinkle of sparks.

Wiping the blood from my fingertips onto my dark pants, I went to work on the controls. A couple minutes later, the door opened. No alarm sounded. I stepped forward only to find Cassie leaning against the wall across from me. A Prigta guard stood beside her.

I had never been that close to a Prigta before. Nor had I ever wanted to be. The beings are sometimes called pig-rocks, and they do resemble huge pigs made of stone. But mostly they're called that because they stink. In the Paraxous they're often used as bodyguards because of their rock-hard exoskeletons as well as their size; this one was about the size of a Volkswagen Beetle.

Cassie shook her head and made a "tsk, task" sound. "Twyla, I thought we had an arrangement." She turned to Daylight, who trudged up the hall toward us, obviously unhappy at being awakened so early. *So, what do you think your sister's punishment should be?* Cassie asked her.

You know best. To me Daylight snorted with disgust. "I can't believe you're so stupid. Did you really think you'd be allowed to just walk out of here?"

That's not the point, Cassie flashed before I could come up with some smart-ass remark. *She broke our deal.*

"I never made any vreking deal with you," I spat, refusing to have this conversation telepathically.

She huffed like a mother dealing with an unreasonable child. "Yes, you did. We agreed: you behave yourself and we postpone your Dashia training until you've completed your basic ed."

"You're a vreking liar, c'assie!" I shouted, purposely slurring the informal use of her common name that she hated. "I never agreed to—" My airway clamped shut.

Cassie stepped forward with a deadly glare. "It is Cassiopeia, Madam DeConnett, or Mother. And I have asked you repeatedly not to use such language. It's unfit for a lady."

I laughed, which with no air came out as soundless hiccups.

"You may not be much of a lady now," she responded, her voice full of loathing. "However, by the time I'm through with you, you will be."

She kept my airway shut. I sank to my knees, telepathically hurling curses in English, Standard and Ruslo at her. When I ran out of those, I resorted to the Katian swear words I'd learned from Nina.

Cassie retaliated with images of me as her brain damaged, Human pet. She wasn't going to let me breathe again until I stopped cussing.

Might as well just kill me, I shot back and started my list of vulgarities over again.

Never!

Why the hell not? Just kill me. It'd make your life easier.

Daylight suddenly took interest. *Twyla, don't be an idiot. She won't kill you. She'll make an example of you. She'll make you feel it as your brain cells die one at a time.*

To our mother she said with a yawn, "So, I'd rather not be awakened in the middle of the night again. Can we, please, just assign her a guard or something?"

Cassie didn't release her mental grip on my throat as she replied sweetly to Daylight. "Of course, dear." She looked at the Prigta next to her. "You're in charge of her guard detail from now on." She crouched down beside me as my vision went gray. "Since you broke our agreement, it's only fair that I make some modifications to the deal as well."

Chapter 11

CASSIE'S MODIFICATION TO OUR DEAL turned out to be adding cooking lessons to my schedule, which hardly seemed like a punishment to me. I loved to cook. However, I quickly learned that food was one of the tools Dashia use to seduce their targets. It was a two-pronged attack. First, the pleasurable smells and tastes placed their target in a romantic mood. Second, the food was laced with drugs that made the victim more susceptible to bonding.

As if that wasn't bad enough, my lessons were taught by HelaShia, the Katian Dashia-in-training who'd hung all over Cameron and later threatened to help me bathe. She hated me almost as much as I hated her. Apparently, she'd gotten in a lot of trouble for letting my friends get away. Fortunately, she was forbidden from ripping my guts out like she obviously wanted to.

Also fortunate was the fact that everyone assumed since I'd been raised on Earth, I didn't know the first thing about cooking. This meant we started with kitchen basics, and I didn't have to worry about trying to drug anyone.

The other modification, my Prigta guard, was more of a problem. It followed me everywhere. One morning it showed up several minutes early to escort me to my lessons. I was facing the window with my back to the door and the cameras, contemplating the inscription on the triple heart pendent my parents had given me.

Usually I kept the necklace tucked in a makeshift pocket I'd slit into my bra. No doubt if Cassie found out what it meant to me, she'd use it as leverage. I managed to tuck the necklace back away without the Prigta noticing. But the scare made me hate the thing even more.

Everything about the huge creature irritated me. The grating sound it made while lumbering on four legs. Its expressionless, pupil-less, gemlike eyes that gave no hint life. Worst of all was its body odor. Prigtas smell like sulfur, and with my recently heightened senses, it made me want to puke.

The Prigta guard brought me to the kitchen even though it was too early for my cooking lesson. HelaShia snarled at the sight of me. Her fingers flexed, sheathing and unsheathing her claws while her tail slashed the air. Her fur coat and mane had been recently dyed in a rainbow of colors that were bright and garish.

"Please, don't tell me you actually paid for such a blixed-up dye job," I said, looking over her neon fur.

She charged forward. Her glittery, neon-blue mane stood on end. She flexed her claws within a few millimeters of my face. I could feel them brush across the fine hairs of my cheek without actually touching my skin. Her top lip curled, revealing freshly sharpened fangs. "Do not provoke me, DeConnett daughter," she snarled. "Your mother has ordered that you assist me with making her breakfast."

I swatted her hand away from my face. "You've got to be kidding. Cassie's not stupid enough to trust me with her food."

"Madam DeConnett trusts me to ensure you don't do anything to sabotage her breakfast with Captain Constantien." She motioned over to one of the counters where a datapad sat displaying a recipe. "Now while you prep the basic ingredients, I'll be right here mixing the special ones. Remember, I will be watching you closely, DeConnett daughter, so don't do anything foolish."

"Stop calling me that. It's Twyla or Splendor. And you can tell c'assie c'onnett to take the first flight to Montara. I'm not about to help with—"

HelaShia backhanded me. I crashed against an open cabinet, knocking a bunch of jars and bottles to the floor. Then she swept my legs out from under me, sending me to the floor with a thump.

She leaned down, leering over me. "You will show respect. And I will address you as your mother has instructed. And since she is the daughter of the third Elder of the DeConnett family, DeConnett daughter is quite appropriate. So as tempted as I might be to call you t'wyla ..." She hit the "t" with a spit in my face. "I will refrain from doing so out of respect for your mother."

She straightened up, towering over me with her chest and mane puffed. "And you will remember that I am HelaShia of Clan Fosh. You will not challenge me again, ch'ild."

She spit in my face again. I couldn't let that go. I spotted a bottle of nably on the floor among the stuff knocked from the cabinet. The sweetener is used to create thick candy coatings on pastries. Once out of the sure-warm bottle, the sticky substance hardens within seconds. I grabbed the bottle and squirted it all over her newly dyed fur.

She peered down at me in disbelief. She was so stunned, in fact, I was able to squirt some in her face before she knocked the bottle from my hands. In that instant, I knew the Katian was about to kill me.

My Prigta guard inserted itself between us. It shook its massive, boulder-like head at HelaShia as she ranted in Ruslo. I caught the word [[kill]] as well as the Katian phrase, [[I'll feed upon your heart while it still beats in your chest.]]

Suddenly she stepped back, sheathed her claws and bowed. There was no way a Katian would ever show a Pig-rock such deference. Cassie's voice came from the doorway behind me. "Really HelaShia, are you completely incapable of handling my daughter? I'm so disappointed."

Cassie stepped near, waving the Prigta out of her way. She inspected HelaShia from mane to tail. Her noses crinkled with disapproval. "You're a mess. Get out of my sight."

HelaShia hurried away like a freshly cuffed kitten.

Cassie called after her, "Oh, and I do hope you have some decent clothes to wear."

HelaShia turned at the door and regarded Cassie with a quizzical look, but didn't dare speak. Cassie laughed at her as she explained. "You'll have to shave your fur to get that off. We can't have you running around here with your shameful nakedness showing for all to see. While you're at it, you might as well shave your face and mane just to make sure you get it all. That way you'll remember never to disappoint me again."

HelaShia wanted to protest so badly, she shook. There were other ways to remove the nably, and to be mane-free was a horrific humiliation for a Katian. Her lip twitched, but she carefully resisted showing fang to the daughter of the Third Elder DeConnett.

Cassie cocked her head as if daring her to say something. HelaShia just bowed and started to slink away. A young Katian girl rushed up to her. HelaShia started to shoo her away, with nervous glances back toward Cassie.

[[No. Let your daughter stay,]] Cassie ordered in Ruslo. [[It would be good for her to learn …]] I didn't understand the rest of what she said. However, the joy in HelaShia's eyes made it clear I wasn't going to like what was coming.

Cassie sent HelaShia off with a wave. I stuck my tongue out at her as she left. Mistake. Now Cassie's attention was focused on me. Slowly, somewhat theatrically, she pulled a metal chain from her pocket. "Are you simply incapable of behaving yourself?" She continued before I could give her some smart-ass answer. "Never mind. It doesn't matter. This will help you learn."

The chain had a cluster of small spikes on one end, and she intended to put the damn thing around my neck. A melter had fallen to the floor next me. I grabbed it, flipped it to max heat and scrambled to my feet, brandishing the melter like a weapon.

The Prigta and Cassie's two Katian guards rushed forward. Cassie motioned them back. "Don't interfere. My daughter obviously requires a lesson in obedience."

She turned back to lock gazes with me. *Lesson one: Power … struggle. I have all the power, and you have all the struggle.*

Suddenly, it felt like an artery in my head exploded. My arms fell limply at my sides. Cassie held me frozen. The melter hung from my fingertips, singeing my pants and burning the side of my thigh. The anguish of my flesh frying surpassed anything I'd ever known. The smell made me sick to my stomach.

"Now stop being so stubborn and put that thing away," she said, putting on her concerned mother routine. But she refused to release me, so I could obey.

HelaShia's daughter came forward looking from where the melter burned its way into my thigh to my frozen face covered in sweat. In a high pitched, prepubescent, kitten of a voice, she pleaded with me, "What are you doing? Put it away! Put it away! Holy Makers!"

The poor girl had no clue what was going on. Even though she had to be at least part Kobbi for her mother to be a Dashia-in-training, she was too young for her telepathic powers to have manifested yet. Her ears went flat. Her bright green eyes bulged, and her tail tucked tightly as she begged me to do what Cassie ordered. Finally, I couldn't take her desperate cries anymore. *All right, Cassie. Enough is enough.*

She placed the metal chain around my neck and fastened it. *Now, enough is enough.*

She stepped out of reach and released the link. I dropped the melter and let out a choked groan of pain. In that instant, the metal collar adjusted to an uncomfortably tight fit. With a stab that drove the air from my lungs, it inserted a spike into my spine. I tried to yank the collar off, but it was now a solid metal ring with a rod embedded into the back of my neck.

Cassie ordered one of her bodyguards to call for a med-tech and sent HelaShia's daughter to fetch the med-kit. To me she asked calmly, "Are you ready to listen?"

When I only glared at her, she sighed. "This is important, Twyla. I'm through fighting with you. I simply don't have time to deal with your tantrums. From now on we'll be using the obedience collar."

A steak of pain rushed down the center-line of my body making me forget about my burnt thigh. I sank to my knees. *That was the first level. I can ignite it with just a thought. So think twice before misbehaving again.*

I plopped down on floor in the middle of the mess I'd made and curled into a ball with my back against the cabinet, totally defeated. Cassie ordered the house-bot to clean up the area around me. HelaShia's daughter returned with a med-kit. Cassie took a small bottle from it and crouched down beside me. She placed a hand on my shoulder as if consoling me.

"This will help until the med-techs get here. Just hold still." She sprayed the charred area. The fabric of my clothes bubbled away, and a pink layer of fake skin covered the red and black injury. "Better?" Cassie asked softly, almost tenderly.

I nodded numbly. A warm wave of empathic energy washed through me—the pain of the burn completely forgotten. In fact, all my pain, both physical and emotional, vanished. Cassie's approval made the hurt go away. As long as I did what she wanted, it would remain that way.

Beneath the surge of empathic energy, I felt Cassie's sense of victory. She really believed that she'd be able to control me from now on. The worst part was, she might very well be right. All I cared about was not returning to the pain. Nothing else mattered. Even my grief at the loss of my mom and dad had begun to fade.

At the thought of Bill and Tina, something in me snapped. "Get out of my head," I growled through gritted teeth. I batted the little house-bot at her.

She dodged the thing as it flew by and smashed into the wall. She ignited the collar. I lunged at her despite the pain.

I swiped at her sparkling shoes and finely tailored slacks. She jumped back and increased our link and the collar's pain level.

I won't cooperate! You're going to have to kill me! I screamed telepathically since she'd shut off my airway.

At first, she assumed it was a bluff. She scanned deeper only to discover that I really did want to die. For some reason that pissed her off even more. In a flash, her mind betrayed the fact that she was not allowed to kill me. The DeConnetts had invested a fortune in my development. Cassie cranked up the pain level on the collar in response to my trespassing on her thoughts.

Yes, my dear daughter. You are not only a Kobbi. You are an experiment meant to create the perfect DeConnett. With your added abilities, you could be the greatest Dashia of all time.

I clung on to the fact that she couldn't kill me even as she suffocated me.

Do not assume the fact that we need you alive will help you. There are things worse than death. With a shrug, she said, "Well, if you're not going to cooperate, you're of no use to us." *Except as breeding stock.*

She was considering cutting off my air until I was brain dead. She didn't need my brain to use my body for breeding. There were indeed some things worse than death. Despite my resolve not to beg, I found myself doing just that. *Please, no. Please. Not that.*

My chest heaved with breaths that could suck in nothing. The hypoxia made me drowsy despite the continued electrical shock from the collar, but I refused to pass out. I had to know if I'd still have any of my brain left when I woke up. *Please, Cassie. Not that. Anything but that.*

She released me with a smile. "I knew you could be reasonable," I heard her say as everything went black.

●　　　●　　　●

The next morning, I lay awake in my bed, afraid to move. My stomach heaved like an angry ocean. My body felt like it'd been hit by a Prigta at full roll. My everything hurt.

Speaking of pig-rocks, my damn guard began to take shape at the edge of my still blurry vision. It extended its gelatinous neck to look at me with its sapphire eyes from across the room. I wondered how hard it would be to pluck those gem-like eyes out. They'd be worth a fortune on the black-market. I'd probably have to kill the thing in order to escape anyway. Why not make some credits while I was at it?

Cassie's voice came over the comm. "I'm glad you're awake. If you agree to attend your classes without causing trouble, I'll offer you a truce, again." There was no challenge in her tone. Even so, I wanted to tell her what she could do with her truce. Then she added, "Just for today, Twyla. Or are you too stubborn to admit you need time to recover?"

"Fine. Truce. But just for today," I heard myself saying. I did need a break, and she'd said "attend my classes" not "participate." So I went to the office of each of my tutors and napped while they droned on.

After my last lesson, I headed for the lift that would take me to my room. My ever-annoying Prigta guard motioned for me to go the opposite direction. I crossed my arms over my chest and stood my ground. "I'm done with my lessons. I'm going to my room."

It swung its head toward the opposite corridor and pointed with its front pincher-like claws. I ignored it and marched toward the lift. It tucked and rolled past me, blocking the lift door. This close, its sulfur body odor made my eyes water. I plugged my nose with one hand and fanned the other in front of my face. "Holy Makers, don't you ever bathe?"

It remained tucked and rolled a bit toward me. I stepped back, afraid the stupid thing would squash my toes. It edged forward some more. "You wouldn't dare," I stammered in disbelief, taking several more steps back.

Then it began to roll in earnest. Slowly at first, but picking up speed until I was forced to turn and run. That damn 350 kilogram living-rock herded me at a full roll from one end of the fetshous to the other. I looked over my shoulder, sure the thing would miscalculate and run me over. I smacked right into the door at the end of the corridor.

The Prigta came to a stop a couple meters away. It untucked its head and all its extremities. If it had been possible for the creature's stony face to smile, I would have sworn it was smirking at me. The comm display for the door read, "Sir VerVum." To be referred to as a "Sir" or a "De" within the DeConnett's fetshous meant the guy had to be damned important. Was Cassie already done with Captain Constantien? Was I about to meet her next victim?

I pressed the comm, ready and wanting a fight. Instead of the normal door buzzer, a beautiful melody played. The door opened to reveal a fully-equipped music studio. Seated at a triple-layered synthesizer-like instrument was Sir Venor VerVum, premier Cantor of the Paraxous Cluster. I may have returned to the Cluster only a few weeks ago, but even I'd heard of him. Truth be told, I loved his voice and music so much he'd become one of my singing idols. The Katian had more hit songs than he had whiskers—and he had a lot of whiskers.

Chapter 12

SIR VENOR VERVUM WAS by far the most flamboyant Katian I'd ever seen in person. I'd assumed that his outrageous costumes were just that—costumes. Apparently not. Here he was wearing a piece of holographic art instead of clothes. It swirled with a spectacular galaxy-scape that dazzled the eyes. His obviously cosmetically-enhanced whiskers reached a good two feet in length and stood straight out, which was the current style for Katian entertainers. Instead of a natural gray coat, his fur was shiny and metallic. The same silver fur crowned his head in an outrageously huge, puffed-out mane and majestic ruff that glittered.

"Are you staring at me, ch'ild?" Sir VerVum's glare implied I'd be his next meal if I didn't stop.

Though I knew staring was considered a challenge in Katian culture, I couldn't help myself. After all, this was *the* Venor VerVum. It seemed impossible that he was really here.

He leaned back from the synthesizer and appraised me with a sneer. I regained my senses and lowered my gaze respectfully. [[You're late,]] he snapped.

I felt compelled to apologize though I'd known nothing about the appointment. I gave the damn Pig-rock a glare for not telling me who it was that had been waiting for me. Then again, it was possible the creature had never even heard of Sir VerVum. The nearest thing to singing Prigtas have is seismic vibration, which is banned from public places on most worlds as noise pollution.

[[Are you coming in? Or do you intend to merely darken my doorway?]] Sir VerVum growled the common Katian phrase in Ruslo.

I hurried in and postured submissively: hands out, palms up and head bowed. I decided not to risk offending him with my poor Ruslo and replied in Standard. "So sorry, Sir VerVum. No one informed me of your arrival. I am humbled and honored by your presence." I had been taught the proper way to greet a Katian superior but had refused to use it until now.

His lip twitched in distain. The phrase didn't translate well into Standard, and most Katians disliked using the fairly guttural language. Having to speak something so ugly was considered demeaning for a high-ranking artist like Sir VerVum. "I have agreed to listen to you sing, child. If you are worthy, I'll teach you. But I will not waste my time on a sour voice. So be sure to impress me."

Holy Makers! This is an audition. My mind screamed in panic. Here was my chance to have private lessons from one of the best singers in the entire Cluster. Cassie was obviously up to something. It should have worried me. But I couldn't get past the awe of meeting such a celebrity.

"Well, child? Your mother claims you have a tri-level voice. Sing something."

I stood there like an idiot, jaw flapping. Sir VerVum threw his hands in the air. He glared at the camera on the wall. [[The child has no tongue. How can she possibly sing? Our deal is done. She had her chance.]] He waved me away dismissively.

Cassie's voice came over the comm. [[Oh, she has a tongue. A very sharp one when she chooses to use it.]]

I flinched at hearing her voice, but my fear turned to anger. More to the camera than Sir VerVum, I snapped. "Sure I've got a tongue. I just refuse to perform for m'adam c'onnett."

With parental frustration in her voice, she sighed, "I'm trying to do something nice for you. Does everything have to be a battle with you?"

"Well, yeah."

If Cassie wanted me to learn to sing, that meant she thought it'd make me a more effective Dashia. On the other hand, music had always been my haven. I'd be getting something I needed out of this deal. To Sir VerVum, I resumed a submissive posture and said humbly, "It would be my honor to audition for you, Master Cantor. Just as soon as the comm is off."

Venor tapped the comm control, then motioned to me with exaggerated flourish. "So sing, child."

"A cappella?"

"How else am I supposed to judge your cords? Now sing."

There were only a few songs I could sing without the music. They were all Earth folksongs. They wouldn't work in Standard, so I sang in English. By the chorus, memories of my parents completely overwhelmed me. A tear rolled down to my chin—the first tear I'd managed since their death.

I stopped singing.

"What am I doing?" I turned to face the camera sure Cassie would still be watching. I made the rudest gesture I knew. It depicted grabbing someone's genitals and yanking them. It meant the same as "vrek you."

I stalked toward the door, but Venor's voice caught me. With no lead up, he sang in a full cantor. The effect of his perfectly harmonized voices touched something deep within me. Since cantors are rare and their effect can't be recorded, I'd never experienced it before. I'd heard a few partial cantors. Compared to Sir VerVum, their efforts sounded like stray tomcats yowling.

This was pure beauty that hypnotized and healed the soul. All the tension left my body. It didn't matter that the lyrics were in Felniez, a Katian language I'd only learned a few curses in from Nina. The melody carried my spirit far from this prison. For a moment, I was free. The rush of being in love—though not with anyone in particular—gave me the strength to want to live again.

He stopped and I crashed like a ship that lost its grav-repulser. "I'm not here to entertain you, child," he snapped. "I'm here to judge whether or not you're worth teaching. Now, why did you just insult me by trying to walk out?"

"You're here to help my bemfornte of a mother turn me into a Dashia!" My volume increased with every word.

Sir VerVum sat back and folded his arms across his chest, unimpressed by my temper. "You're as hot-headed as your flame-red mane, aren't you?"

"She killed my co-parents!"

"And because she killed them, you won't sing for me?"

"I won't have any part of becoming a Dashia!"

He snarled. His midnight blue eyes sparked and fixed on me as prey. "So you think *I'm* a Dashia?"

I gasped. "No. No, sir. Of course not."

"Good." He let the snarl relax. "Cantoring and being a Dashia are two totally different things. Few Kobbies have the gift, just as few Katians have it." He stretched, flexing his fingers causing his claws to show and gave a big yawn that revealed his dagger-like teeth. Then he fixed me with a glare. "Child, your anger has you so twisted up, you're fighting all the wrong battles."

He grabbed a datapad, jabbed at the settings, then thrust it at me. The screen displayed the lyrics to a Katian folksong I'd heard a few times while working in the kitchen. It was the Ruslo version instead of the Felniez. It was a fairly simple song, and he played the melody on the synthesizer, so I decided to give it a try.

After just a few lines, Venor snatched the datapad from me. "Your Ruslo is atrocious."

He changed the selection back to Standard, handed it back, and motioned for me to try again. Halfway through my next attempt, he stopped me again. "Not nearly what I'd hoped for … But not as bad as I feared."

His next words cut my growing hope short. "However, there's no way I can teach someone who cannot pronounce Ruslo properly. Surely, you can't expect to split your voice in Standard? That's simply too much to expect from even an expert coach like me. How on Montara did you manage to grow up in the Cluster without learning proper Ruslo?"

They were rhetorical questions, but I heard myself answering anyway. "I didn't. I mean I didn't grow up in the Cluster. I grew up on a planet out in the Halo." The truth was Cassie had tried to teach me Ruslo when I was a little girl, but I just didn't get it. Not that I was about to tell him that. Let him think I was just ignorant and could be taught.

I became desperate for this chance to escape from reality. Then the memory of Mom singing "You are my Sunshine" played in my head. While it might not have been in Ruslo, she made the melody beautiful. I opened my mouth and let her voice sing through me.

When I finished, Sir VerVum blinked his midnight-blue cat eyes and asked with an amused lilt, "Well, why didn't you just sing like that in the first place?" He gave me a firmly dismissive wave. "All right. Go away. Your mother and I have terms to discuss."

Chapter 13

CASSIE FIRED MY RUSLO INSTRUCTOR the next day and had Dovain take over teaching me the soft, flowing language I could never wrap my tongue around. A standard Paraxous month passed with me going through the motions, biding my time. It was pretty much impossible for me to escape on my own. My only hope was contacting the Dashia Hunter without Cassie finding out. So, the next forty days of my captivity passed in relative calm.

Besides biding my time, there were other reasons I cooperated with my lessons. First, as long as I attended my classes, Cassie kept her promise and left me alone. Second, I didn't want to lose my singing lessons. Third, I actually enjoyed working with Dovain on my study of Standard Literature and Critical Writing Skills. He made the subject interesting enough to let me forget reality for a while. Even the Ruslo lessons weren't as painful with Dovain as my teacher.

The timid Sian became the closest thing to a friend I had in the fetshous, though I was careful not to show it. I hoped he might eventually become an ally. Between my time with Dovain and my singing lessons, life was almost bearable. Those golden hours with Sir VerVum did a lot to help me recover from the nightmares I had nearly every night.

Besides reliving my parents' death, I started having dreams about turning into my mother. The revelation that I was the product of some DeConnett experiment messed with my head pretty bad. I was a freak among freaks. Worse, the DeConnetts obviously planned on using me to further their interests. No matter what that plan was, it had to be bad. Very bad. I had to get away before that happened.

I wasn't sure how to recall the Hunter's contact code without tipping off Cassie. Her mental invasions had become fairly rare, but accessing my eidetic memory might draw her attention. Then one night after reliving my parents' murder, the dream continued. It flashed to the library in San Francisco when Vance had checked for messages from the Dashia Hunter, and I saw the information I needed to make contact. However, the dream also reminded me that this Hunter had ordered me killed if capture was unavoidable. Would he or she help me, or simply execute me along with the other DeConnetts?

Does it matter? Death's better than becoming a Dashia. I decided I'd take the chance. Anything to get the hell out of there.

Thankfully, Cassie no longer paid any attention to my nightmares, so she didn't bother scanning my thoughts that night. I committed the contact info to memory then buried it. If I was careful not to let it come to my surface thoughts, maybe sooner or later I'd get a chance to access an interplanetary comm-line. At least then, there'd be some hope of rescue.

Okay, no doing anything to attract Cassie's attention, I promised myself.

My promise lasted until that night. I cut through the dining-room on my way to the kitchen. Constantien sat alone at the dining table. His spiritless eyes were a haunting reminder of my father's.

Don't get involved, I warned myself. *He's not your problem.* Yet I couldn't help but wonder: if someone had tried to help Ebon, would he have been able to escape Cassie's control before she'd destroyed him?

Keep walking, I told myself. I owed it to my parents to get myself rescued or at least die in some sort of escape attempt. I couldn't throw away my best chance at getting away by doing something stupid. And interfering with Cassie's target, who'd already been bonded, definitely qualified as stupid.

I reached the kitchen door but couldn't keep myself from looking back. Captain Constantien sat silent and stone still. Tears streamed down his face and dripped onto his perfectly pressed uniform.

"Are you all right?" I asked and immediately regretted it. Of course, he wasn't all right. He'd been telepathically raped and stripped of his will.

"She won't be joining me for dinner, will she?" His flat, emotionless tone belied the anguish that reached me.

My mental shields snapped on. *Walk away,* I told myself. But I went to him anyway. "Look. This is going to hurt like hell. But if she's done with you, you should be glad. Get the hell out of here while there's still something of you left."

He gaped at me like I was insane. "I—I can't live without her. She made sure of that."

Was that bitterness in his voice? Perhaps there was something of him left to save after all. I glanced around the room, glaring at the Prigta and the cameras that monitored my every move. "Why don't we take a walk?" I suggested, taking Constantien by the arm.

The captain pulled away. He sounded like a stubborn, pouting child as he said, "She said to meet her here."

"Fine. Wait here all night for all I care." I intended to leave it at that, but for some reason I added, "Meanwhile she's out in the garden with some new flame she's kindling right under your nose."

He sprang from his seat. "No! You're lying!"

I was, but was careful not to show it. "Come see for yourself."

Once we were outside, the Prigta hung back far enough to allow us some privacy. I kept my voice low, hoping it wouldn't be picked up by any monitors. "Listen, Captain. I'm only going to get one chance to say this. My real father was bonded just like you. My mother chewed him up and spit him out. But he survived. He made it through mental reconstruction and is back on active duty. You still have a chance ..."

Constantien started shaking his head and backing away. I grabbed him by the arm and stepped closer. "The sooner you get away, the better off you are."

He stammered denials and tried to pull his arm free. The Prigta moved in to intervene. Before I let Constantien go, I added, "She's just about done with you anyways. Believe me, you don't want to give her the chance to recoup the energy she spent bonding you. It's brutal."

He jerked his arm away and ran for the door. "You'll end up a mental vegetable!" I yelled, no longer caring who heard. I was getting through to him, I could feel it.

He disappeared down the hall. I went to follow, but the Prigta blocked me. It stared at me with unblinking eyes glittering in the sunlight. As far as I knew, Prigtas were incapable of facial expressions, but I could have sworn there was disbelief in its gem-like eyes.

I glanced back down the hallway as the Pig-rock shook its head in warning. With a dejected sigh, I let my shoulders sag. There was going to be hell to pay, and it might all be for nothing. There was nothing else I could do but hope Captain Constantien kept on running until he was long gone.

Chapter 14

I SPENT THAT NIGHT WAITING for Cassie's punishment. The penalty for interfering with her target was bound to be bad. By the time the Prigta came to escort me to my morning lessons, I'd worried myself sick. Then the Prigta led me to Sir VerVum's studio instead of the kitchen for my cooking class.

Okay, here we go. She's going to take away my singing lessons, I thought, bracing myself.

To my surprise, the Cantor Master sat relaxed at his synthesizer, and Cassie was nowhere in sight. "Tell me, please, why your mother felt it necessary to schedule your lesson this hour of the morning," Sir VerVum demanded by way of a greeting.

"How should I know?" I answered with a shrug.

He quirked a whiskered brow at me. "Really? Your mother gives me the rest of the week off, and you have no idea why?"

The blood drained from my face and I had to sit down. "Holy Maker, what do you think she's going to do to me?"

"How should I know?" he said, throwing my words back at me. Then he folded his arms across his chest and twitched his nose, making his long whiskers wave. "Just what kind of stupidity have you indulged in, child?"

My cheeks flushed. "I tried to help Captain Constantien," I muttered.

His whiskers went into a frenzy as he drew back in shock. His eyes went wide in disbelief and then rolled in disgust. "While I knew you weren't the brightest star in the Cluster, I never dreamed you were that foolish. Holy Makers child, what possessed you to do such a thing?"

"Seemed like the right thing to do at the time."

He released a huff and gave his fur coat a good shake. The holographic seascape he wore went into a roll. "Hopefully you realize you risked your life for nothing. Next time, think before doing something so reckless."

With that, he began my lesson. Nothing else was said on the subject. When we were done, I gave the traditional bow of respect from student to master, but then hesitated. I didn't want to leave the relative safety of his studio. Sir VerVum waved me away, but under his breath he muttered the traditional Katian parting given before battle.

I recognized it from the bootleg Paraxous holo-vids Vance and I used to secretly watch. In essence it meant, "May the Makers grant you the strength to stay true to yourself."

Though he might not have expected me to understand the words, I clung to them as the Prigta escorted me to Dovain's office.

The office was empty, so it seemed I was safe for a little longer. My Prigta guard took its usual position just outside the door. I sat at the desk, wondering how a nice guy like Dovain had gotten himself tangled up with the DeConnetts.

The guy sure was no Dashia in training. The Sian didn't have a drop of Kobbi blood. I'd discovered soon after my arrival that I could sense other Kobbies. Their mental energy made my skin prickle. Dovain also wasn't wealthy or powerful enough to merit being a DeConnett target. So what did that leave?

Why would the guy have possibly agreed to serve the DeConnetts? Next to Vance, Dovain was one of the most open and unassuming people I'd ever met. In fact, his mannerisms were so Vance-like it wrung my heart. But based on his constant state of alarm, he knew what and who Cassie was. Maybe he was just an ordinary guy trying to scrape out a living in the middle of a Cluster-wide, war-induced depression.

After five minutes of waiting, I buzzed the comm to the door that divided the office from his apartment. Maybe he hadn't been told about the schedule change. No one answered.

After pacing for a few minutes, I stopped and peered out the clear door leading to the balcony. I pictured Dovain fluttering in for a landing, apologizing profusely for his tardiness. I wished I could just fly out that door. Of course, without a thruster pack, the opening was only good as a means of suicide. I tried it anyway. Locked.

I stared at the huge wall that made up one side of the nearest fetshous. Only about the width of a two-lane highway separated the buildings, but it might as well have been miles away. Sians glided between the buildings; hover-cars zipped by above them. I thought about trying to signal one of the Sians for help, but it probably wouldn't work. And if it did, I might get my would-be rescuer killed.

On the other hand, the instructor's computer terminal hadn't been shut down. It was obviously a trap, yet it might be my one and only chance to access the interplanetary comm-system. *Hell, she already set aside the rest of week to punish me. How much worse could it get?*

Ignoring the cameras I was sure were hidden in every room, I brought up the comm system. Not wanting to reveal my skills and knowledge of Paraxous tech, I did a sloppy job of bypassing the login and pretended not to realize I'd tripped an alert.

Still no one came. I wondered just how far Cassie would let this go. She obviously hoped that I'd give something away. Did she know I had the Hunter's contact code? Well, I wasn't about to give her that. I sent a distress message to my father instead. It was such a predictable, futile move I could picture Cassie's disappointed frown.

This way, she'd have no reason to believe I had any way of contacting the Hunter. Besides, maybe the Hunter was monitoring Ebon's messages as I assumed Cassie did.

A noise from Dovain's apartment made me jump. I did an illegal shutdown of the operating system and waited. But nothing happened. I buzzed the door to Dovain's apartment again. A muffled squawk came from inside. I opened the door to find him lying face down on the floor, his feathers fluffed like a sick baby bird. His breathing came in short gasping coughs.

I hurried over. He was unconscious and burning with fever. Sweat soaked his face, clothes, and feathers. I knew all too well how dangerous fevers were for Sians. Vance had almost died from a febrile seizure a few years ago.

I yelled for help while struggling to roll Dovain onto his back without injuring his delicate wings. Once I got him positioned so he could breathe easier, I went to tell the Prigta to call for a med-tech. The door to Dovain's office was now locked. I pounded on the control panel, then tried the intercom and then the computer's comm-line. They were all dead.

I banged on the door. "Hey, there's a medical emergency in here!" Still no response. "I know you're out there, you stupid pig-rock! Open the door!"

My gut sank. This was Cassie's punishment. She had obviously decided to take her vengeances out on Dovain. Would she make me watch him die like she had Terrel?

Dovain went into a seizure. His head whacked against a table-leg several times before I managed to pull him away from it. It took me a couple of minutes to find the furniture controls and order the table and chairs retracted into the floor. By then, Dovain's beautiful blue skin had turned grey. He wasn't breathing.

The nearest thing I had to a friend was dying and I didn't know how to save him. I forced down my panic and tried to recall some of what I'd learned from the medical manuals I'd read while hiding in the safe room on Earth.

I ran to the bathroom, found the emergency med-kit and grabbed the oxygen mask. I set it to Sian specs and pressed it onto his face. It made a good seal around his beak, but an error message flashed. His airway was blocked.

I wrestled with his head, yanking it back and forcing his beak open. His tongue was so swollen it kept the breathing tube from being inserted. I pressed his tongue out of the way. He gagged and bucked, but the tube finally slid into place.

My next priority was bringing down the fever. I ran back to the bathroom and filled all the absorbies—space age towels— with several gallons of cold water. I wrung them out over Dovain, drenching him from head to talon-like toe. Soon the convulsions subsided. He started breathing on his own again. I switched the 02 mask to demand mode.

He had a huge lump on each side of his neck just under his jaw-line. No doubt it was an important clue as to what was wrong. If only I could recall the information from those medical texts. Being part Kobbi, I'd inherited an eidetic memory. Unfortunately, I wasn't very good at using it.

In desperation I guessed at where one of the cameras might be hidden and called out, "All right, Cassie. You've made your point. I promise never to interfere with one of your targets again. Just let him live."

No response. Cassie wasn't even scanning me empathically.

I brought the absorbies to the kitchenette's sink and refilled them. This time I placed them on Dovain, hoping to keep the fever down. Then I closed my eyes and pretended to be back in the shack with the Vance's holographic imager in my hand. Like a hologram, an image of the text on Sians appeared.

It took me a while to find the flowchart for Sians and fevers. The only thing that seemed to fit Dovain's symptoms was tyathyn withdrawal. Besides fever, swollen tongue and lymph nodes, the text listed a buildup of brownish mucus in the eyes that could be mistaken for an eye infection.

I brought myself out of the trance and lifted one of Dovain's eyelids, hoping with all my might to be wrong. A murky, brown gunk clouded his gold-flecked avian eyes. The guy I'd thought was so nice, innocent, and honest was a drug addict.

Of course, now was no time to judge. But being a tyathyn addict meant saving him was going to be damn near impossible. The text clearly stated that Sians couldn't survive being suddenly cut off from the drug. They needed professional medical intervention. It surprised me that Cassie hadn't contacted me yet in order to bargain for his life.

I forced myself to return to my trance and envision the text. But the end of the section on Sians and tyathyn addiction was a blur. No matter how hard I tried to see the treatment protocols, they refused to come into focus. I'd skipped that section since I never expected to deal with the problem.

If Sians couldn't survive abrupt withdrawals from the drug, then Dovain needed a dose. I scoured his apartment without finding anything that might be the tyathyn. To make matters worse, all the fever reducers were missing from the med-kit.

With no other options, I gave in and reached out telepathic to Cassie. *What do you want?*

She laughed in my head. *Please don't tell me you're not smart enough to figure that out. Since punishing you doesn't do any good, from now on those around you will suffer every time you misbehave.*

I began searching the apartment again. Cassie laughed in my head. *You won't find what you're looking for. My people confiscated all of his tyathyn.*

I kept searching anyway. *What's it going to take to get him treated?* I asked, fearing the price I'd have to pay.

This isn't a negotiation; it's a lesson. You're learning not to cross me.

I threw all his clothes out of the closet and went through every pocket. They were all empty, of course. The auto processor would have cleaned them out. I checked the catch bin that held items removed before clothes were auto-washed and hung in the closet. Among the pile of debris was one little pill. I was ecstatic.

Cassie couldn't have cared less. *If you can pull him through, fine. If not, I'll simply hire another instructor. And you'll have even more blood on your hands.*

I broke the pill in half, hoping that would be enough. Removing the O2 mask, and pinching open his beak, I dropped the pill down his throat and hoped he'd swallow it without choking.

Cassie continued to taunt me as I waited for Dovain to respond. *You were there when the Splendors died, weren't you? You could have offered yourself in exchange for their lives. Yet, you did nothing.*

You bemfornte! I couldn't do shit! The memory of Dad injecting me with something flashed to my mind.

A medication that blocks telepathic scans? Interesting. She wanted to know more and probed deeper. However, I was trapped in the flashback of my parents' death. As she tried to get past it, I became aware of her own memories of the event. She'd planned on killing Bill and Tina all along. Even if I'd surrendered myself, she still would have executed them.

The weight of the guilt I'd carried over their deaths lessened just a little. And she could never use it against me again. Cassie broke our link. Before she did, I sensed her intention to have her people on Earth search for the medication.

Not wanting to give anything away, I refused to think about that. Instead, I gathered Dovain's long, lanky body into my arms the best I could and just cradled him against me. "Come on, Dovain. Hang on. Please don't die."

His eyes rolled open only to shut again. Brown pus-like goo oozed from the corner of his eyes. I pulled a redi-wipe from my pocket and cleaned it away. He groaned and shifted restlessly. His groans escalated into cries of pain. Then he called my name.

"I'm here. I'm here, Dovain."

He tried to look up at me, but couldn't keep his eyes open. "Get help. Med-droid. Med-tech. Hurry."

"My mother isn't going to let that happen," I said flatly. "I'm sorry." There was no time for tact. "Dovain, I know about the tyathyn. I found some and gave it to you. I think that's what brought you around."

He grimaced. His glossy-white cheeks found enough blood to flush blue. He tried to say something, but his voice failed. He went into a coughing fit. Moving him off my lap, I went to get him some water. When I returned, he was curled into a fetal position and sound asleep. His breathing was steady and the fever wasn't nearly as high.

His reprieve wouldn't last long though. As soon as the half dose of tyathyn wore off, we'd be right back where we'd started. Cassie undoubtedly hoped I'd reach out and support him telepathically. But making mental contact, even with the best of intentions, could backfire and bring me one step closer to becoming a Dashia.

Mom and Dad had taught me that the Kobbi race had been created with the best of intentions. My hybrid race was supposed to bring peace to the Cluster. Unfortunately, some of them just couldn't resist abusing their powers. I wouldn't make that mistake.

Dovain rested peacefully for a few hours then started writhing in pain. Cursing myself for not thinking of it sooner, I got several trans-dermal analgesic patches from the med-kit and placed them on the nape of his neck and forearms. I settled myself against the wall next to him to keep an all-night vigil. His temperature spiked a little before dawn. I tried re-soaking the absorbies and spreading his wings to increase heat loss, but the fever kept climbing.

I broke the half of the tyathyn dose in half again and slipped the tiny piece under his tongue. A few minutes later, his eyes fluttered open. I used the ready-wipe again to clear some of the brown goo from around his eyes. It took several minutes before he was coherent enough to ask, "What happened?"

"You don't remember?" He just shook his head, so I explained, "My mother cut off your tyathyn supply. You went into withdrawals."

He lowered his eyes and looked away. He tried to speak, but the words stuck in his throat. I handed him a cup of water. His hand shook so badly, he spilled more than he drank. I reached out and steadied his hand while he held the cup to his beak and sipped.

When he finished, he whispered, "Please try not to judge me too harshly. One dose of tyathyn and we ... Sians are hooked."

I propped him up a little, trying to make him more comfortable. "Let's see about getting you unhooked, okay?"

He twisted his head around like an owl and tried to read my expression. "I'm not sure that's possible. I'm so sorry."

I forced on a smile and said, "We've gotten you this far."

He bowed his head and tears rolled down his face. "Yes, yes you did, Twyla. Surely, the Fates sent you to me. Thank you for all you've done."

"Don't thank me," I snapped gruffly. "You're in this mess because my mo.... because Cassie is getting back at me for trying to help Constantien."

He struggled to sit up and looked me in the eyes. "You did? How? What'd you do?"

Until then he'd had no reason to trust me. Now he watched me with desperate hope. He wanted to believe he'd found an ally.

"Nothing that did any good," I said dismissively. He waited to hear more, so I continued, "The guy was already bonded. But I thought if he got away, he'd have a chance at recovering."

"It was brave of you to try."

With a scoff, I got up and went to the kitchenette. "It wasn't brave. It was stupid. And now you're paying the price." I ordered a bowl of barley broth from the dispenser. It was what Mom had made for Vance when she went to the vault to help care for him while he was sick.

I set the furniture controls to create a small table next to him and put the bowl of broth down on it. Then Dovain said quietly, "Twyla, you saved my life."

I shoved a spoonful of broth into his mouth. He went into a coughing fit, spitting it everywhere. Purposely putting humor into my voice, I said, "Yeah, sure I did. Then again, with my fabulous nursing skills, I might just kill you yet."

He smiled at me. A wide, open-beak grin. Oh Makers, he really did remind me of Vance. I pulled a throat spray out of the med-kit and read the label. He opened his mouth and waited like a baby bird. I put the bottle into his hand and said playfully, "I'm not your mama. Spray your own throat, unless you're really such a chickling."

He took the bottle and gave his throat a spritz. "I mean it. I would have died without your help. I was stupid enough to fall for one of your sister's romantic dinners laced with tyathyn. I had no idea how I was ever going to recover. Treatment's expensive, and I have to help support my younger brother and sister."

Now it all made sense. I'd been so obsessed with Cassie, I'd forgotten about my sister's career in the family business. "You're just lucky she didn't bond you," I said. Then it hit me that maybe she had. My heart thudded in my chest.

"Cha-shaw," he made the distinctively Sian sound of dismissal. "I wasn't important enough for that. Apparently, I was just practice."

"Bonding someone takes a lot of empathic energy," I said as if I knew anything about empathology. "In fact, bonding anyone that's not Kobbi costs more energy than they can recoup from the victim." The thought made me wonder why Cassie had bothered with Ebon Milett. What had she gained from it? It didn't matter. The bottom-line was I was the product of my father's ruin.

"How can you even stand to look at me, knowing what I am?" I demanded of Dovain.

He squinted his hawkish brows at me, confused by the sudden turn in the conversation. "I don't blame you for what your family is."

I let the conversation drop and forced more broth down him. He asked if we had any more tyathyn. I lied and told him no to avoid a fight. With only a quarter of a dose left, we needed to wait as long as possible.

He eventually fell into a fitful sleep. When the fever spiked a short while later, I couldn't rouse him, so I decided to drag him to the shower hoping a cold soak would work instead of using up the last of the tyathyn. Naturally there were no 0-grav lifters in his quarters. So I pulled a blanket off his bed and rolled him over onto it.

As I tugged the blanket toward the shower, his pain invaded my senses despite my best efforts to raise my shields. Beneath the pain, his fear of dying gripped me. It wasn't so much that he was afraid for himself, but he worried about the brother and sister he'd leave behind.

My muscles trembled with exhaustion even though Dovain wasn't very heavy. With their hollow bones, Sians are extremely light for their size. He couldn't have weighed more than 70 pounds. But I hadn't eaten or slept, and the mental contact hurt like hell, which sucked the life right out of me.

I got him into the shower and turned the water on full blast. The shock from the blast of cold water hitting me in the face broke our empathic contact. It occurred to me that empathic shields probably required a lot of energy. I needed to eat something to keep my strength up.

Once Dovain had cooled down enough to be out of immediate danger, I shut the shower off and went to the food dispenser. I downed a nutrition bar and vitamin drink without really tasting either. The sedative hit me almost immediately. One or both of them had been drugged.

I went to the toilet to gag myself, but it was too late. My muscles went limp and my eyelids shut.

The next thing I knew, I was reliving memories of a sky dance. Many of the non-Sians wore thruster packs or anti-grav belts. Some just enjoyed the dance as spectators from one of the many balconies. Among them was my sister, Daylight. It didn't take a genius to figure out these were Dovain's memories, especially when the scene jumped to him sky-dancing with her in his arms.

The memory jumped again, this time to when my sister had invited him to her apartment for a home-cooked dinner. He'd been flattered. What came next consisted more of feelings than a particular scene. Just shades of anguish and disbelief.

The contact began to fade. I was relieved at first. Then I realized that it wasn't our link fading; it was Dovain himself. If I didn't do something, he'd be dead in a minute or two.

I can show you how to save him, Cassie's mind invaded mine.

Get the hell out of my head, I flashed automatically.

Are you sure that's what you want? In my mind, two lighted tunnels appeared. Cassie explained, *One tunnel will lead you back to reality. In so doing, your connection with Dovain will be broken, and he will die. However, the other leads you to the part of his brain affected by the tyathyn. I can show you how to repair it. Now do you want my help?*

Chapter 15

THE SAFEST THING TO DO would have been to let Dovain die. I could take the mental tunnel back to reality and not risk being turned into a Dashia. Or I could simply do nothing, refuse to take either path, and let us both die.

I'll have you revived. No matter how brain damaged you are, I won't let you die, Cassie flashed telepathically.

All right. Whatever. Just get out of my head!

You won't be able to save him without me, she taunted and then was gone.

Cassie had offered only two options: Go deeper into his mind or return to reality without him. I figured there had to be another way. In the physical world maybe I couldn't travel down both tunnels at the same time, but this was a mental plane of existence.

I pictured myself facing both tunnels like a split screen in a video game. Then I visualized the telepathic image of me splitting in two. One stood in front of the tunnel that angled down, which represented death in my mind. The other me stood in the tunnel leading up to life.

I moved them forward slowly. *Dovain*, the me in the downward tunnel called. *Try to come to me. I can lead you out of here.*

I can't move, came his very distant and weak reply.

Both images of me ventured a little farther. The me in the upward tunnel tried to open her eyes to the real world. Nothing. I moved the figure forward. The other me automatically moved the same distance down the other tunnel. The translucent image of Dovain hung onto the edges of a doorway that seemed intent on sucking him in.

I ran toward him.

No! he shouted mentally as he fought to keep from being pulled in. *You can't help me if you get yourself trapped too.*

I could feel the tug of death's door. Instead of bitter cold, it was gentle, warm, inviting. To keep from being sucked in, I pictured the floor becoming a metal surface and my shoes morphing into magnetic boots, anchoring me. Next, I imagined my arm stretching out like a cartoon character and grabbing him by the shirt to prevent him from being pulled through.

I'm going to give you a little tyathyn, I thought to him. *When you feel it take effect, throw yourself forward.*

I thought you said there wasn't any more.

Do you really want to discuss this right now? I asked, but then ignored his answer. The me in the upward tunnel opened her eyes. Without letting go of the two empathic versions of myself, I pulled the tiny tab of tyathyn out of my pocket. I dragged myself toward Dovain's body, which looked dead.

I stretched my arm out, straining to reach his beak and stick the pill in. Back in the downward tunnel, I shouted to Dovain's fading image. *It's now or never. Throw yourself forward. I'll catch you.*

He flew forward. I visualized the door closing, hoping to cut off death's pull. It worked. He plowed into me and we tumbled to the nondescript black bottom of the tunnel. I lost contact with reality and the other empathic me.

All was dark. I couldn't make out the walls of the tunnel anymore, and I didn't feel any slope. We got to our feet. *Which way?* I asked my Sian friend. But this wasn't the physical world with magnetic poles, celestial bodies or breezes to guide his avian senses.

He shook his head. Then he froze and jerked his head from side to side. *Do you hear that?*

From across the empathic plane, HelaShia's daughter, FreaShia, called to us. An invisible paw patted my cheek. I grabbed Dovain's hand. *Come on. We can follow her voice out of here.*

As her voice became louder, the pats turned into slaps. Dovain's head snapped to the side. He put his free hand to his cheek and rubbed. *Did she just hit me?*

She's trying to wake us up. I kept a firm grip on his hand as we rushed toward FreaShia's voice. The next slap knocked me awake. I raised an arm, blocking yet another blow. "I'm awake! I'm awake. Check Dovain."

FreaShia moved to Dovain as he opened his eyes. Her purr rumbled loud enough for me to hear. "You're okay!" she cried with joy and threw herself onto him with an unrestrained hug. "My mother finally told me why my lessons had been suspended. I came as soon as I could. Holy Makers, I thought you were dead." She spoke to Dovain like some heroine in a Hollywood love story. Our unexpected ally had a pretty big crush on her language tutor.

"I think I was," he mused.

She pulled away and showed him the med-kit next to her. "I brought some stuff: fever reducers, anti-seizure meds ..." She paused and glanced over at me. In a whisper, she admitted, "tyathyn."

Dovain sat up, his gold flecked eyes grew big and bright. In disbelief and frustration, I snapped, "Dammit Dovain, I did not just bring you back from the cosmic black hole, or celestial plane—or wherever it is dead Sians go—just so you could go right back to being an addict."

He panted through his open beak-like mouth like an overheated chick would. "You don't understand. I need it."

He reached for FreaShia's med-kit, but I blocked him. FreaShia glared at me. Her ears went flat. Her green eyes bulged, and her black mane bristled. She actually hissed at me before saying, "Sians have to be weaned off, you idiot!"

A sickly feeling crept across my senses. Cassie was on her way, and she was pissed. FreaShia's act of kindness was about to get her killed. "Oh shit. FreaShia, run! Get out of here! Don't take the south lift. My mother's coming."

She seemed taken aback. "Why should I be in trouble for helping Dovain detox?"

"Because he wasn't detoxing voluntarily." I said it loud enough to make sure the monitors picked it up. If Cassie knew FreaShia hadn't intentionally interfered with my punishment, maybe she wouldn't be too hard on her.

Then I had an idea of how to get her back in Cassie's good graces. I pretended to make a break for the door, knocking FreaShia over in the process. Into her flattened ear, I whispered, "You've got to stop me from escaping."

She threw me back. "You're crazy. No way on Montara I'm helping you escape." She bared her teeth at me. "It's your fault

Cassie almost let Dovain die. She was using him to punish you, wasn't she?"

I tried for the door again. She slammed me against the bathroom wall a little harder than necessary. In a blur of motion, she bounded out of the bathroom, across the common room and out the door. I heard the lock set after she left.

Dovain and I locked gazes; then we both scrambled for the med-kit.

I snatched the bag from his grip, found the tyathyn, and dumped it down the toilet. Dovain collapsed to the floor. "Oh Twyla, Fates preserve me. I know you meant well, but you just killed me."

I knelt beside him. "No, Dovain. We broke the hold that stuff has on you. As long as you stay away from it, it can't hurt you anymore. You're going to be okay."

He stared into my eyes. It was one of those gazes that happen in the movies right before the couple kiss for the first time. We started to lean toward one another, but then I felt Cassie waiting outside the door. No doubt she hoped for a romance between us so she could use Dovain against me. I pulled away, stood and turned to face the door.

Cassie entered. "Congratulations. You managed to pull him through." She paused long enough to give me hope this was over. Then she added, "But at what cost? Surely, you didn't think I'd let you win?" She turned to one of the guards and ordered, "Kill him."

"No. Wait!" I jumped in front of Dovain and played the only card I had left: total defeat. Careful to keep my tone contrite, I bowed my head and begged, "Please don't kill him. I've learned my lesson. You have all the power, and there's no way I can ever beat you. I get it."

My show of submission was enough to make her reconsider how to best use Dovain. Her mental probe suddenly stabbed at my mind. My shields snapped on out of reflex. *This is the price for his life. Drop your shields.*

My knees buckled. She'd force her way in either way, but if I allowed it willingly, she'd let him live. *Okay. I'll cooperate. But I don't know how to control my shields. They're a reflex. I can't just shut them off.*

Well, this would be an excellent opportunity for me to teach you. Cassie smiled—a predator going in for the kill. She overwhelmed my senses, drowning everything else out. All I knew was a Dashia's sense of joy at my pain.

•   •   •

I was back on Earth. Cameron and I sat in the courtyard of our apartment complex talking. I recognized the memory as one of the many times I'd almost told him how I felt about him. After a particularly nasty fight with Nina, he was thinking about breaking up with her. I asked him if he was still in love with her.

In reality he'd not only said yes, he'd gone into great detail about just how much he loved her. But here in Cassie's blixed up telepathic torture he said everything I wanted to hear. He didn't love her anymore. There was someone else.

I gave up my grip on reality and surrendered to the fantasy. My heart pounded as I pretended not to get his insinuation. We recited corny, cliché lines from our favorite rom-coms until he finally told me it was me that he loved. We kissed, and it was wonderful.

Wonderful, but not real. I sensed Cassie's manipulating my dreams. She had hoped to awaken my sexual desires by kindling my feelings for Dovain. Instead, she'd stumbled upon my weakness for Cameron. She decided it had been a mistake to let him go. A mistake she planned to rectify.

My complete surrender or death were the only things that would prevent her from going after Cam. So, I'd have to kill myself the first chance I got. Cassie became aware of me reading her thoughts. Her shock at my telepathic trespass turned to rage. *Don't you ever try that again.*

The collar ignited at a level beyond comprehension.

As for killing yourself, I'll gladly kill your mind. Your body would be more useful to me anyway. Think of all the new, younger targets I could bond using your body as bait.

My head exploded. I was sure I was having a stroke.

Chapter 16

I WOKE TO FIND MYSELF in a psychedelic fog. The equipment in the med-unit swirled around leaving colorful trails of lights. Cassie had obviously pumped me full of some pretty potent drugs. At least I wasn't a mental vegetable—yet.

Cassie sat in a windowed booth overlooking the med-unit. She scrutinized the readings on several monitors, not even bothering to look at me. Was she killing my brain one cell at a time like she'd threatened to do?

The med-droid in the alcove across from me whirled to life and floated toward me. I tried to jump off the bed, but my head, arms, legs and waist were all strapped down. One of the droid's six appendages was an injection rod. Despite my efforts to twist and pull away, it slammed a shot into my shoulder.

In desperation I called out to the med-droid. "You're supposed to help people. You're not even supposed to be capable of harming them." My speech was slurred, and my tongue felt like it was sealed in insta-wrap. "This is hurting me. Please, you have to help me!"

Don't be ridiculous, Cassie chided. *Of course, I had the droid reprogrammed. It's not going to help you. No one is going to help you.*

The sedative dragged me under. The next time I woke, I was back in my room with no idea what Cassie had done to me. All I knew was I felt so sick I wished she had killed me. Since my body was too weak to stand, I had to crawl to the bathroom. When the vomiting finally stopped, I curled up right there on the floor next to the toilet and slept.

Nightmares invaded the darkness. I experienced the murder of my parents over and over. Then a new nightmare struck. I was making out with Cameron and suddenly went all Dashia on him. My own scream woke me. The tile floor was damp with my sweat.

The door to my room opened and the Prigta skittered across the floor. The grating sound of its stony body made my head throb. All I could do was raise my hand and shake my head as it scooped me up in its front pinchers.

The Prigta's sulfurous body odor hit my gut. I heaved; nothing but a mouthful of bile came up. When the thing dumped me on the bed, I spit the bile at it. The Pig-rock leaned in, trapping me with the weight of its body and holding my arms with its pinchers. For a second, I thought it'd squash me.

A med-droid floated in with several injection rods ready. I went wild, bucking and thrashing. My hands fought to swipe at the Prigta's sapphire eyes. One of the droid's metallic claws clapped onto my arm; another jabbed several shots into me. It released its grip, set a cup of something on the bedside stand and floated out the door.

Some of my strength returned. My stomach no longer writhed. Whatever the droid had given me worked pretty fast.

The Prigta let go and backed away. I glared at the thing. "Don't expect me to thank you, you vreking, sadistic p'ig-rock!"

It pointed at the cup the med-droid had left. I knocked the cup from the stand and sent it flying at the Prigta. "Do you actually think I'm stupid enough to drink that? Get the vrek out of here. Go take a bath. Get yourself deodorized! You vreking stink."

"You heard her," FreaShia's voice came from somewhere down the hall. The Prigta withdrew as FreaShia rushed in.

"Is Dovain all right?" I asked.

Her tail drooped. "I don't know. My mother won't tell me. My Ruslo and Standard lessons are still suspended. So, they haven't replaced him. That has to be a good sign, right?" She offered me the cup in her hand. I hesitated.

"It's safe," she said. "I ordered it from the food dispenser myself." She glanced back at the door that was now closed. "I don't blame you for not trusting anything that pig-rock gives you. I hate those things. Disgusting, stupid creatures. It's too bad my people didn't wipe them out when they had the chance." She shoved the cup under my nose. "But from the looks of you, you could really use some bismuth water."

After how she'd helped Dovain and me, I decided to trust her not to drug me. I took the cup of fizzing water and sipped. "Aren't you going to get in trouble for this?"

She growled. With a switch of her tail, she sat down beside me. She unsheathed her claws and ran them through her thick black mane. "Actually, I'm here under orders. Sir VerVum sent me to get you on your feet and get your ass back to your lessons."

"Oh," I said, disappointment clear in my tone. I'd hoped she'd come as a friend.

"Hey! You're lucky I don't beat the dung out of you for putting Dovain in danger."

"You really like him, don't you?"

She shrugged. "He's cute. And no one can deny that he's a nice guy. Maybe too nice. I'm not sure if I want to bed him," she commented casually. Her gaze narrowed, and she jabbed a clawed finger at me. "You'd better pray to the Makers he's okay. Now, are you ready to go to your lessons?"

"You've got to be kidding," I scoffed. "FreaShia, I'm still half dead."

"But you have to go. It's the only way to find out what's happened to Dovain."

I tried to get up, but the room swayed and I nearly threw up. "I'm sorry. I can't. Not yet. Not unless you want to carry me."

She bounded off the bed and out the door. "I'll be right back," she called over her shoulder.

She returned with another cup. This time the fizzing liquid inside was green. "Bismuth and nutrica drink. My own invention. The nutrica will help you get back on your feet. The bismuth will help you keep it down."

I tried to wave her off, but she huffed, "Don't make me force this down your throat."

Everyone in the Cluster knew there was no arguing with a mission-minded Katian. I took the cup and sipped. It went down surprisingly well. With a smile of gratitude, I drank some more.

"I brought you something else." FreaShia produced a nasal spray applicator. "This will block the stench of the pig-rock."

I snatched it from her hand and inhaled the medication. The lingering smell of sulfur vanished. "Thanks, FreaShia. You're awesome."

She looked at me confused. "Awesome?"

The Ruslo equivalent of the word meant awe-inspiring due to great power or might. "Wonderful," I corrected.

She laughed. "Oh no. I like being awesome. Better awesome than memfed."

It felt so good to be having a normal conversation, I grabbed at the chance to keep it going. "What in the universe does that even mean? Memfed?"

She rolled her eyes at my ignorance. "Really? Memfed ... as in considered a memform. It's basically the bottom of the Clan hierarchy. Just one step from being outcast."

"Are you memfed?" I asked.

Her growl came from deep in her throat and was clearly a warning. Apparently, it was considered rude to ask a Katian such a thing. Still, I couldn't stop myself. "But why? Why would you be considered ... that?"

Her ears went flat and she bared her fangs as she hissed at me. "Don't pretend to be so stupid. Mother's not exactly in Madam DeConnett's good graces, thanks to you." Then she bowed her head and mumbled, "And interfering with whatever Madam DeConnett had planned for Dovain didn't help my case any."

There just didn't seem to be any way to win. No matter what I did, someone always got hurt. "I'm sorry," I offered lamely.

"You should be. Maybe for once you should stop to consider how your stupid little rebellion affects everyone around you."

I snapped right back. "Well, I promise you the effects will be a hell of a lot worse if Cassie has her way. Just what do you think would've happened to Dovain if I'd given in? He'd be bonded."

Her green eyes flicked a glance toward one of the "hidden" cameras. She cleared her throat. "Speaking of Dovain ... Let's get your ass going and find out what happened to him." She went to the door and ordered the Prigta to carry me to my class.

I protested loudly and angrily as it picked me up in its two, front claw-like hands. I continued protesting all the way to Sir

VerVum's studio. When the door opened, I shouted one last time, "Dammit! Put me down, you pig-rock!"

The thing dumped me on the floor at Venor's feet and left. Sir VerVum stood up from the mixer. His silver mane stood on end. "Fur balls, child. You look like the remnants of a memform's last meal."

He extended a hand and helped me to the bench. "You can't possibly sing in this condition."

I gave him a "no shit" expression and a snort of bitter laughter. That was enough to send my gut into another spasm. I doubled over in pain.

Sir VerVum dismissed FreaShia then knelt in front of me. He took my face in his hands. The soft tufts of fur around his wrists and between the pads of his fingers felt warm and comforting. "Twyla, your mother has given me just one month to get you to split your voice. If you don't, she's going to have your vocal cords surgically altered."

I couldn't have cared less. She'd been threatening me with the surgery ever since I'd begun my singing lessons. Vocal cord alteration was no big deal. It sure didn't compare to what she'd just done to me.

Venor began sniffing the air. He traced the unpleasant odor to me and took a whiff. "By the Makers, child, you're in need of a thorough scrubbing." He waved his hand in front of his face. "And you complain about how the Prigta smells."

He led me to the bathroom and turned on the shower. I tried to pull away, panicked at the thought of him washing me. He released an annoyed growl. "Relax, child. I wouldn't demean myself enough to wash my pupil. Just sit down. I'll call a nanny-bot."

The nanny-bot came and peeled off the clothes that seemed encrusted onto my skin after so many days. I lingered in the shower long after dismissing the bot. Finally, Venor knocked on the door. "Twyla?" His voice was soft and full of concern.

When I gave him a gruff, "Yeah, what?" he switched back to his typical Katian persona. "The nanny-bot brought you a change of clothes. I ordered the others incinerated. Now hurry up."

I dressed only to find my clothes were now two sizes too big. I glanced at the 3D holo-reflector. My image was gaunt and sickly looking. There wasn't anything pretty about me. Cassie would be very unhappy with my appearance. That gave me a grim sense of satisfaction.

Venor spent the remainder of our time demonstrating how Cantors split their voices. His demonstration did a lot to heal my battered body and spirit. It was like drinking a cold cup of water after feeling like you were about to die of thirst.

By the time the Prigta came to get me, I was able to walk to Dovain's office with just a bit of a wobble. *Please let him be okay,* I chanted inwardly the entire way.

The door opened to reveal my Sian friend standing there. Dovain lurched forward as if to embrace me but stopped short when he spotted the Prigta. Yet another reason to hate the thing. I wasn't usually a touchy-feely person, but I could have really used a hug.

Dovain motioned me inside and told the Prigta to wait in the hall. Once the door closed, he took my hands in his. We both glanced at the cameras and sighed in frustration. His wings sagged as he fidgeted, unsure what to say. "I'm glad to see you're all right."

I was hardly all right, but there was no point in worrying him. "I'm glad to see you, too. I was afraid I'd show up to find I had yet another Ruslo tutor." Meaning I was afraid he'd been killed.

He cocked and then bobbed his head in understanding of my double meaning. He gave that imitation of a Human smile that showed his dimples and reminded me of Vance. Then the smile dropped and his expression became serious. "Oh, I'm not going anywhere. Your mo— Madam DeConnett has decided I'm too useful to her. In fact, she has requested that I not leave the fetshous."

I cringed. Now that she no longer had his addiction to keep him under her control, she'd placed him under house arrest. That made using him to get a message to the Dashia Hunter pretty much impossible. On the other hand, it also meant she *hadn't* gotten him hooked on tyathyn again.

I studied my friend's appearance. He was all knobby knees and elbows. As with all Sian, he'd been skinny to begin with, but he'd lost a lot of weight during detox and hadn't gained an ounce back. No doubt he was trying to avoid eating anything that might be laced with tyathyn.

My breathing became sobs. My eyes stung from the lack of tears. "I'm so sorry, Dovain."

"Cha-shaaw, Twyla. As I've already told you, this is not your fault. I got myself into this mess."

The unspoken question was: How were we going to get ourselves out of it?

Chapter 17

D AYS SLIPPED BY one after another with no viable plan for escape. After three weeks, I'd also failed to even come close to cantoring. During my last singing lesson before the weekend, Venor expressed his frustration at my lack of progress. "Ch'ild," he snapped, "pay attention. You're so pitchy; you're making my ears bleed."

I pretended to check his ears for blood. With everything else at stake, cantoring just wasn't high on my priority list. He swatted me away and gave me a predatory glare with russet eyes that matched his sunset holo-garb.

"Sorry."

He got in my face, revealing a fang still blood-stained from his lunch. "I don't want your apology. I want you to merge with the music. Your half-hearted attempts are a waste of my time." He began ranting to himself in Felniez.

When he paused to take a breath, I risked asking, "What's gotten into you, Venor? You're madder than a pregnant memform."

He raised a clawed hand at me. For a nanosecond, I feared he'd actually strike me. Instead, he froze in frustration. "It's Sir VerVum to you, child," he announced in a bone-chilling tone. "And if you ever compare me to a bemfornte again, I'll claw your eyes out. You don't need them to sing."

I cringed and carefully kept my gaze fixed on the floor as he scolded, "And I have every right to be angry. I had no desire to take on a student, and now I risk being disgraced because my pupil has to have her pipes sliced."

My gaze snapped up to meet his. "Disgraced?" I asked, confused. "I get that in Katian culture only natural cantors are considered genuine artists, and altering your voice is seen as fraudulent. But none of the other races have a second set of vocal cords. Katian half-breeds have been getting their 'pipes sliced' for decades. So, why would you be disgraced? It'd be my failure, not yours."

Venor gave a humorless snort and shook his head. "You really are naïve." He methodically smoothed his fur from mane to tail making a show of making me wait. Finally, he explained, "I will not be party to a fraud, and your mother knows that. Yet, if I refuse … Well, it would not be good for my career." His feline pupils narrowed to slits. "See, child, you are not the only one here with something to lose."

I nodded, dumbfounded. It terrified me to think that anything bad might happen to Sir Venor VerVum because of me. "Sorry. I'll do my best. I promise."

Satisfied, he played the opening to the song we'd been working on. It was the only Ruslo one in my repertoire that didn't make me stumble. Venor sang with me in a full cantor. His voices coaxed me deeper and deeper into the music until I was almost in a trance.

Warmth spread through my chest. It grew into a wave of energy that washed through every cell of my body. I was about to cantor. I was sure of it.

"Can you hear me?" Venor's third voice asked. It was low enough to hide beneath his first two voices, but it brought my ecstasy to a mind-wrenching halt.

I gave a discreet nod, shocked that he'd separated one of his voices from the lyrics and spoke in Standard. Such a thing wasn't even supposed to be possible. He gave me a firm swat with his tail. "Keep singing," he hissed.

I hadn't even realized I'd stopped. I resumed our duet but nowhere near the euphoric split.

"The operation," his third voice continued in the same low tone, "it's not just for your voice. Your mother believes she has found a way to permanently link your minds so she can control you. She intends to turn you into her puppet."

My voice faltered. Venor cuffed me lightly with the back of his hand. I let out a startled yelp. He hadn't hurt me, but anyone watching would figure my subsequent meltdown was due to his discipline. My breathing came in short hiccupping gasps. I brought my knees to my chest and rocked back and forth on the bench.

"That's it!" he yelled, "I'm through with you. And to think I was going to give up my weekend to work with you."

I took the proper Katian submission stance: arms out with palms up, bowed at the waist, but with my head tilted back exposing my neck for easy slashing. "P—Please Sir VerVum, if I c-cantor, do you th-think she'll c—cancel the surgery?" I stammered.

"How should I know?" Venor tried to maintain his mask of anger, but it slipped a bit as he sighed, "Maybe."

"Then please give me another chance. I'll do whatever it takes to cantor without having my cords split."

He started to refuse, and his experience acting in a few holo-vids really paid off. I almost believed him myself. [[Why should I? You can't even converse with me in Ruslo. And your pronunciation of it when you sing offends my ears.]]

[[Please. I'll do better,]] I begged in Ruslo. [[With your help, I know I can cantor. I came so close this time. I could feel it. I won't disgrace you. Please, don't give up on me.]]

He puffed his chest and his glittery golden pink mane. [[I'll demean myself enough to give you one more chance on two conditions: first,]] he growled, shoving a clawed finger in my face, [[not one vreking word of Standard comes out of that mouth of yours until you cantor.]]

I nodded eagerly.

[[Two,] he said, unsheathing a second finger and flexing the claws in front of my eyes threateningly. [[Two, you put everything into your lessons for the next three days. You'd best show proper gratitude to me for sacrificing my weekend by ditching that attitude of yours. Understood?]]

What he couldn't say was that my continued existence as an autonomous being depended on convincing Cassie to cancel the surgery, and he believed cantoring was the only way to do that. For some reason, seeing me cooperate and progress as a cantor would buy me some time before she tried turning me into her puppet.

[[Yes, Sir VerVum. Thank you.]]

The Prigta came in to collect me. I glanced at Venor, hoping for some sort of reassurance. Instead, the Cantor Master just raised a challenging brow as if to say it was up to me to get myself out of this.

The Prigta lumbered alongside me as I contemplated my fate. I glanced at its rock-like exoskeleton as it crawled. In order to escape,

I'd probably have to kill the thing. Their gelatinous joints were the Prigtas' only weak spots. However, they could retract their heads and limbs into the contoured spaces of their shells, becoming a solid mass of death as they rolled over you. To kill my captor, I'd have to chop its head off before it knew what was happening.

I didn't have to wonder what my pacifist parents would think of such a plan. Even as stupid as the creatures were, Prigtas were considered sentient beings. Would that make it murder? Wouldn't it be self-defense? And what about Dovain? I had to save him. And there was no way to do that with this thing following me around all the time.

If I did manage to get away though, I doubted my mom and dad would be proud of what I'd become in order to do it. It felt like the floor was yanked out from under me. I leaned against the wall for support and cried out to their memory, "What am I supposed to do?!"

The Prigta stared at me with unblinking sapphire eyes. It swung its head toward the lift and waited for me to comply with the silent order. I gripped two fists full of my auburn hair and yanked with a scream. "Don't you get it? You stupid, ugly, stinking, pig-rock! She's going to turn me into a Dashia!"

The few people who'd been about to approach the lift saw that I was pitching a fit and went the other way. My tirade continued until I'd worn myself out. "Oh, what's the use? You're too stupid to understand a word I say, aren't you?"

I gave it a swift kick and immediately regretted it. While the creature didn't even seem to notice, it felt like I'd broken a toe. I hopped up and down holding my foot, swearing every curse I knew in Standard, English, Ruslo, and even the few I knew in Felniez.

The Prigta herded me into the lift one hop at a time. The door closed. The Prigta pressed the hold button. [[Now DeConnett daughter, are you too stupid to understand the words I am saying?]]

It was a decidedly masculine voice. I shook my head in stunned silence at hearing the Prigta's rumbling voice for the first time. [[Good,]] he continued. [[I will only have enough time to tell you this once. I have the means to disable your obedience collar. When your mother sends you to the surgery center, I can arrange for you to get away.]]

My first reaction was this had to be a trap. Instinctively, I went to reach out empathically, but stopped myself. I had no more right to invade someone's thoughts than my mother did. [[Why should I believe you?]]

[[If you have another option, I beg you to take it.]] I wasn't sure if I heard fear in his voice or if I was sensing it. He took my lack of response as confirmation. [[I thought not.]]

Suddenly, I grabbed for the only lifeline offered. This really might be my only chance. [[What if she cancels the surgery?]] I asked, thinking of all the things that could go wrong.

[[She won't.]]

I'd known it wasn't likely, but I had hoped. Then something occurred to me. [[What's going to happen to you if you help me?]]

He postured upright on his hind legs, extending his gelatinous neck forward to look eye to eye with me. [[So now you care what happens to this stupid, ugly, stinking, pig-rock?]]

I bowed my head and felt my cheeks burn. [[I'm sorry for the things I said. But you're helping Cassie keep me prisoner,]] I said in stammering Ruslo. [[I'm still not sure I should trust you.]]

[[Perhaps you shouldn't. You are right: you know nothing about me. Did it even occur to you that I might have a family that would be put in jeopardy if I fail in my duty to Madam DeConnett?]]

[[Family?]] I gasped. I'd learned how Prigtas reproduced in my basic science class, but I'd never thought of them as having families. [[Ah Makers, what are you going to do? You can't risk your family's life for me.]]

He moved its boulder-sized head to within a few millimeters of mine and stared until I looked away. Then he came back down on all four legs, making the lift shake. [[No, I would not risk my family for you. Not even to keep another Dashia from being created. However, I will risk myself. My family is now safely off Oweena. I do not know where they've gone, so Madam DeConnett can no longer use them as leverage against me.]]

[[But how will you ever find them?]]

[[I won't.]] He cut me off before I could tell him how sorry I was. [[Just be ready to make a run for it when your transport breaks down.]] He moved to release the hold button on the lift.

"Wait! Please! Dovain!" I switched to Ruslo, pleading. [[We've got to find a way to save Dovain, too.]]

[[That's not possible. Even if it was, I don't trust the addict.]] He jabbed the release and the lift resumed. I was about to beg for my friend's life, but the Prigta glanced at the camera. I had to assume they'd been off while the lift was on hold but now had resumed recording.

Once we were out of the lift, I tried to talk to him. In response, he tucked and started to roll at me. I took the hint and ran all the way to Dovain's office with the Prigta at my heels.

I rushed through the door only to run smack-dab into Cassie. *Oh shit.* I focused on my intense hatred of her to mask any thoughts of escape.

[[You're late,]] she said.

[[I was fighting with this stupid pig-rock again,]] I said, trying not to feel guilty at using the racial slur.

She glanced over at the Prigta. If she scanned him, he was dead and so were our chances of escape. I had to distract her. "I'm vreking sick of smelling the damn thing. Assign me a different guard. A Katian ... anything but a Prigta."

She stepped closer, her gaze narrowed with displeasure. Of course, I knew there was no way she'd give me what I wanted after the way I'd demanded it.

[[Aren't you supposed to be speaking Ruslo, young lady?]] she asked. It was her way of letting me know she'd been monitoring my singing lesson and suspected that something was up.

I managed to keep myself from panicking. If she'd known about Venor's warning or the Prigta's offer to help, she wouldn't be worrying about me speaking Ruslo. [[Yeah, sorry. Venor's determined to force me to cantor by Firstday. He says he'll quit if I have to have my vocal cords surgically split.]] I tried to ignore the way Cassie smirked and Dovain cringed at my lousy Ruslo pronunciation.

[[Did he tell you the surgery is scheduled for next Finday?]] Finday is the last day of the Paraxous Standard calendar's work week. That meant I had ten Owenian days before she turned me into her puppet.

[[You know he did,]] I said, hoping to make her think there was nothing I needed to hide from today's lesson. [[And you know I promised to do my best not to disappoint Sir VerVum. I'm going to cantor by your deadline. Now please let me get to work on my Ruslo.]]

We glared at each other. Dovain cleared his throat softly, drawing our attention and ending the standoff. [[If I may, Madam DeConnett, I have an idea that might improve Twyla's Ruslo substantially.]] Belatedly, he added, [[Which of course is crucial to her ability to cantor.]]

[[Of Course.]] Cassie folded her arms over her chest and raised a brow.

Cantoring in Standard is nearly impossible because the language is so guttural. The native Katian language of Felniez is ideal; however, few non-Katians can pronounce it. So Ruslo was my only chance.

[[And what is this extraordinary idea?]] she prompted when Dovain hemmed and hawed.

[[Allow me to work with Twyla and FreaShia together ... Just for this weekend.]]

[[I've kept my daughter isolated from the other youths in the fetshous for a reason, Dovain. Besides, what could you possibly achieve in the next three days that you haven't managed in as many months? And why do you need FreaShia in particular?]]

I wished Dovain hadn't made the suggestion. I didn't want a third person around us, and I didn't want to get FreaShia into more trouble. Yet if I protested, Cassie would agree to Dovain's request just to spite me.

Dovain explained, [[FreaShia is proficient in Ruslo and Standard. And it would be helpful for Twyla to converse with someone other than myself.]]

[[Find someone else for her to practice with. Preferably an adult. I fear my daughter would be a bad influence on any of the other children. Especially FreaShia.]]

Cassie caught my relieved expression and scanned me. I had to come up with a plausible reason for not wanting her around. I focused all my thoughts on how much I hated FreaShia's mother. Cassie smiled. [[On second thought, perhaps HelaShia's daughter would appreciate a chance to redeem herself.]]

She turned to Dovain, [[I'll grant your request. In fact, I'll even take it a step further. Twyla will room with FreaShia. That way she'll get even more practice.]] With that, she left.

The Prigta lingered.

[[You can wait outside,]] Dovain told him. [[Oh, and please have FreaShia sent to us.]]

The Prigta looked to me. Would he refuse to help me if I told Dovain? To make sure he understood that I wouldn't desert him, I said, [[Yes, please go. Dovain and I have a lot to talk about.]]

His mammoth body shook so badly, it clattered. He gave me a slight shake of his head, but said nothing as he backed out of the office.

The second the door closed, Dovain was at my side. [[Are you all right? You're so pale.]] He sat me down, then took a seat beside me. He draped a wing over my shoulders.

His caring, gentle nature reminded me so much of Vance. I wondered if my friends back on Earth were okay. Would Cassie go after Cameron? There was one way I could think of to make Cassie decide it wasn't worth the effort: make her think I'd fallen for Dovain.

He was still waiting for a reply, so I explained, "I'm just scared that I'm going to lose you if I can't do this."

[[Ruslo, please,]] he reminded me softly.

I smiled at him and handed him my datapad. [[Speaking of, I need your help with some of the words in this song.]] I reached over and started the music.

Dovain had never heard me sing before. The poor guy took it as a come on. He blushed a deep purple as he listened.

As I finished, I braced myself for what came next. He pulled me closer. I cuddled against him. Though I was mildly curious what it would be like to kiss him, I had no intentions of letting things get that far.

"Careful not to react," I whispered into his ear.

He tensed and began to pull away, confused. I pretended like I was in a movie and looked up at him with Caldaxian-mooring-pup-eyes. [[I really like you, Dovain ... but ...]]

He bobbed his head in understanding. [[It's all right. This isn't the best of circumstances.]]

I hugged him and he wrapped me in his wings. I nestled my head in the crook of his neck and whispered again. "The Prigta is going to help me escape. I want you to come with me."

He gripped me fiercely. He buried his face in my hair. We both breathed in heavy pants. Hopefully anyone watching would figure it was due to us being freshmen when it came to romance.

"When?" he said in a sigh.

I didn't like how his breath on the back of my neck made me feel. It was too similar to how I'd felt whenever Cameron touched me. "On the transport to the surgical center."

"So we don't want you to cantor?"

"Yes, we do. She'll do the surgery no matter what. If I don't try my best to cantor, she'll get suspicious. The problem's going to be getting you aboard the transport undetected."

Finally, I couldn't stand the closeness anymore and had to pull away. As if on cue, FreaShia entered. She suffered through a couple hours of boring language exercises making a show of brushing every bit of her short, tan fur that wasn't covered by her black vest and trousers. Once she'd finished, she declared, [[These practice conversations are stupid. I'm hungry. Come on. Let's get some dinner.]]

Dovain and I exchanged uncertain glances. When we didn't respond quickly enough, she grabbed us by our arms and hauled us to our feet. [[I said let's go. You both could use some food, and I happen to be an excellent cook. Plus, I can make sure your meal doesn't contain any unwanted extras.]]

We decided to chance it and followed her to her clan's private kitchen and dining room. I looked around the smaller version of the master kitchen. Immaculately clean, and fortunately completely deserted.

FreaShia caught my quizzical glance. [[Looks like we've got the place to ourselves. Awesome! The guards must have seen us coming and cleared the place out.]] She seemed awfully pleased with her newfound power.

Though I wanted to believe she might become a friend and ally, I did keep an eye on her while she ordered ingredients from the dispenser and baked them in the insta-oven. We were rewarded with the first meal either of us had been able to truly enjoy since Dovain's detox. As we ate, FreaShia and I compared our lessons with Sir VerVum.

She had a natural set of dual cords and could use them well. She only needed to master the art of harmonizing them into a true cantor. The topic moved on to the music of the different races. Dovain set the computer to play the top ten Owenian songs.

FreaShia made a show of being unimpressed by the Sian whistles and trills. Halfway through the second song, she changed the setting to play the top ten songs from her home world, NelSeca. The Katian music was incredibly powerful, while at the same time quite melodious.

As we debated the merits of the different musical styles, Dovain commented on how much my Ruslo had improved. FreaShia chuckled. [[Of course, we're talking about something a lot more interesting than those stupid Ruslo lessons.]]

She went on mockingly, [[Allow me to introduce my family; dog-faced mother, fat-ugly brother, whiney-annoying sister. I see your family is here, too. How droll.]]

We all laughed. FreaShia said to Dovain, [[See, she understands insults just fine.]] Then she asked me, [[What else do you like besides insults and music?]]

"Poker." Of course, neither of them knew the term so I chose the closest thing to poker the Paraxous had, a game I used to play with Terrel. "Rochi," I ventured.

[[Excellent. I'll go order a deck.]] She jumped up from the table and went to the nearest replication terminal.

When she returned with a standard rochi deck in her hand, Dovain admitted, [[I've never played.]]

FreaShia licked her lips and twitched her whiskers. [[Fresh meat. Even better.]] She sat down and started dealing. [[Okay, what should we bet?]]

I hadn't played rochi since being smuggled out of the Cluster. [[Let's just play for points.]]

[[Boring!]] She gave it some thought then said, [[Secrets. Let's play for secrets.]]

Dovain fluffed like a baby bird. I scoffed. "Just how stupid do you think we are? Either you're a really bad Dashia-in-training, or you've got the brain of a zee-nat. We're prisoners. We're not about to say anything Cassie can use against us."

She yawned at my show of temper. [[Ruslo. Remember to speak Ruslo.]]

I repeated myself, translating it word for word without the slightest stammer. FreaShia seemed truly pleased. [[That was perfect. And you're the one with the brain of a zee-nat. Of course, I shut off the audio. They can watch, but not hear us.]] She took in our shocked expressions with the typical air of Katian superiority.

I got up from the table and checked the nearest terminals. It was true. The audio was off. [[I didn't know you could do that,]] I admitted, astonished at the flood of relief having some sense of privacy triggered.

[[The video can't be turned off without your mother's permission.]] She stretched and yawned, displaying her wide jaw and sharp fangs. [[Now are we going to play or what?]]

[[You mean I could have shut off the audio whenever I wanted?]] I stammered, returning to the table.

She rolled her big cat eyes. [[Don't be stupid. Of course not. Only long-term residents in good standing can. And it only lasts an hour. So can we get this game started?]]

With a sigh, I said, [[Sure. But for points. I'm not slipping any secrets.]] I glanced at my Prigta ally, but he remained at his post by the door as impassive as a statue.

[[Oh, stop worrying. The stupid creatures can hardly even speak,]] FreaShia said, misinterpreting my glance. [[That's why Cassie uses them. Besides, I'm talking about funny secrets like the time I was supposed to give my first recital and threw up all over the judges.]]

We both gave sympathetic grimaces, but couldn't help chuckling. [[I guess that kind of stuff couldn't hurt,]] I found myself saying, then quickly added, [[But let's stick to points for now. At least until Dovain learns how to play.]]

[[Coward,]] FreaShia huffed, tossing down her first discard and starting the game.

When the hour was up, my Prigta came to collect me. [[I guess play time's over,]] I said, honestly disappointed.

[[Over?]] FreaShia asked, puzzled. [[I thought you were staying with me for the weekend?]]

The Prigta swung its head to look at me. For the first time, I could sense and interpret his feelings. He was terrified and frustrated. I wondered how badly he'd freak out if he knew I was considering inviting FreaShia to escape with us.

Chapter 18

FREASHIA HAD LED DOVAIN and me back from death, which had to count for something. That, and her crush on Dovain, made her a potential ally. As FreaShia and I headed to her room, with my Prigta guard trailing behind us, I considered ways to test her reaction to the idea of escaping without giving away anything.

My guard stationed himself across the hall, facing her door. We entered her room only to find it inhabited by seven young Katian females. FreaShia introduced her sisters, including two of her littermates with the same black manes and tan fur. I tried, but couldn't keep all their names straight.

[[Five of my brothers share the adjoining room,]] FreaShia said.

[[The rest are in the nursery,]] one of her littermates chimed in.

[[Or old enough to have their own places,]] the other littermate added.

I wondered if that meant they were practicing Dashias, but didn't ask. Instead, I greeted each of FreaShia's sisters with a nod as Katian custom required. The younger ones seemed tickled to have a proper guest.

It wasn't surprising that FreaShia had so many brothers and sisters. The fact that Katians breed like rabbits was one of the reasons they'd been able to conquer the Cluster not once but twice. But having her sisters around meant I didn't dare mention anything about escaping.

The girls surrounded us, prattling in Ruslo so fast I couldn't catch a word of it. Finally, FreaShia shouted over them, [[Hey! Shut your yaps. We have a guest who speaks the Ruslo of a nursery cub. So s l o w it d o w n.]]

[[Thanks for making me feel like an idiot,]] I growled playfully, the Ruslo flowing off my tongue for a change.

The first littermate took me by the hand and led me to their entertainment area. [[We're about to VR. Join us.]] It sounded more like a command than an invitation.

[[VR?]] I asked.

[[Virtual reality,]] FreaShia explained with a roll of her eyes. [[Holo-grams? Cyber-world? Oh yeah, I forgot you grew up on a Halo-world. They probably didn't even have VR. But don't you have a system in your room?]]

Now it was my turn to roll my eyes. [[No. Of course not. Like Cassie would trust me with a computer terminal in my room.]]

This aroused her sisters' curiosity. Before they could ask why I wouldn't be allowed such a basic necessity, FreaShia changed the subject. [[Where would *you* like to go?]]

A little escape from reality sounded pretty good. And there was a whole cluster of planets out there that I knew nearly nothing about. Hell, there was so much about Oweena I didn't know. I'd hardly ever even been outside the fetshous.

[[It's my turn to choose,]] FreaShia's littermate complained.

[[And we were going to go to NelSeca. We miss home,]] the second littermate whined.

FreaShia cuffed them both. Her littermates crouched with a sparkle in their feline eyes and leapt at her. The three of them tussled about the room. Soon the others joined in. When the brawl ended, FreaShia announced, [[We have an honored guest. The Code says we must let her choose the night's entertainment.]]

[[I'm no honored guest. I'm just crashing here for a few nights,]] I protested.

They all gave me an odd look. [[Crashing here?]] FreaShia asked, and I realized the phrase didn't translate into Ruslo well.

[[Plopping at your place,]] I corrected. [[Anyways, no big deal. The Code doesn't apply. I definitely do not qualify as an *honored* guest.]]

FreaShia jerked her head back in surprise. [[You are the daughter of the Third Elder of the DeConnett family. How is that not an honored guest?]]

I pinned her hard against the wall. Even as a Crean Kobbi, the Katian should have been stronger than me, but my anger made me more than a match for her. "My parents were Bill and Tina Splendor. They raised me. They cared for me. They taught me to be a good, honest person. The fact that Cassie DeConnett is my biological mother is a sick cosmic joke!"

To my surprise, she laughed. It was a full and hearty belly laugh that made me let her go. [[My mother warned me that you're even more hot-headed than most Katians. But damn, you put the fire in fiery redhead.]] She shrugged and said to her littermates, [[NelSeca it is then.]]

She draped one arm across my shoulders and guided me over to the squares on the floor that lit up when one of her sisters activated the system. Into my ear, she whispered, [[Careful what you say, some of my sisters are very loyal to the DeConnetts.]]

•   •   •

The next morning, I stopped by the kitchen to grab some food before heading to Dovain's office for my Ruslo lesson. I started loading a 0-grav tray with some of our favorites to take with me. I'd need plenty of energy for the vocal workout Venor was going to put me through later. He was determined to make me split my voice. To be honest, part of me felt a thrill at the idea of me actually cantoring.

HelaShia stepped in my way, ruining my good mood. Her fur had regrown some, but was at the stubble stage that must have itched like crazy. Needless to say, her mood was as dark as mine. [[Listen to me, DeConnett daughter,]] she warned in a rasp. [[Just because your mother has ordered that FreaShia allow you to stay with her does not mean you are friends. Understood?]]

"Whoever said anything about being friends?" I asked, trying to deny her any fuel for her fire.

[[Shouldn't you be speaking Ruslo?]] she challenged.

[[Fine,]] I said.

[[No. It is not fine. That is exactly the kind of flouting of the rules that gets those around you into trouble. I will not allow you to bring more shame upon my family. FreaShia is young and naïve. She doesn't understand the ways of The Paraxous yet.]]

I finished loading the tray and started to leave. She grabbed me by the arm and swung me around. Only the tray's stabilizer kept food from flying everywhere. [[You do not seem to be taking me seriously. So I'll rephrase: If FreaShia blixes up again like she did with that tyathyn addict, she is through. I'll disown her.]]

That sounded like a good thing to me. Then HelaShia continued, [[Once disowned, she will be handed over to the DeConnetts as Dashia practice.]]

I gasped. Even as I said, [[You wouldn't. Not to your own daughter,]] my empathic senses told me she wasn't lying.

She shoved me into the tray so hard that despite the stabilizers the drinks spilled. [[Do not presume to tell me what I would or would not do with my daughter. I have many children, several of whom are quite successful. However, it would only take one outcast to ruin it for all of us.]]

I took the tray and marched out of the kitchen, leaving her to deal with the spilled drinks. Her threat had exactly the opposite effect of what she'd intended. Now, I was absolutely determined to help FreaShia escape.

•　　　•　　　•

After my Ruslo lessons, Dovain and FreaShia accompanied me to Venor's studio per the Cantor Master's orders. We entered to find Venor seated at the mixer, wearing nothing except the socially mandated loin-cloth. There was nothing flamboyant about him today. His fur was a soft, natural tannish-grey. His eyes were a common feline green.

He pointed at Dovain and FreaShia then motioned to the chairs against the wall. [[You two, take a seat.]] Then he pointed at me. [[You, get your tail over here.]]

I refrained pointing out that I didn't have a tail, but it was hard. I forced myself to bow to the Cantor Master and rushed to take my place beside him at the mixer.

[[Sing,]] he ordered. [[Sing to them as if you were performing back on Earth with your friends.]]

My expression darkened at the mention of my friends. He gave me a snarl meant to keep me in my place. [[Your mother was able to obtain a recording of you performing at some local event. And, it is far livelier than any performance you have given me thus far.]]

[[Maybe that's because my parents hadn't been murdered yet.]]

Venor held two clawed fingers in front of my eyes threateningly. [[I've told you before: do not bring the burdens of your past into this place. Leave them at the door.]]

[[You're the one who brought it up.]]

[[Shut up and sing, child.]]

I almost said I couldn't shut up and sing at the same time. But Venor seemed honestly upset. He was trying his best to prevent Cassie from butchering my brain. He had no way to know Madam DeConnett intended to send me off for the surgery whether or not I managed to cantor by the deadline, so I put everything I had into the warm-up.

When he began the first song, he sang with me, pushing me deeper. The same warmth spread through me that had the last time I'd almost split my voice. I looked over at Dovain. He leaned forward in his chair, watching me with such intensity it was as if he thought he could will me to cantor.

The energy within me continued to build. When the chorus came, Venor split his two voices into four. My emotions went off the chart. My second voice emerged, making it sound like I was two people singing. Unfortunately, one of them was off key.

Venor cocked his brow and gave me a warning swat with his tail. I tried to get control of the second voice, but it disappeared.

[[You'll get it on the next chorus,]] FreaShia called.

The chorus came again. My second voice broke out—still off key. As soon as the chorus ended, I went into a coughing fit that threatened to expel a lung.

Venor reached into a drawer on the side of the mixer's stand and pulled out a throat spray. He tried to administer it, but I couldn't stop coughing long enough get any of it in my mouth. Dovain rushed forward. My friend, who was usually so gentle, grabbed me by the hair, yanked my head back and pinched my jaw open with his other hand. Venor sprayed my throat and the coughing stopped.

[[What ... what the hell was that?]] I croaked.

[[A laryngeal spasm,]] FreaShia said, seemingly unconcerned. [[It used to happen to me all the time when I first learned to split my voice.]]

Venor ordered Dovain back to his seat. Dovain gave me a quick smile before rushing off. I couldn't help smiling back.

Venor cleared his throat, demanding my attention. [[It's a common mistake freshmen singers make.]]

When we came to chorus on the next try, my voices harmonized pretty well. I sensed the joy this gave my friends. No, not friends plural. I was only picking up Dovain's feelings, and there was something more than joy there. It felt familiar. It felt like how I felt about Cameron.

I choked. Face flushed and chest heaving, I faked another coughing fit to cover my embarrassment. Venor sprayed my throat again. When I recovered, I gasped, "I did it!" I took a deep breath and repeated, [[I did it!]]

I threw my arms around Venor, hugging his soft fur. He tolerated the display for a few breaths, then pushed me away. [[Do not thank me, child. I was only doing what I've been hired to do. However, you *can* thank Sir DeNorial.]]

To my unasked question of why I should thank Dovain, Venor explained, [[Many freshmen Cantors need a focus to inspire their second voice. I'd heard of your relationship with Dovain and used it to bring out your ability.]]

I was mortified. [[We're just friends,]] I blurted defensively, worried how FreaShia would react.

She waved it off. [[It's okay. You two make a cute couple.]]

Her reaction seemed strange for a Katian. From what I knew, there was no way she should be okay with me moving in on her territory.

She smiled at my look of concern. [[Don't worry. I found myself another bed-warmer. That's all I was looking for. I'm way too young for an intended, and Dovain's a bit too serious for me.]] She turned toward him, adding, [[No offense.]]

[[None taken,]] he said, sounding more than a little relieved. Apparently, my Sian friend didn't have a clue how to handle a female Katian experiencing her first heat.

•　　•　　•

That night I snuck out of FreaShia's room, hoping to talk to my Prigta. [[I'm going back to my room,]] I told him for the sake of the monitors. [[I can't sleep with all those cubs in there.]]

We got into the lift. He hit the hold button, then tapped a different control and explained, [[Anyone monitoring will be treated to a recording of one of your previous tantrums. Now listen. Things are ready for Finday. I think we have a good chance of setting you free, but only you.]]

[[No. Please, Dovain has to come with us.]]

[[I told you, that's not possible.]]

[[There has to be a way. Please. I can't live without him. I love him!]] I didn't, but I hoped the declaration would be enough to convince the Prigta. For dramatic effect, I threw my head into my hands, jabbing myself in the eyes. When I looked up my cheeks were soaked with tears. [[I won't go without him.]]

[[That's makes things much easier for me then, doesn't it?]] he said, unmoved.

I folded my arms across my chest, my fake tears forgotten. [[You gave up your family to keep me from being turned into a Dashia. If you don't help me, it'll have been for nothing. Besides, I already told him.]]

He released the hold on the lift. [[Fine. I'll smuggle the addict aboard.]] He changed some settings, presumably to shut off the recording, and pressed the button to return us to the level with FreaShia's room.

The door opened. FreaShia stood in the hall, looking around wide-eyed and panicked. With obvious relief, she ran up to me. [[Where on Montara have you been?]]

[[Trying to go back to my room.]] I jerked a thumb at the Prigta. [[But this stupid pig-rock won't let me.]] I hoped he understood me continuing to use the racial slur for the sake of our cover. [[Would you please tell it to let me go? I'm so tired. I just want to sleep in my own bed tonight.]]

Her eyes narrowed, but she kept her tone casual. [[With the way my sisters snore, I don't blame you. As a matter of fact, I wouldn't mind a good night's sleep myself.]]

She walked to the room across the hall from hers and opened the door. [[This is our extra room for when any of us don't feel well enough for communal bedding or when we have a bed-warmer.]] When I hesitated, she waved me forward. [[Come on. No one's using it tonight.]]

I followed her into a lavishly furnished bedchamber. My Prigta took his position outside the door. Once it shut, FreaShia silenced the audio as she had done in the kitchen the other day. [[I know you're planning an escape. Take me with you.]]

Chapter 19

F INDAY CAME. I DRESSED in a double layer of clothes and put a few rings on my fingers to hock in case we actually managed to get away. When the Prigta came to escort me from my room, he gave me a subtle nod. Somehow he'd smuggled both Dovain and FreaShia onto the transport.

I was supposed to believe since I'd cantored, Cassie had canceled the vocal cord surgery. So I did my best to act surprised when my guard brought me to the hangar-bay. [[What the hell? Where are we going?]]

I spotted my mother standing by a transport and ran up to her. [[What's going on?]]

[[I have a surprise for you,]] she answered, all smiles.

[[What kind of a surprise?]]

She gestured toward the closed door of the transport. [[Why don't you go in and find out.]]

I pretended to panic and tried to back away. An enforcer droid moved behind me, blocking any retreat. [[But I cantored,]] I protested. [[And see, my Ruslo's gotten better. No. Please. If you slice my cords, Sir VerVum will quit.]]

Cassie released the transport's door. Dovain knelt just inside. Blood trickled from a swollen bruise on his cheek. A Katian guard held a gun to his temple. FreaShia stood frozen on the other side of him.

There was nothing to do. We'd been caught and there was going to be hell to pay. Something flashed across FreaShia's expression. Just a glint in her cat-like eyes; the twitch of her whiskers. But it was enough to make me suspicious.

"What have you done?" I asked her, hoping I was wrong.

She swaggered down the steps of the transport with her tail straight and proud. [[Did you really think I'd make friends with someone who'd disgraced my mother and stolen my target?]] She sounded so different. The prepubescent meow she'd always spoken with before was gone.

Cassie gave her a sideways glance. No doubt she'd hoped to continue the charade and use my supposed friend as a spy. With a shrug, she switched tactics. [[This is an important lesson for you to learn. If you'd bothered scanning FreaShia, even just superficially, you would have known right away it was all a lie. She doesn't have the ability to project false feelings or thoughts, yet.]]

Now FreaShia seemed worried. She adopted a submissive posture, only glancing briefly at her mother who'd just arrived. Cassie caught the flick of her gaze and looked back at HelaShia. Cassie reached out and ran her fingers through FreaShia's mane. [[Don't worry, little one. You did well enough to restore your family's place of honor.]]

"Honor?" I couldn't help but scoff. "What the hell do any of you know about honor?"

That was a mistake. Now Cassie's attention was focused on me. "I told you others would pay if you disobeyed." She turned to look Dovain in the eyes. [[Kill him,]] she ordered the guards. [[Right here. Right now. Do it slowly and make sure my daughter watches as he dies.]]

I lunged at Cassie. The collar didn't activate, which gave me the chance to grab her by the throat. The Katian in the transport moved to protect Madam DeConnett, turning his back to Dovain. My gentle Sian friend shoved the guard so hard he fell down the steps and smacked the deck face first.

My Prigta's booming voice echoed through the bay. [[Get in the transport!]]

Another Prigta tucked and rolled toward my Prigta. Everyone scrambled to get out of its way. The Katian guard on the floor didn't make it. The two-ton mass of rock rolled right over his legs, squashing them. His scream lasted only a few seconds before he either passed out or died.

Dovain took advantage of the distraction. He yanked me off Cassie and into the transport as the Prigtas collided.

"We have to help him!" I protested.

"We can do a lot more for him from in here," Dovain said, shutting the door.

He was right. I followed him up to the controls with a groan. Dovain set the transport into reverse, trying to get to my Prigta as the two collided with a boom. They bounced apart and the enforcer droid fired its pulsar cannon. Pieces of granite-like exoskeleton and gelatinous goo hit the back of our transport. My Prigta ally was dead.

Cassie tried to force her way into my mind, but my outrage and guilt over the Prigta's death left no room for her to whittle her way in. I concentrated on my emotional pain, pictured it as a laser bolt, and shot it at her. Out the side window, I watched her drop to one knee grabbing her head.

Then the bay doors slammed shut on us. Dovain frantically tried the remote release. Nothing happened. "The doors aren't responding," he squawked in panic.

"Back up as far as you can!" I ordered.

He did. I found the weapons system and activated it. Dovain cringed as I fired at the bay doors. The laser seared a hole nearly big enough for us to get through. I fired again.

So far, no one had shot at the transport. They must have feared harming a DeConnett daughter, no matter how much trouble she was in. Then the enforcer droid fired at the anti-grav drive in the rear. The transport dipped a bit but then stabilized. Activating the weapon's system had automatically brought the shields on line.

Dovain glanced at me in surprise.

"Don't look at me," I said. "Go!"

He slammed the accelerator to full speed. We flew out of the hangar and away from the fetshous. We were out. But it had cost the Prigta his life. He had sacrificed himself for me, and I'd never even asked him his name.

"Okay, now what?" Dovain merged our vehicle into the traffic that flowed between the rows of gigantic fetshouses. "Which way?"

"How should I know? This is your planet!"

The rear-view monitor showed three hovercrafts coming through the hole we'd created in the bay doors. They turned and headed straight for us. Dovain took a sharp left between two fetshouses. "Even if I could lose them, you know this transport has an auto-tracker," he said.

"Maybe we should ditch this thing and find another way. What kind of public transportation does Oweena have?"

"There are transport and hovercar stations at every fetshous. But they'd catch us before we'd finished checking one out."

"If you've got a better idea, I'd love to hear it," I said, watching the hovercrafts approaching. They were a lot faster than our transport.

Dovain swerved onto a busier route, as if that could hide us. "We could try going to the nearest security station."

I just glowered at him. He ducked slightly and sighed. "Yeah, you're right. Never mind." He looked around at the metal mountains of buildings we passed between, hoping for an idea.

Our pursuers flew over the traffic and came back down right behind us. "On second thought," I said near tears. "Maybe you'd better drop me off at the next security station we come to." Over his squawking protests, I explained, "They'll be too concerned with rounding me up to bother chasing after you. I'll keep them busy as long as I can. You just drop me at the next rooftop and hightail it out of there."

"No way on Montara I'm deserting you!"

A local security vehicle, hovering to the side of the flow of traffic, pulled in behind us and ordered us to land. Cassie's henchmen flew on by as we descended. Dovain sat back against his seat sighing with relief.

I ducked out of sight. "We're not out of this yet. The DeConnetts keep the local authorities on their payroll. Besides, it won't take those hovercrafts long to come back around."

I snuck to the back door of the transport as the Sian officer approached Dovain's door. "Just keep her distracted," I whispered.

The female security officer came to his window. [[Please, shut off the engine and step out of the vehicle.]]

[[Greetings to you, Madam Peacekeeper. I am so terribly sorry, was I going too fast?]] Dovain could have won an Oscar for his acting job as he stalled. He hadn't shut off the transport yet and "accidentally" revved the motor instead. The Sian crouched and reached for her weapon. That gave me a chance to slip out the back door unnoticed. Dovain turned the transport off, apologizing.

[[Please step out of the vehicle, sir.]] The peacekeeper repeated. [[We have a report of a kidnapped juvenile, Human female.]]

[[Oh! How awful. Who would do such a thing? Of course, feel free to check the vehicle.]]

I reached the passenger side door of the officer's hovercraft. With a quick prayer to no deity in particular, I tried the release. It wasn't locked.

[[Sir, step out. Now.]]

[[Sure. Sure,]] he said quite agreeably. [[It'll just take me a second. You see I've got this old knee injury …]]

I couldn't hear the rest of the exchange. I just hoped he'd figured out what I was up to and would be ready when I swung the craft around to pick him up. There was one problem with my plan: I didn't know how to drive. I hadn't even started Driver's Ed before being kidnapped. Not that it would have helped much. The controls of the hovercraft bore no resemblance to cars on Earth. There wasn't even a steering wheel.

I took a deep breath and examined the control panel. The computerized system seemed pretty straightforward, kind of like a videogame. And there might not have been a steering wheel, but there was a joystick. I engaged the 0-grav drive and squeezed the trigger on the joystick hoping it controlled the thrusters.

The craft popped up several meters too high and shot forward passing over Dovain and the officer. I over-corrected and almost put the nose of the craft into the ground. They dove out of the way as I backed up, nearly hitting them. I came to an abrupt halt and opened the passenger door.

"What are you doing?" Dovain shouted.

The officer had rolled to one side. She brought her weapon to bear and ordered us to halt in three different languages. Dovain dived in. The peacekeeper and I locked gazes. *Please don't!* I instinctively broadcasted my thought.

She hesitated. It was clear to her that I was no kidnap victim. She noticed my resemblance to Cassiopeia DeConnett and figured out the truth. She hated the DeConnetts. *Go kid. Run away! Get out of here.*

I broke the contact. Dovain closed the door, and I jumped out of the driver's seat. "Now what are you doing?" he squawked.

"Obviously, I don't know how to drive."

He shifted into the seat and engaged thrusters. Once we were safely in the air, the peacekeeper fired and missed.

"I can't believe we're doing this," Dovain panted. "Stealing government property."

"They can put it on my mother's tab." I brought up the computer interface. "Right now, we need to find a way to call the Dashia Hunter. Then we need to find a place to lay low until arrangements can be made."

Dovain looked at me, panic-stricken. "You do realize the comms of this thing will be monitored, and it'll have a tracking device. It won't take them long to locate us."

"Working on it," I replied, punching away at the computer controls. "But it's going to take me a while."

He muttered a curse, something I'd only heard him do during his fever. He shifted forward in his seat to adjust his wings and give them a good fluff. "I'm climbing to suborbital and engaging the overdrive. That should buy us some time."

The navigation system brought us up to a sub-orbital flight path, and the maze of fetshouses dropped far beneath us. Part of me registered that it was a hell of a view, but I was too busy working on shutting down the tracking system to enjoy it. Instead, it registered that if I screwed up and shut the transport down by accident, we'd be dead. And we'd likely kill a few innocent people when we crashed.

"Once we send the message, where are we going to hide?" Dovain asked. "It's not like we can go to any of my family or friends."

"No, that'd be way too obvious," I agreed. "First things first. Once I get the tracking system offline, we'll change directions and jump continents. Then we'll find a safe place to ditch this thing."

I entered the last piece of code needed to turn off the tracking system. The security system tried to send a message to its command center, but I'd already disabled the comm. A red warning light started flashing on the dash. "Overdrive shut down in five minutes," the control system announced. "Please reduce altitude to cruising level."

"Change directions first," I ordered. "Go over that ocean." I pointed at the map on the screen. "Hopefully, it won't force us to crash into the water. With the tracker off-line, even a few minutes at suborbital will give them a hell of a big search area."

As we sailed over the ocean, I tried to bring the overdrive back on-line. But the computer had locked out all access to the controls. Its dispassionate voice announced, "Reducing to cruising speed. Complete shutdown two minutes after landfall. Prepare for emergency landing procedures."

"Do you think shutting down the tracking system is what's causing the craft to shut down?"

"Yeah, but if I bring the tracking system back online, we're blixed."

We passed the coastline and flew over a mountain range. The auto-pilot function brought us gently to the ground in a small meadow. "The comm-system is currently off-line. Do you wish it restored for automated assistance call?" the computer asked.

Dovain looked at the wilderness surrounding us and then at me. I shook my head frantically. He closed his eyes and squeezed the bridge of his beak just above his nostrils. "No. Leave the comm-system off-line and cancel the call for assistance."

Chapter 20

"NOW WHAT?" I asked Dovain.

"Our only two options seem to be either getting this craft working, without the tracking system, or abandoning it."

I looked through the window at the steep mountainous terrain surrounding us. "You might be able to fly out of here, but without wings, I'm not going to get very far."

We rummaged through the storage compartments. No thruster or 0-grav packs. "I hate to state the obvious," Dovain said, glancing out the window, "but we can't stay out here in the open much longer."

The computer had chosen a clearing to land in. That was fine for making a safe landing, but not so great for hiding. Whether we were going to work on the craft or ditch it, we needed the distinctive peacekeeper's hovercraft out of sight.

I brought up the diagnostic program, reviewed the 3D schematic and scrambled out of the rig. I crawled underneath and located the 0-gravity drive. Dovain squatted down and twisted his head to peer at the underside of the rig. "What are you doing?"

"This thing would be a lot easier to push into the brush with the 0-grav on, right?"

"Out of curiosity, how do you know how to do all this, Twyla? It was my understanding that you came from a low-tech halo-world."

Now wasn't the time to explain to Dovain how Vance and I had made a hobby of studying forbidden Paraxous tech and hacking in general. "It's a long story."

He understood that to mean I needed to concentrate and left me to it. After several agonizing minutes, I got the 0-grav working. "Time to push," I announced proudly as the craft began floating nearly a meter off the ground.

When we reached the tree-line, Dovain stopped. He stared at me as I continued shoving the thing on my own. "What the vrek are you gaping at?" I snapped. "It's not like you didn't know I was Kobbi."

Dovain wasn't the least bit offended by my outburst. In fact, he smiled at me. "Chaw-shaw, Twyla. Knowing you are Kobbi and seeing such a demonstration of strength are two different things." He came over and put a hand on my shoulder. "Such strength is a gift."

I shrugged his hand off and stepped away with a rude snort. "Whatever. Let's stick to the problem at hand: do we stay and try to fix this thing or head out on foot? Or maybe you should fly on ahead, get a transport of some kind and come back for me. It'd be a lot faster."

He dropped his gaze and shuffled his feet. "I did consider that possibility. But I can't leave you out here all alone." He held out the datapad we'd found. "Let's look over the map and see what's around before deciding what to do."

The "you are here" icon flashed in the middle of the screen. There was nothing but forest surrounding it. Dovain increased the area shown. The nearest city, Gyfa, was over a hundred miles away. "That can't be right," I protested. "There's got to be something else around here."

Dovain surveyed the map closely. "There is a mining camp fifteen miles south." Then he pointed at a symbol and consulted the key. "Ah, that explains it. We've landed in the middle of a reservation. This land belongs to the Brassaud. They're a group who rejected technology and maintain a simple lifestyle. They might have a comm-system or a vehicle, but their aviaries aren't even marked on the map."

"Well, getting the craft flying without the tracking system could take a couple hours, or couple days. Or worse, I could give away our location by even trying."

"So we walk to the mine? It's not too far."

I gathered branches for covering the craft. With it powered down, it shouldn't show up on most scans. But it'd be just our luck for someone to spot it. Meanwhile, Dovain packed up whatever supplies he thought might be useful.

A few minutes later, we set the last of the branches over the door, and put on the 0-grav backpacks he'd loaded with stuff. He handed me a utility belt with a snack pouch on one side and a filtering/condensation unit on the other with a large canteen. The canteen was full, and even in this gravity it was fairly heavy. It didn't have a 0-grav unit.

Dovain usually made such an effort to be a gentleman, so it surprised me that he didn't insist on carrying it. He caught my expression and blushed a sweet purple. "Sorry. I need to be able to take to the air and scout the terrain in order to find a passable route for you. I can't do that with the weight of that belt."

So my hopelessly romantic friend had a practical side. My estimation of our chances increased a bit. I strapped on the belt with a nod. "Makes sense. Let's go."

"First," he said, producing a couple of bracelets from his pack. He handed me one and slapped the other onto his own wrist. "They're heat signature blockers."

"This is fantastic!" I said with delight and hugged him without thinking. He blushed again, and I pulled away. "You didn't happen to find any guns, did you?"

"The weapons cabinet was locked. I couldn't get it open."

I turned back toward the transport. He reached out, just barely brushing my shoulder. "Let's leave them. It's not like I'd know how to use them anyway."

"Neither would I, but we'd better learn."

"I thought you told me your parents were pacifists," he remarked. He caught my pained expression and apologized.

"They were. I'm not." I picked my way through the brush and reentered the craft. After smashing the lock's control panel, I reemerged with a peacekeeper's pistol tucked into my utility belt.

Dovain didn't say anything about it. He just handed me the datapad and made sure I was clear on the location of our rendezvous, then prepared to make his first scouting flight. It occurred to me that this would be his first flight since recovering from his tyathyn addiction. I held my breath as he climbed high up into a tree on the hillside that overlooked the meadow. Did he have enough strength for launch?

He spread his wings, testing to make sure he had enough clearance, then leaped from the thick branch. Even knowing this was how Sians often launched themselves on their native planets, I still cringed, half expecting him to hit the ground before getting enough lift. He flapped his great golden wings hard and began to rise. He soared across the sky. I watched in wonder until his form shrank to a small silhouette against the sun.

I started toward the fetshous-size boulder that marked our agreed-upon rendezvous spot. At first, my legs muscles burned as I worked my way up the steep mountain's slope. But soon, the physical exertion felt darn good. After a while, my head cleared enough to take in the scenery—dramatic and beautiful, but so different from Earth. Forests were supposed to be green, but most of the vegetation here was autumn maroon, though it was springtime. Some of these maroon trees had palm-tree-like fronds and bore some kind of nuts. The shells crunched under my feet and occasionally made me slip. The only thing familiar were the few pine-like trees, but they were twice the size of even the Giant Sequoias back on Earth.

I reached the boulder where we were to meet just as Dovain's silhouette reappeared over the ridge of the next mountain. He landed with a smile and took the offered datapad from my hand. He traced the route on the map with his fingertip. The scribe function marked the route for me to follow.

"It's not going to be easy," he admitted. "I had hoped to find a road, but there doesn't seem to be one."

"Do you think we can make it to the mine before nightfall?" I asked, still panting from the hike.

He shook his head. "We'll be lucky if we make it over that ridge before it gets dark."

"Who's we, kemosabe?" I heard my mom in my voice. Her mom had been a huge Lone Ranger fan and the line was an inside joke in the family. A joke Dovain obviously wasn't in on.

"Kemosabe?" he asked, cocking his head in a way that reminded me of Vance. Damn, I was really getting homesick. Only, I had no home to return to. Even if I ever made it back to

Earth and some relatives of the Splendors were willing to take me in, I could never put them in that kind of danger.

Dovain still waited for an answer, so I explained, "It's an Earth term for friend. My point was that I'm the one stuck down here climbing over this mountain."

He looked hurt and offended. "Cha-shaw. We already talked about this. I'm staying with you. I've scouted far enough for now. I'm going up that ridge with you, kemosabe."

I stuck my thumbs into the straps of the utility belt, my hands on my hips. "That's just plain stupid. There's no reason for you to expend all that energy when you can just fly."

He motioned for me to give him the canteen and took a long drink before answering. "I'm way too visible up there. At least down here there's cover. We should limit my flights to short scouting expeditions."

We crested the ridge at sunset. Dovain launched himself and circled the area ahead. He glided through the air so gracefully it gave me wing envy. The sound of a hovercraft came from behind me. I dived behind a rock. It would cross the ridge that blocked Dovain from view in just a few seconds. I didn't sense Cassie, so at first I thought we'd be okay. Then I did sense something. Whoever they were, their intentions weren't good.

Dovain, get down! I flashed, trying to target the thought directly at Dovain so no other telepaths would pick it up.

His silhouette tucked its wings and fell from the sky. As much as I wanted to charge down the mountainside to get to him, I forced myself to remain hidden until the hovercraft moved away. The terrain was steep and treacherous. I stumbled a lot before making it to where the craggy ground leveled out. By then it was getting dark.

I ran by the light of Oweena's four moons until I reached the area where I thought Dovain had crash landed. I found him crouched under the curved top of a big boulder. "You okay?" I asked.

"Yeah, fine. But what in the universe was that? Did you send me a telepathic message? I had the overwhelming urge to land right before the hovercraft flew by."

I waited while he came out from hiding and got to his feet. "It wasn't telepathy. It's more empathic. I can sense and send feelings." I felt compelled to add, "Anyways, I'm sorry. I didn't know what else to do."

"You probably saved my life. No need to apologize. In fact, I should be thanking you." He noticed all the bruises and dirt from my many falls. "Are you all right?"

"Fine. But we'd probably better set up camp and call it a night."

Since we had no tent and didn't dare build a fire, "camp" consisted of nasty nutrition bars for dinner and sharing a thermal blanket. Dovain made no attempt to be romantic, so sharing the blanket wasn't as awkward as it could have been. But the night passed very slowly with us jumping at every noise.

We got up at the first wisps of dawn. Dovain stretched the kinks out of his wings. "I should do another flyby. I never got a chance to map out a path last night," he said with a yawn.

"Sounds good. I'll try to fix us some real breakfast."

"May the Fates bless your efforts. I'm starving," he said before heading up to a ledge. Unlike my rather blasphemous references to God, the Makers, or the Fates, Dovain sounded quite sincere. I wished that I had some kind of faith to hold onto.

Vance and I had debated religion and politics a lot, but Dovain wasn't Vance. And I didn't want to offend my new ... my new what? Friend? Romantic interest? *Oh man, I wish Vance was here.* Our relationship was so easy. I never had to worry about what to say or do.

Get your head back in the game, I told myself and pulled the food analyzer from the utility belt. I set it for both Human and Sian specs. The scanner showed that those nuts I kept slipping on were edible, and extremely nutritious. The guide recommended boiling them to reduce their bitterness before roasting.

Dovain ran headlong for the ledge, making a low drop launch. He swooped down halfway to the river below, gave his enormous wings several powerful strokes, caught the updraft, and sailed down the river toward the mine. As he banked to follow the bend in the river, the springtime sun caught his golden wings, making them shine. Part of the river ran glass smooth, reflecting his image.

Once he was out of sight, I got to work on breakfast. I couldn't risk a fire, but the utility belt had a couple reusable insta-heat packets. With no tools for cracking the nuts, I smashed them with a rock. More times than not, the meat flew into the dirt along with the nut's thick shell.

After starting two handfuls of nuts boiling in a packet, I roamed the banks of the river, scanning the plants and fish. It must have been spawning season because hundreds of fish were bottlenecked in the crook of the river. The scanner showed these large black fish were safe for both of us. *Meat!* My mouth watered. Dovain was a vegetarian, as most Sians are; however, that's a cultural choice, not due to their physiology. I hoped he'd make an exception given the situation. We'd both need the energy.

None of our supplies included any fishing gear. But the river was full of the things. How hard could it be to spear a couple of them with a sharp stick? After all, they did it all the time on the survival reality TV show we used to watch.

I fashioned a long, straight stick into a spear and positioned myself on a large rock that jutted out over the bank. I jabbed my spear at what seemed like a solid mass of black fishes several times but somehow managed to miss. Finally, I got so frustrated that I thrust my spear so hard it struck the bottom and stuck. I slipped into the icy river, which was no doubt runoff from melting snow.

Despite the cold, I waded over to recover my spear only to find a fish on the tip. The slippery sucker wriggled off when I brought the spear out of the water. It flew a couple feet into the air. I batted the big fish with all my might then sloshed my way to shore, teeth chattering.

Dovain appeared just in time to find me awkwardly trying to pull myself onto the bank. "You decided to take a bath ... in your clothes?" he teased, offering me a hand up.

"Very funny." I splashed a token bit of water at him before accepting his help. "Just please tell me there's a fish flopping around somewhere up here."

"Um," Dovain said, glancing about. "Twyla? I don't know anything about fishing, but I'm pretty sure you aren't supposed to go diving in after them."

"Really? Thanks for the tip. Now help me find the damn thing ..."

He pointed to my right. The fish had nearly flopped its way back to the river. I scrambled over the rocks between me and my breakfast and pounced. A few minutes later we sat eating the roasted nuts while chunks of fish cooked in an insta-heat bag. Dovain noticed me shivering and retrieved the thermal blanket.

"Thanks," I said, as he draped it over my shoulders.

"Chaw-shaw, it is I who should be thanking you. It was kind of you to go to so much effort to make 'a real breakfast' for us."

He suddenly blushed and looked away. "Speaking of thank-yous: I can never thank you enough for what you've done—"

"Forget it," I warned. "Let's just hope Cassie doesn't catch us. Once we make it to civilization, we're going to have to split up."

He drew back in surprise. I rattled on, trying to make him understand. "In case you haven't noticed, people who try to help me don't tend to live very long. And she'll never stop hunting me. You, on the other hand, have a chance, but only if you're nowhere near me. So it's better if we go our separate ways."

"If that's what you want," he said in a soft, sad voice.

"Of course, it's not what I want, but it's too dangerous for you to come with me."

His expression brightened. He spoke firm and sure. "Twyla, do not think to leave me for my own good. I believe we have a much better chance of making it if we stick together."

I caught a whiff of the fish. "Oh thank the Makers!" I grabbed the packet and ripped it open. The steam scalded my fingers, but I didn't care.

Dovain handed me a safety sleeve. I snatched it from him and dumped the contents onto a travel tray with shaking hands. He gave me a strange, puzzled look. "And I thought my tyathyn addiction was bad." He took the canteen and poured water over my red fingertips.

"I need meat. It's a … protein thing." No doubt he knew I meant it was a Kobbi thing. Damn Katian genes. I shoved a forkful of the fish into my mouth, savoring the sensation of my body soaking in the nutrients it desperately needed.

"Since you're that hungry, it's all yours." He said, popping a handful of nuts into his mouth.

Movement in a tree across the river caught our attention. A young Sian male was perched on a thick branch at the top of the tree. A flood of adrenaline dumped into my system, making my whole body pulse along with my heartbeat. I got ready to run, but then the guy waved and called out a friendly sounding greeting.

Dovain and I looked at each other and then waved back, unsure what else to do. The guy took this as an invitation and flew over. He landed gracefully and stood before us as straight and regal as most mature Sians. However, I guessed him to be a young adult like Dovain, roughly twenty standard years old.

His skin was a healthier shade of blue than Dovain's. And his golden wings were really something to behold—larger than any I'd ever seen and somewhat sun bleached. They almost seemed to glow. Their accompanying musculature was so well developed that he could probably launch from the ground given enough room to run.

There was nothing threatening about his demeanor. Just the opposite. He seemed quite friendly as he chattered at us in what I guessed was an archaic form of Ruslo. Dovain cocked his head from side-to-side listening. He apologized and asked the fellow if he spoke modern Ruslo.

The newcomer blinked then took a second to reply. [[I speak modern Ruslo some. Please answer: for you this is better?]]

[[Yes, thank you,]] Dovain replied.

[[My intrusion, please excuse. I did not wish to interrupt your conversation.]]

[[Not at all. It is a pleasure to meet you. I'm Vin and this is Twilight.]]

I glanced at my friend but said nothing. He'd simply used a common nickname for Dovain and given the proper Ruslo translation of my name. They were aliases without lying. I'd just have to get over my dislike of the name Twilight and the image of sparkling vampires it conjured up in my mind.

[[I am Ter'ue of the Brassaud. Now my bluntness, please excuse. However, please answer, Miss: You are all right?]]

It suddenly occurred to me how awful I must look. My hair was one big, wet tangled mass with leaves and twigs in it. My face was scratched from where Cassie's fingernails had dug into my skin during our wrestling match. I had numerous bruises from all my falls, and my clothes were caked in mud from pouncing on the fish.

I met his gaze and set my chin. [[I'm fine. I just fell into the water.]]

Ter'ue didn't press any further. He just stood there patiently waiting for one of us to say something. In contrast to my disheveled appearance, his red-brown crown feathers were preened to perfection. They flowed to his shoulders, then ran across his chest to form a decorative ring. Most Sians in developed society had their chest feathers removed to allow for more comfortable wearing of front shirts. But since this guy only wore pants, I guess it wasn't a problem.

Dovain asked, [[Answer please, which is closer: your aviary or the mine?]]

[[Chaw-shaw.]] Ter'ue waved dismissively in the direction of the mine and said something about [[closed]] and [[years.]] He noticed me looking to Dovain for a translation and slowed down enough for me to understand him. [[You come to my aviary. You both very welcome. It is not far. I'll show you the way.]]

While Ter'ue went back to gather his tools, I asked Dovain, "How much of our conversation do you think he overheard?"

"He's Brassaud. They don't eavesdrop. He just waited until our conversation was over before making himself known. Interrupting is the height of disrespect in their culture. I've always found Brassaud culture interesting."

I'd spent some of my restless night skimming though the information the datapad had on the Brassaud. They'd turned their backs on all the new technology after first contact and lived off the land. Since the invading Katian forces didn't consider them a threat, many of the groups had survived the centuries of Katian occupation relatively intact. Once the Katian Empires ended, they simply chose to continue their way of life.

After Ter'ue had gathered his backpack and tools, he climbed back up the tree he'd launched from before. My vision telescoped in on him instinctually. He didn't seem to have any weapons, but I caught the tell-tale red glows that indicated both the pack and tool belt were equipped with 0-grav. "So much for rejecting technology," I said under my breath.

"They aren't technophobic," Dovain replied. "Their leaders are just selective about what tech they allow in."

Ter'ue returned, touching down lightly. He looked around, clearly puzzled. [[Forgive, please, if intrusive; however, I am most curious. Please answer: How did the Fates bring you here with no transport?]]

[[It's a long story,]] I answered. [[Can we make an interplanetary call from your aviary, Bras-a-red?]]

Ter'ue jerked his head back, cocking it a full ninety degrees at how I'd massacred the name of his aviary. [[Brassaud,]] he corrected. [[I know not of such a need previously. However, our Elders will know.]]

I looked to Dovain to see what he thought of the offer. He, in turn, looked to me. We both shrugged. It wasn't like we had a lot of options. He turned to Ter'ue with a polite bow of his head. [[We are honored by your offer. However, answer please: the mine is completely shut down? There are no workers there? No chance of obtaining assistance?]]

Ter'ue's expression turned somber. [[It was necessary to shut it down to prevent the Cluster's civil war from intruding upon our land.]]

"I guess that settles that," I said to Dovain. "But we should leave their reservation as soon as possible."

"Reservation?" Ter'ue looked to Dovain for a translation. When Dovain did, Ter'ue's hawkish brows furrowed. [[Excuse please. This is our land. We have held it from the time of first contact. We work this land as our ancestors did before us. It was not given to us as charity. Does not reservation imply some type of government charity? We are a self-sufficient people.]]

I noticed how quickly his modern Ruslo had improved. His pronunciation was already better than mine.

Dovain apologized and said something about the term on our map. [[We know nothing of your culture, and ask that you please teach us,]] he said as the three of us started walking.

That made our new friend happy. He chattered on and on all the way to the aviary. They believed that to lead a good life, people only needed the basic necessities: food, shelter, health, love, and purpose.

I soon began to understand everything he and Dovain said, and their grammar became suspiciously Standard. Somehow, I was using my telepathic powers to translate. My mental shields snapped on, blocking the contact.

The two of them prattled on in Ruslo that flowed like a rapid river as we continued down the trail for an hour or more. We came through the lush foliage and into a large clearing. The cliff-side towers of the aviary came into view. The way it was carved into the mountain reminded me of the Anasazi ruins, only these cave walls were made of granite and quartz.

Intricately sculpted murals filled the natural rock walls. The artistry completely contradicted Ter'ue's claim that his people were merely simple farming folk. Ornate garden terraces punctuated each of the dozen levels of the towers.

Ter'ue lifted his chin until his beak pointed to the sky. He let loose a beautiful call that announced us to his aviary. Then he turned to face us, stretched his wings to their full fifteen-foot span and puffed his chest in pride. [[Please answer: it is nice?]] he asked indicating his home.

[[Nice?]] I answered. [[Ter'ue, it's amazing!"]]

Dovain nodded and Ter'ue made a happy trill sound. [[So glad you appreciate what we have here.]] He shifted uncomfortably. [[Before I bring you in, I must ask: do you have any weapons? We do not allow them in the aviary.]]

[[We have a pistol for protection,]] Dovain answered before I could stop him.

Our guide who'd been so happy-go-lucky turned serious. The pupils of his hawkish eyes narrowed and he extended his hand. [[You will need to relinquish the weapon before I can allow you to enter.]]

To my shaking head, he added, [[You will have it returned when you leave the aviary. I promise.]]

Dovain cleared his throat. [[Ter'ue, would you give us a moment to discuss this?]]

[[Of course. However, please know you will have no need for such protection here. I guarantee your safety within the aviary.]] With that, he walked ahead on the trail into the clearing where he was met by a couple of other young males.

They exchanged hearty greetings while Dovain and I discussed the issue. "I just don't feel comfortable without a weapon. We don't know these people," I protested.

His feathers fluffed. "Have you picked up on anything threatening?" He glanced over at Ter'ue who was enjoying telling the others a story as they craned their necks to get a good look at us.

"No," I answered. "But it's not like I make a habit of invading people's thoughts."

He realized he'd accidentally offended me and raised a hand, shaking his head. "No. No. Of course not. I just thought you might be able to sense overtly, negative emotions."

"I'm pretty sure we can trust Ter'ue. But what about the rest of them?"

He took a slow breath through his nostrils, making a faint whistling sound. "There is not likely to be anywhere farther removed from your mother's influence." He took my hand. "Please, Twyla, this might be our best chance."

His eyes were desperate with hope. And he was probably right. The Brassaud might be our only chance for help. With a sigh of resignation, I pulled the pistol from my pocket and gave it to Dovain to hand over to Ter'ue. I just had to hope I wouldn't end up regretting it.

Chapter 21

TER'UE LED US THROUGH the valley of farmland spread out at the foot of the aviary. As we passed, the Sians working in the fields paused, waved and called out greetings, but none of them approached. The other young males he'd met upon our arrival had not been introduced. They had flown on ahead to announce us to the Elders.

We followed Ter'ue to a ladder on one end of the cliff-side dwelling. [[The Elders' chamber is on the top level,]] he told us.

I looked up at what had to be a twenty-story climb. "Of course it is," I sighed.

[[We do have lifts for the old, infirm, and the wingless, if you prefer,]] Ter'ue offered.

I shook my head and started climbing. "Dovain, ask him if we can clean up before going before his Elders."

Dovain did, and Ter'ue cocked his head, bewildered by the request. [[Going before the Elders? Chaw-shaw, you make it sound so formal. It is nothing like that. They simply like to meet visitors. We don't get many.]]

I looked down to Dovain, who followed me up the ladder. "Was that a polite way of saying no?"

"It was," Dovain said then returned to speaking Ruslo, though he made sure to speak slowly so I could follow. [[In many traditional Sian cultures, it's customary to bring guests to the senior member of the group immediately upon arrival.]] He added, [[It's also considered rude to carry on conversations in a language that others cannot understand.]]

Ter'ue cleared his throat and said shyly, [[I do not wish to interrupt.]]

[[Not at all. Please go ahead,]] Dovain responded.

[[Please feel free to talk whatever language best for you two as needed. As for cleaning up before meeting the elders: they merely prefer to meet people exactly as they are upon their arrival. You will have your cleaning afterwards.]]

[[I'm afraid I won't make a very good impression like this. I'm a mess.]] I motioned from my matted hair to my mud encrusted shoes.

[[Chaw-shaw.]] Ter'ue gave a dismissive wave, but there was a definite gleam in his avian eyes. [[You will make the best impression possible ... an honest one. Something highly valued by my people.]]-

By the time we reached the top level, Dovain was slightly purple and sweating profusely. My scholarly friend hadn't been in the best of shape before the tyathyn withdrawals. Now he was coping with the after effects of his addiction. Of course, it didn't help that he'd half-starved himself to avoid being re-exposed to the drug.

A half-dozen mature Sians stood ready to greet us as we each came over the ladder and stepped onto the terrace. Their lightly arched brows and etched faces projected wisdom and alertness. They may not have been trying to be intimidating, but their piercing eagle-like gazes were nonetheless. One of the taller males stepped forward saying something in archaic Ruslo.

In response, Ter'ue ducked his head and bowed deeply. [[Elder Seftan'ue, this Twilight and Vin,]] he said in modern Ruslo. [[They were stranded in the forest and require our assistance.]]

Seftan'ue embodied all the regal dignity one might expect from his avian race. His amber eyes bore an intensity that was startling. Yet, they also held a kindness that reminded me of my dad, Bill. However, it was the deliberate, graceful way he moved and spoke that gave him presence. [[Welcome, strangers. May you soon be considered friends of the aviary.]]

He studied us for some time. It took the courage of two people who'd faced Cassie DeConnett not to flinch under his scrutiny. He gave us a nod of approval and gestured to the vista behind us. [[Please answer: truly lovely?]]

We turned around, taking in the view, and nodded mutely in answer. Directly below us the stair-step design of the terracing gave a breathtaking view of the gardens on each level. Just beyond that the different colors of the crops made the valley look like a gigantic quilt. In the distance, sunlight dappled the treetops of the forest.

I thought I saw movement at the edge of the forest beyond and squinted, trying to make it out. Suddenly my vision telescoped in on the scene. I could see a wandering tracky beast—basically a very long haired cow—as clearly as if it were on one of the terraces beneath us. I grabbed onto Dovain's arm to counter the wave of vertigo such a huge shift in my sight caused. I really needed to get better at controlling my emerging abilities.

Seftan'ue took a moment to enjoy the sight of a pair of Sians out for a flight with their pet sergans—eagles larger than condors. [[It is important that you both understand what we Elders are duty-bound to protect. Our community and our way of life are precious to us.]] He turned and headed toward the large chamber built into the cliff. [[Shall we go inside and talk?]]

Ter'ue ushered us into the dome-shaped room. The Elders took seats at two of the four large tables that appeared to be carved from the same granite that formed the walls, shelves and murals. The curved tables formed a broken four-part circle. Dovain and I were seated at one of the vacant tables across from the Elders. An older Sian woman sat at a small desk outside the circle. She had a scribe-sheet, and from the way her claw-like finger hovered over it, she had an embedded pen.

Scribe-sheets and embedded pens, but no computers. I just don't get these people.

Ter'ue requested permission to have Dovain translate what was said into Standard. The request was granted and Seftan'ue introduced each of the Elders. Then he asked us in perfect modern Ruslo, [[Please, explain your situation and how we may help.]]

Once Dovain finished translating, he waited for me to answer, allowing me to decide just how much to tell these people. I didn't betray their hospitality by lying, but kept my explanation as simple as possible. "The hovercraft we were in broke. We'd be grateful for a ride to Gyfa or whatever city is close by. We can pay you once we get there." I glanced at one of the rings I had purposely worn yesterday, knowing the jewelry would be worth a small fortune.

Several of the Elders chuckled. A female Elder, who'd been introduced as Dreena, explained, [[Close by is a relative term, no doubt. We do not consider anyplace beyond a half-day's flight as close by. However, we do have a hover-car and could give you a ride.]] Then she gave a dismissive waving gesture. [[And we could never accept payment for such a basic act of courtesy. You are, after all, our guests.]]

I sighed with relief and thanked her.

Dreena seemed very kind, almost motherly. She was one of those people who was like a serene lake with a bubbling spring hidden beneath the surface. In fact, her incredibly radiant blue skin could have been a frozen lake and the fire in her amber eyes the warmth of a spring sun melting through. If so, then her golden wings with copper-pink highlights were surely the sunrise.

When did I become so poetic? I wondered. Then I realized those were Dovain's thoughts. I'd accidentally eavesdropped again. I wasn't sure which freaked me out more: the fact that my empathic powers were getting stronger or that my friend thought in poetic verse.

I pulled back within myself as Dreena continued: [[Before we offer aid and involve our aviary, please answer: are either of you wanted for any crimes?]] There was no accusation in her voice.

Dovain spoke up before I could figure out what to say. [[Twilight is a runaway, honored Elders. I'm helping her to escape from an abusive mother. The collar she wears is a pain inducing device used to torture her, and her mother was about to subject Twilight to an experimental, mind-altering procedure.]]

He started to translate what he'd said; I raised a hand to stop him. "I understood just fine. Thanks." I crossed my arms and hunched down a bit, staring at the floor. "You knew about the operation?"

Dovain extended a wing over my shoulder. "There's a lot I know that we have not had the chance to discuss." I looked over at him, confused. "Later," he answered my unasked question. To the Elders he said, [[It's my hope to reunite her with her father.]]

[[Is that why you stole a hovercraft?]] Dreena asked. Once again there was no accusation in her tone. To our shocked expressions, she explained, [[That is why you referred to it as the hovercraft you were in and not your hovercraft. That is also why you are not interested in fixing it, is it not?]]

[[Yes, Elder,]] Dovain answered. [[People with weapons were pursuing us, and we feared for our lives, so we took a craft.]]

[[We can deal with that later,]] Dreena said. [[For now, we must know: do either of you have any intentions of harming the people of this aviary in any way?]] She spread one of her wings in a grand sweeping gesture.

We gave an emphatic no. Seftan'ue stood and consulted with each Elder in turn. Dovain seemed remarkably relaxed while we waited for our fates to be decided. I, on the other hand, sat quaking with fear. My eyes darted around for an escape route in case they voted to return me to my mother.

Dovain reached over and gave my hand a reassuring squeeze. "It'll be okay."

Seftan'ue cleared his throat, silencing the room. [[We would be honored to assist you. However, we wish for you to take respite here with us until arrangements can be made to reunite Twilight with her father. After you have refreshed yourselves and had supper, Dreena will help you place the call.]]

"That's very kind," I started and Dovain translated. "However, it'd be safer to let us make the call from Gyfa. We can't stay. I'd hate to bring … to bring trouble to the aviary."

Seftan'ue leaned forward with his hands folded in front of him. His keen eyes pierced me. [[Answer please, just what kind of trouble is it you fear you'll bring? Local law enforcement? Zartous security?]]

I asked Dovain to explain the best he could without telling them who my mother was. When he finished, the Elders conferred for a few minutes and then it was Dreena who asked, [[Answer please: are you sure you will be safe in Gyfa?]]

Dovain and I exchanged looks that answered her question without a word. She sat back, satisfied. [[That is what I thought. You will both stay here, and someone will go and send your message in the morning. Return here after supper, and I will gather the information needed to make the call.]]

[[It is settled then,]] Seftan'ue declared, ending the conversation.

Ter'ue patted us on the shoulders and puffed his chest. [[Welcome to Brassaud.]] He looked us over with a dramatic scowl. [[Now let's get you both cleaned up. As your host, I couldn't possibly allow you to go to supper looking like this.]] He grinned an open beak grin at me. [[You're a mess.]]

Dreena came over and said something to Ter'ue. Before I knew what was happening, he reached into the pocket of his utility belt, pulled out the pistol and handed it over to the Elder. She caught the panic in my eyes and spoke directly to me in slow, precise modern Ruslo, [[It will be all right, Twilight. You do not need a weapon for protection here. You are our guests. We will not let anything happen to you.]]

Dovain added, "Twilight, please. This is the one place we might be safe. Dreena's right: if we go to Gyfa, we're bound to be spotted."

I looked around the chamber. By the way Dreena and Ter'ue bobbed their heads, encouragingly I felt sure he was right. A heavy weight fell from my heart. We could and would risk trusting these people. For the moment, and maybe just for this moment, we were safe.

Chapter 22

ONCE THE ELDERS EXCUSED US, Ter'ue brought us to their head mechanic, an older Flagoan female with brown bark and autumn leaves. Of course, as one of the majority races of the Paraxous Cluster, there had been plenty of Flagoans at Cassie's fetshous. In fact, two of my tutors had been Flagoans, but I'd written them off as enemies.

On the other hand, this nine-foot-tall tree-woman who knelt beside me reminded me of Sam's mother back on Earth. As she worked on removing the collar, she explained everything she was doing in a slow, calming patter. Her four hands with their ten fingers set about their tasks seemingly of their own volition.

Her shop actually housed an impressive array of tools and equipment. When I asked about some, she took obvious pleasure in teaching me about them. She and her small team of Sians were entrusted with maintaining all the mechanized devices allowed in the aviary. This included their transport, hover-car, lifts and everything else they had in this supposedly primitive village.

The mechanic said something that Ter'ue translated into modern Ruslo. [[They found an implant and want to have a med-tech check it over before extracting it. However, it does seem the entire unit was already deactivated.]]

A med-tech. Yet another contradiction in this "primitive village." Then it occurred to me, I'd been trying to compare them to the Amish, and that just didn't work. But figuring out their culture would have to wait; I needed to get back to the conversation about the implant. "I was counting on the fact that my guard had deactivated it," I said. "Otherwise, my mother would have tracked us down already."

Dovain went pale. Ter'ue noted Dovain's reaction, but the med-tech arrived before he could ask about it. Though the tech's med-scanner had to be at least a hundred years old, it seemed to be in good working order. The med-tech extracted the implant without any problems then placed a dermal patch over the small incision.

[[What would you like done with this?]] the Flagoan asked holding out the collar with a small bloody spike showing.

I stared at the thing that had tortured me so. "We should dispose of it far away from here, just to be safe," I said and Dovain translated for me.

Ter'ue volunteered to fly the thing far from the aviary and drop it into the river.

The mechanic nodded in approval. [[If your objective is to ensure it cannot be traced back to us, then I suggest placing it in something that will float for a while so the river will carry it even farther away.]]

With that settled, Ter'ue led us to the bathhouses in the courtyard on the valley floor. He loaned Dovain a set of his own clothes before flying off with the collar.

Dreena met me at the female baths with a large piece of cloth. I'd seen many of the Brassaud dressed in similar cloths folded, wrapped and tied in various designs. Dreena helped me replicate the simplest wrap pattern before we stepped out of the bathhouse and met up with Dovain. She went ahead of us to the ladder, giving us some privacy.

Dovain noticed my necklace. Since I'd always kept it stashed in a slit in my bra, he'd never seen it before. He eyed the heart-shaped pendant with the three diamonds and commented on how beautiful it was. It felt good to be able to wear Mom and Dad's gift without worrying about it being taken away. I clutched the pendant and forced a smile. "Thanks," was all I could manage.

"I take it *that's* not one of Cassie's trinkets like the other stuff you took." He caught my pained expression and sighed. "Ah Twyla, I am sorry. I didn't mean to bring up a painful subject."

I shook my head. "No, it's okay. My parents—my real parents, the ones who took care of me before Cassie killed them—gave it to me right before they died."

"It is very beautiful. They must have loved you a great deal."

I nodded vigorously, but couldn't speak. There were no words for how they'd cared for me, how they had sacrificed for me. Not in English, Standard or Ruslo. Dovain draped a wing over my shoulders in silent comfort. I looked up into his sympathetic eyes and felt the need to change the subject. "You said there was a lot you hadn't had a chance to tell me. Like what?"

Dovain looked stricken. He took a long breath before answering. "Yes. I should tell you everything. But there's no way I could even make a start of it before supper. And it should be someplace private, so we can talk without interruption."

We reached the ladder. We were to dine with Dreena and Ter'ue on the sixth level. I looked up at the petite bird-woman as she climbed to the third level with just a few flaps of her wings. Apparently, she felt it would be rude to leave me behind and just fly up.

"Something tells me I'm going to hate ladders by the time we leave here," I said with a groan.

"You could always take the lift," Dovain pointed out.

"And you could fly," I shot back playfully.

We reached the sixth level where Ter'ue and Dreena greeted us. They led us to a grand dining chamber where nearly two hundred Sians stood around, apparently waiting for our arrival. They turned toward us with open curiosity.

[[This is Vin and Twilight. They are our guests. Ter'ue will be acting as their guide,]] Dreena announced.

Ter'ue took great delight in introducing us to dozens of the residents from this level, including several non-Sians who were either on sabbatical or had come to live with the Brassaud. I found myself a bit overwhelmed by the time we sat down to dinner. Most of the Sian names were a mile long. I'd never be able to pronounce them, let alone remember them.

Several junior members brought out the communal meal. The crowd cheered. Ter'ue proudly served us large goblets of soup with a delicate broth that reminded me of Mom's cooking. To my surprise, the mash served on the side contained the same nuts I'd cooked in the woods, but these were almost sweet.

A dozen or so children hung around asking us questions. Ter'ue noticed that they weren't giving us a chance to eat and shooed them away. However, as soon as they left, he turned to me and asked, [[Answer please: Your father, he will come from where? He will take how long?]]

Since there was no spoon for the soup, I picked up my goblet and drank, stalling. Every mention of my father hurt. [[It depends on where he's stationed.]]

Ter'ue raised the goblet to his beak, tipped his head back and swallowed with pleasure. [[So you do not know how long you will need to stay here?]]

[[No. But it shouldn't be long. We'll leave as soon as possible.]]

[[Ch-Sha,]] Ter'ue said sounding insulted.

[[What she means,]] Dovain intervened, [[is that we would not want to impose and dishonor your hospitality.]]

[[You would only dishonor it by refusing it,]] Ter'ue said flatly. Then he leaned back and relaxed. In his usual playful tone, he added, [[Besides, you have no place better to go. I am sure of it. There is no finer place than the one my people have created here. So it is settled: Vin, you will stay with me, and Twilight, you will stay with Calian until you are reunited with your father.]]

I wished Dovain hadn't mentioned my father. It wasn't like the guy could help me. It was the Dashia Hunter I needed to contact, but now I wasn't sure how I was going to explain that to Dreena.

[[I was kind of surprised that you have a comm-system capable of interplanetary messaging,]] I said. [[For people who rejected technology, you sure seem to have a lot of it.]]

Ter'ue launched into another lecture. [[We rejected a life dependent on technology. That is different. However, we are a practical people.]] He gestured to the glowing stones that illuminated the chamber. [[We use that technology which can be used for good but carefully monitor it to make sure it does not become harmful. As you saw, we use 0-grav belts and packs to allow us to carry our tools. There are many advances we embrace wholeheartedly. Our medical care is second to none.]]

Dreena stopped by our table on her way out. [[Please meet me in my office once you're done. Do not rush. Be sure to enjoy dessert.]]

I moved to follow her, but Dovain informed me that it had been a polite way of saying she needed some time before we joined her.

[[Besides,]] Ter'ue chimed in, [[it would be a scandalous insult to the cooks if we walked out before dessert. You'd never be allowed on this level again, and we'd have to find you a new guide.]]

[[Really?]] I asked, pretending to believe his obvious exaggeration. [[All that over a dessert?]]

[[Nah,]] he laughed. [[I just want a jam-filled nut log. They're my favorite, and my mother spent most of the day working on them.]]

After dessert, which was actually quite delicious, we climbed back up to the Elders' Chamber. Ter'ue led us through the great chamber to Dreena's office. Her door was open, but she was absorbed with whatever was on her monitor. It faced away from the door so we couldn't see the display.

We both stood quietly waiting for her to notice us. When she did glance up, Ter'ue said, [[We do not wish to interrupt.]]

She waved us in, [[You are invited. Thank you, Ter'ue.]] She gave him a nod that he took as a dismissal and left. With a cock of her head and a very reedy accent she said, "You wasted small time in coming."

"You speak Standard," I gasped.

"Only a small."

I wasn't about to correct her grammar. However, she caught something in Dovain's expression, and trilled a question in Ruslo. He responded, [[The correct phrases are:]] "Wasted little time and only a little."

[[Ah, thank you. Perhaps, while you two are here, you can help me practice my Standard.]]

[[It would be an honor,]] Dovain replied with a bow.

[[Excellent,]] she said. [[Now it is time for honesty between us.]] She turned the monitor so we could see what she'd been looking at. The news report listed me as kidnapped and Dovain as my kidnapper. The reward offered was huge.

[[It's not true!]] I swore.

She laid a gentle hand on my shoulder and spoke in soft musical Ruslo. Dovain flushed a little, fidgeted his wings, then interpreted. "She says, 'That much is obvious.' She can tell we are … friends."

Dreena furrowed her hawkish brows and released a low whistle. "Friend?" She began smoothing her wing feathers absently. "Dovain, your skills at Standard more than mine. Answer please: the correct translation is friend?"

"Pardon, honored Elder," he said with another bow. "Good friends or perhaps special to one another."

Then she asked her next question in Ruslo and I thought Dovain was going to pass out. He swallowed back his panic and cleared his throat before translating. "She asked if your mother is Cassiopeia DeConnett."

Chapter 23

*O*H, WE'RE SO BLIXED. No one in their right mind would harbor someone on the run from the DeConnetts. More than that, knowing Cassie was my mother meant knowing I was Kobbi. With a resigned sigh, I told Dovain, "Tell her, I'll leave right away. But I want the gun back, and see if they'd still be willing to give me a ride to Gyfa. I don't want to be caught anywhere near the aviary."

He made the translation but substituted the pronoun [[we]] for "I". Dreena replied in river rapid Ruslo. By her firm, negative tone, I assumed she was telling us to get lost, and I couldn't blame her.

To my astonishment, he interpreted her words as: "Young one, the council's decision is that you must remain here until your father comes for you. We cannot allow you to set foot in Gyfa or any city. You'd be caught and returned to a group we know to be without honor or mercy."

I cried with relief. Tears didn't fall, but I sobbed just the same while fumbling with phrases of gratitude in Ruslo.

Dreena took my face in her gentle, talon-like hands and peered into my eyes. "Chaaaw-shaaaaw, child. We could do nothing different." She released me and pulled a datapad from a drawer in her desk. "Answer please: we should encrypt the information the messenger will need, should we not?"

In Ruslo, the phrase [[Answer please]] is one quick questioning cluck. In Standard, it sounded rather cumbersome. I couldn't help but smile at it coming from this high ranking elder of the aviary. Then I realized it was time to tell her about the Dashia Hunter.

Dovain placed a hand on my shoulder and bobbed his head encouragingly. I took a deep breath and explained, "There is something you should know, Honored Elder. My father will not be able to ... reclaim me without help. I was going to contact the Dashia Hunter he worked with before. The one who helped me escape from the DeConnetts when I was just a kid."

She clasped her hands together. "Excellent." She switched back to Ruslo. [[A Dashia Hunter is the logical solution to a DeConnett problem. We must take every precaution. We will encrypt.]] She handed me the datapad, [[Now please enter the contact information.]]

I did, choosing to trust her and resisting the urge to scan her empathically. She considered for a moment then said, [[The messenger will send it to someone we trust off-world and have it relayed through several people before going to the Dashia Hunter. We'll make it as hard as possible to trace. In fact, we'll have the messengers set up an anonymous message site for you. One you can check from here, but will appear to be being accessed from Gyfa.]]

I was impressed. With Dreena on our side, maybe, just maybe, we had a chance.

•   •   •

That night Calian, the young female Ter'ue had volunteered to be my host, introduced me to her family. By the way they greeted me with several head bobs and trills, I guessed they were excited to have a guest staying in their home. They probably had a million questions, but her mother saw how tired I looked and sent me straight to bed. They had an extra one already set up in the room Calian shared with her little sister.

I fell into an exhausted sleep. Sometime later a nightmare forced me awake with a scream. Calian told her sister to stay put and came to my bedside. [[Answer please: you all right? Can I be of help?]]

[[I'm fine. Just a bad dream. Sorry I woke you.]]

[[Cha-shaw. It is nearly dawn anyway. Mother and I leave soon to prepare the breakfast. She is a head chef, and I recently promoted to cook's assistant.]] She regarded me with concern but did not press. Instead, she offered, [[You are invited, if it would please you.]]

I got up. A chance to cook instead of lying in bed pretending to sleep sounded great. Calian showed me how to use the juicer and brought me a pile of fruit. The level's kitchen soon bustled with activity. They spoke mostly in archaic Ruslo, but I listened contentedly to their friendly banter.

Calian pulled a platter of fish out of the oven and called to me, [[Please bring a couple pitchers of juice. We're done here. Let's go eat.]]

We entered the dining hall and found Ter'ue and Dovain. Ter'ue stood to greet Calian with a warm gaze. He scooped up a fillet for himself and then one for the empty plate beside him. Calian gave the platter to Dovain and sat down next to Ter'ue.

To my surprise Dovain took a serving. [[So I gather meat is not forbidden here, as it is in most Sian cultures,]] he said.

Ter'ue perked up at a chance to serve as our guide or [[shepherd]] as they called it. [[We monitor the wildlife within our territory. We only hunt when a species population becomes unsustainable. These fish, as you might have noticed when you fell in the river,]] he said looking at me, [[have far exceeded their habitat's ability to support them.]] Between mouthfuls he added, [[Out of respect for the life taken, we make sure nothing goes to waste. What is not eaten is used to fertilize our crops.]]

Before he could start another lecture, I asked him if the Serga-Sians we shared the table with were visitors or residents. Ter'ue gave a dismissive wave. [[Chaw-shaaw. Their family has resided here since the second Katian Empire. They are Brassaud.]]

There were about a dozen of them ranging in ages from elderly adults to chicklings. Ter'ue made introductions, and I regarded them with the same intense curiosity they showed for me. I'd met very few Serga-Sians, and they apparently hadn't met many Humans.

During the early days of first contact, the Katians had mistaken them for Sergans, their favorite food. They'd hunted them nearly to extinction. It had taken centuries for their population to even begin to recover.

Despite the misnomer, the name Serga-Sian had stuck, and it was easy to see why. Serga-Sians are only slightly bigger than Sergans, about two-thirds the size of Sians, making them between three to four feet tall. Feathers cover their torso, and they come in a much wider range of colors than the trademark Sian gold feathering. And like Sergans, they have large beaks and beautiful tail feathers with dazzling patterns.

Once finished with introductions, Ter'ue started explaining the Brassauds' beliefs when it came to dealing with the world beyond the aviary and outsiders. When he paused, the eldest of the Serga-Sians said with a duck of her head, [[I do not mean to interrupt.]]

[[You are invited, Oreewa]] Ter'ue replied with a merry chirp. [[Twilight was wondering whether you and your family were guests here. I was setting her straight,]] he said in a somewhat stern tone.

I blurted, [[I'm sorry. I meant no insult,]] before catching the gleam in Ter'ue's eyes.

[[No insult taken,]] Oreewa said. [[It is a common misconception that Brassaud is a closed society. However, as you can see, visitors and newcomers are welcome. Just as you have been welcomed.]]

She waited for Dovain to interpret, then continued, [[We have Ateolies, Tyberians, Serga-Sians, Quelexonites, and Flagoans both as aviary members and guests.]]

Ter'ue refilled our juice cups though they weren't empty. For once he remained silent, obviously deferring to Oreewa as she explained, [[Newcomers do have a shepherd who is responsible for assisting with the transition to aviary life, as Ter'ue is doing for you. You must forgive his exuberance. This is his first time as a shepherd.]]

Ter'ue shot back, [[I may be a probationary adult, but I am adult.]]

Many Sian cultures consider the years between twenty and twenty-five to be a test period. From what I'd read, the Brassaud took this very seriously. If probationary adults, or "fledglings" as they were called, failed to live up to the responsibilities of adulthood, their rights were revoked.

Oreewa teased, [[You, Ter'ue, an *adult*? But you're such a hatchling to my aged eyes.]]

I wasn't sure how to react to such banter. The others at the table, including Calian, all chirped with amusement. Ter'ue squawked with a laugh. [[Chaaaw-Shaaaaw,]] He extended his wings to show they were full-sized and gold, not prepubescent white stubs. [[I'm old enough to take Calian as my intended at the quad-lunam. Besides, even our eldest of Elders are mere chicklings compared to you. Please answer: how many quad-lunams does this make for you? Five-hundred?]]

[[Four-hundred and fifty,]] she corrected.

Dovain gave a startled jerk, spilling some of his drink. He apologized repeatedly as he wiped it up. To me he explained, "Quad-lunams are when the four moons are spread evenly across the night sky. They only happen three times a year, making Oreewa nearly one-hundred and fifty years old."

Though Oreewa was the oldest non-Flagoan I'd ever met, nothing about her seemed old. Not the way she held herself. Not the quick intelligence in her eyes. And certainly not the way she rolled those eyes whenever Calian and Ter'ue gazed at each other like lovesick Caldaxian-mooring pups.

The conversation went on in Ruslo that I couldn't keep up with. Dovain's usual grave expression slowly faded away. He laughed and chatted as if we were safe—as if our ordeal was over.

Maybe it could be for him, I thought. Eventually, I'd have to let him go so he'd be safe. This seemed as good a place as any to leave him. Maybe he could even bring his siblings here.

[[Answer please: what do you think?]] Ter'ue asked.

I jumped a bit. [[About what?]]

Dovain cocked his head. "Ter'ue has invited us to come see his special day-greeting place. It's considered quite an honor."

Oreewa slapped Ter'ue on the back and said, [[The girl was paying so much attention to Dovain, she didn't even *hear* you, my hatchling.]] She glanced at me and gave me the same damn roll of her eyes she'd given Ter'ue and Calian.

The insinuation of a romance between Dovain and me made

me uncomfortable, but I purposely kept my tone teasing, [[Not at all. Ter'ue's just talked so much, my head is full. I simply can't absorb anymore.]]

Several Serga-Sians at the table chuckled, including Oreewa. Not wanting to hurt Ter'ue's feelings, I added, [[However, I'd be honored to see your day-greeting place.]]

He sprang to his feet and motioned with his wings. [[Come then. It's almost sunrise, and we'll need to check out a thruster pack so you can fly with us.]]

Chapter 24

W E CHECKED OUT A THRUSTER PACK for me and launched from the balcony outside the mechanic's storeroom on the sixth level. The dark of night was giving way to predawn light. My thruster pack was set for novice, so it was pretty much idiot proof. That kept me from crashing. It didn't mean I was graceful like the other non-avians flying to their day-greeting places. At first, I watched them swooping about among the Sians and Serga-Sians with a twinge of jealousy. But soon the thrill of defying gravity and the feel of the wind whipping through my hair cleared my mind of any thought. For those few minutes, I just let myself feel pure freedom.

We left the farmlands behind and glided over the surrounding forest, landing in a valley to one side of the aviary. On this side, the granite that made up the aviary walls was mixed with much more quartz and was heavy in iron pyrite or gold. The sculpted murals on this nine-hundred-foot cliff face gleamed.

They were even more intricate than the ones on the front side of the aviary.

A waterfall divided the end of the aviary from the adjacent mountain top. Rays of sunlight peeked over the opposite horizon, bathing the scene in soft lavenders and pinks. The mountainside glittered. The rays of light caught the overspray from the waterfall, creating a rainbow that spread from the top of the aviary to the peak of a quartz boulder across from it.

Dovain and I gasped in admiration. Ter'ue nodded in subdued agreement. He whispered something to Dovain, who struggled with a translation. "Now we sit and silently contemplate the forces of nature and our purpose in this ... world ... universe."

Ter'ue seated himself on a fallen log. He gazed at the vast panorama, settling into deep contemplation. I found a rock to sit on and tried to just enjoy the beauty of the dancing light with its many reflections.

For a few breaths, I became part of the beauty of a new day dawning. I understood the hopes my father had for me when he named me Twilight. In that moment, I could remember the man I'd so loved as a child and forgive the man who'd ultimately abandoned me.

Sunrise blossomed into full daylight before Ter'ue rose. He spoke slowly so I could understand without Dovain interpreting. [[Answer please: you understand the importance of a day-greeting place?]]

[[Yes, I think so, Ter'ue,]] Dovain said. [[Thank you for sharing this with us.]]

[[Your day-greeting place is incredible,]] I added. [[I'm surprised the whole aviary doesn't use it.]]

Ter'ue cocked his head from side to side, confused. [[If everyone used the same day-greeting place, it would no longer be special. I shared my place with you to celebrate our new friendship. It my hope that tomorrow you will begin searching for your own special place.]]

My Ruslo might not have been very good, but I did catch that he'd used the plural form of [[you]] but the singular of [[place.]]

Dovain and Ter'ue spoke briefly. Then Ter'ue excused himself and ran full speed along the bank of the river, flapping his wings furiously until he was airborne.

"I take it we're not going with him?" I asked Dovain. "I thought the guy was supposed to be our shepherd."

"Shepherd doesn't mean keeper. We're free to roam around. Ter'ue has chores to do."

"I guess this finally gives us a chance to talk," I said as we started walking through the woods toward the farmland. "You said there was something you needed to tell me."

His steps faltered and he grimaced. "Twyla, what I need to say will be hard for you to hear. It will be equally hard for me to tell you. I do not wish to hurt you."

"Just tell me."

"Apparently the DeConnetts designed you to be some kind of Dashia weapon."

My shoulders sagged. "Yeah, I already knew that. I'm a freak among freaks."

I started walking, but noticed Dovain wasn't following. I turned to find his face purple. He tucked his head down into his shoulders. "There is more I'm afraid. You are part of some DeConnett plan to bring down Sovereign Zartous himself. You apparently have some ability they need in order to succeed."

No punch in the gut could have hit me harder. *Me? How could the fate of the Cluster come down to me?* Sovereign Zartous had taken over when the Cluster was in chaos. Dashias controlled almost every Kobbi in power. Mass destruction and starvation were the norm. Bernine Cole Zartous changed all that. He banned the Kobbi and brought the Paraxous Cluster back from ruin.

Now the DeConnetts wanted to use me to destroy him. My head spun. This was just too damn big; my mind couldn't get a grip on it. With the New Federation's rebellion, the loss of Sovereign Zartous could plunge the Paraxous back into chaos.

A dozen questions tried to come out all at once, making me stammer. Finally, one of the questions made it out of my mouth. "How did you find out about this?"

"Someone sent me a copy of a message between your mother and the Elder DeConnett." To my obvious question he said, "I do not know who."

"It had to be the Prigta," I guessed, feeling even guiltier about his death. "Lucky thing we got away."

I tried to process what this revelation meant for Paraxous and for myself...and for Dovain. I watched the orange grass of the meadow, now visible through the trees, swaying with the breeze for a couple minutes. Dovain came and stood next to me. He unfolded then refolded his wings a couple times but remained silent.

"At least now I've got some idea what they'd planned for me. Do you remember exactly what the message said?" I asked, resuming our walk along the river toward a field of red grain in the distance.

He shook his head as we started up a steep incline, working our way around several fallen trees. "Not really. Tyathyn withdrawal still had my brain a bit fuzzy. But I'm sure I know the access code to the original message, so the Hunter can read through it him/herself."

Standard has gender-neutral pronouns, but his comment made me realize how little I knew about the Dashia Hunter. In fact, about the only thing I did know about the Hunter was that he/she ordered Vance's father to kill me if I was about to be captured. And this information wasn't likely to tip the scales in my favor. Then again, I had escaped and was going to hand over valuable intel. That had to be worth something.

"Okay. We'll just give the info about the message to the Hunter and let him/her handle it." The statement was as much for me as for Dovain. Even if it meant risking my life, this intel belonged in the hands of a Dashia Hunter. Trying to lighten the mood, I added, "I can't imagine how much trouble my mother's in with the Elder DeConnett for letting their weapon get away. If the Dashia Hunter doesn't get her, maybe the Elder will do her in."

But then it hit me: the DeConnetts would have a plan B. They wouldn't leave something this important to chance. They'd have back-up after back-up. In fact, they could be initiating one of those plans right now. The realizations rattled my brain even more. "We...we n...need to send this information to the D...Dashia Hunter. R ... right away."

"Yeah, we just said that. We'll add it to the message when we meet with Dreena." Dovain regarded me with concern. "Are you okay? You're stammering."

I took several deep breaths and forced myself to get control of my emotions. Once I could trust myself to speak clearly, I answered, "Yeah, like I said, I knew I was a freak among freaks. Just sucks that my own mother wants to use me to take down Sovereign Zartous. Come on, we'd better get back. I can thruster pack once we reach the clearing."

We found a trail and my pace became a double time march. Dovain had to hurry to catch up. He gently touched my arm. "Twyla, we have plenty of time before we meet with Dreena. If it's all right with you, I'd rather walk. That way we can talk."

I continued on the trail. "Not much more to say. At least not until we get instructions from the Hunter."

"Okay then. I'm enjoying the company."

"Chee-shawd." I tried imitating the avian sound but failed miserably. "Speaking of enjoying the company, you seem to like it here."

"I do," he agreed. "In many ways they have an advantage over most modern societies."

He tried to lend me a hand when the trail crossed a shallow part of the river, but I waved him off. He shrugged his wings, then hopped lightly from rock to rock, crossing the stream with a few flaps of his wings for balance.

I made my way across the stream, splashing a foot in the water several times as I went. Once near the bank, I decided to jump for it, but underestimated my own strength. I ended up tumbling to the ground several yards past the riverbank.

Dovain ran over, but soon saw that I wasn't hurt. He gave me an open-mouth Sian grin of amusement and offered me a hand up, which I accepted with a groan of embarrassment. In the next instant, he trapped my arms with his wings and just held me. It took me a second to figure out that he was hugging me. He looked at me the way Ter'ue had looked at Calian. My breath caught.

It would have been easy to play into the moment. He waited for the slightest sign from me for permission. I wondered yet again what it would be like to kiss the guy.

Dovain leaned in, then stopped and stepped back. I followed his gaze over my shoulder. Ter'ue was watching us with obvious amusement. Dovain's cheeks purpled as Ter'ue approached.

[[I do not mean to interrupt,]] Ter'ue announced, though his expression said otherwise.

My own face warmed with a blush. I waited for Dovain to give the standard response. When he didn't, I gave it myself. [[You are invited.]]

Ter'ue didn't even try to keep the chuckle out of his voice. [[Our annual dance of passage is not far off. Perhaps you two should plan to attend.]]

[[You can tell us more about it later,]] Dovain said. My friend was annoyed, and he was actually showing it.

I surveyed my wet and muddy pant legs and started brushing off the dirt, grass, and leaves that clung to them. [[I should probably get cleaned up before we meet with Dreena.]]

[[You two go ahead. I need to bring our herd of tracky to the lower field,]] Ter'ue said. [[Unless you need a chaperone, that is.]]

[[How kind of you to offer, but completely unnecessary,]] Dovain replied in a polite, yet rather clipped tone. He excused himself and headed toward a nearby launching ramp.

Before following him, I tried to think of something to say to Ter'ue to get his mind off the idea of Dovain and me being couple. "Uh ..." I started. Ter'ue just stood there smiling at me. Of all the times for him not to go into one of his long-winded lectures.

Dovain launched and circled above, waiting for me.

[[Uh, got to go. See you later,]] I said, lamely.

I found a clear spot and launched. Dovain came in beside me and we flew toward the aviary. "Ter'ue does know I'm a minor, right?" I called over, wishing we had comms, so we didn't have to yell back and forth.

"Well, just for a few more months," he yelled back.

"A few months? I turn sixteen in a few weeks. Even by Katian law, Humans aren't adults until seventeen."

"You're fifteen?" Dovain slowed, then had to flap like crazy to catch up to me. "Your mother told me you were seventeen."

"She lied," I snapped before going in for a landing on the sixth level. The auto-pilot took over and set me down with only a slight knee bend needed to absorb the impact.

Dovain circled then changed the angle of his flap to slow his descent. The sun gleamed off his golden wings as he touched down. For a second, as he was silhouetted, he looked for all the world like an angel.

"Why would she lie about that?" he asked.

I gave him a "no duh" expression. I wasn't about to explain to him that Cassie had planned to use him to deflower her virgin daughter. "How old are *you*, anyways?" I asked.

"Twenty-one."

"So by Sian standards you're barely an adult yourself," I said, somewhat relieved that our romance seemed to have been nipped in the bud, as my mom would say. Dang, how I wished she was around to guide me. She always listened and knew just the right questions to ask to help me figure things out.

Dovain tucked his wings and readjusted them a few times before answering. "I was emancipated young because our parents died, and I needed to support my younger sister and brother."

"What's going to happen to them now?"

His eyes glistened and his voice caught. "When I realized I'd become a tyathyn addict, I relinquished custody. Our aunt and uncle were kind enough to take them in."

There was really nothing I could say. His family was another in a long list of families torn apart by the DeConnetts. "I'm sorry," I offered lamely. But inside, it just confirmed that Cassie DeConnett had to die. Maybe the Dashia Hunter would let me help take her out. It was something to hope for.

Chapter 25

L ATER THAT MORNING, we arrived in the courtyard outside the Elders' chamber to find Dreena waiting for us.

She hurried us to her office saying something in Ruslo about a large problem. "She says getting you off-world is going to be nearly impossible," Dovain translated.

Dreena turned the monitor to face us and changed the settings to Standard. All Humans had to apply for a new visa before being allowed to leave Oweena. That meant going through a basic medical exam, which would reveal those with Kobbi physiology.

The Kobbi Containment Unit claimed that a group of armed and dangerous Crean-Kobbi Humans had escaped from one of the relocation camps. I wondered if it was true or if Cassie was manipulating the system. Not that it mattered. Either way, getting away had just become a whole lot harder.

My father had always counted on Cassie's connections to provide us with false medical reports so we could obtain travel visas. Of course, I had no idea how to go about acquiring such false documentation. And without it, we were blixed.

Dovain shirked his wings and unruffled his feathers. [[I'm sure the Dashia Hunter will take care of that part.]]

Dreena went into a long explanation I couldn't understand. Finally, I asked Dovain, "What's she saying?"

"Her uncle-in-law works at the docks in Gyfa. He is the one who is sending the message. It will be diverted several times before being sent to the Dashia Hunter. And we have no way of knowing what precautions the Hunter will take. Therefore, we should be prepared for it to take a while to receive a response. Perhaps several weeks."

"We can't stay here that long," I said firmly.

Dreena placed her slender talon-like hand on my shoulder. "I know it is a tall time to wait. But where else can you go? Here you both are well concealed. Anywhere else risk exposing both of yourselves. You risk those relaying the message, and this aviary. Please trust me. You must not leave."

Staying put went against my every instinct. Dreena read the indecision in my eyes. [[That does not mean we should not modify our plans,]] she said reassuringly. [[I suggest we have someone off-world send a message to your father. Let's make the DeConnetts believe you already made it out. That will give them an entire cluster of planets to search.]]

•   •   •

Two weeks went by with no response from my father or the Dashia Hunter. I'd hoped including the information about a DeConnett plot against Sovereign Zartous would get a quick reply from the Hunter. No such luck. So, I was left stewing in my own fear.

Nightmares made it hard for me to sleep. I learned not to make a sound when they came, since I didn't want to disturb Calian or her little sister. But since I couldn't get up without waking them, I spent hours each night lying there waiting for dawn. I worried about what would happen if Cassie found me at the Brassaud aviary. Just as scary was what would happen if the DeConnetts succeeded in taking down the Sovereign.

All that worrying led to me having panic attacks. When any hover-car, craft or transport flew by my entire body shook with terror. It didn't matter that they were outside of the reservation's no fly zone. I freaked out so bad it took several minutes for me to pull myself together.

On the other hand, Dovain was the happiest I'd ever seen him. A friend of the aviary had discreetly checked on his siblings, without risking contact. She reported that everyone was fine. With his biggest worry relieved, Dovain cheered considerably and embraced aviary life.

We were both given jobs, and he loved teaching modern Ruslo to the chicklings. I helped out at the medical center, which was a good distraction. Half my day was spent sterilizing equipment and treatment areas or assisting the med-techs. I found I enjoyed the work and even imagined myself becoming a med-tech someday. The other half of my day was spent on general education classes, something I didn't enjoy nearly as much. However, Dreena insisted, and parts of my classes did directly tie in with my work at the med-center.

One afternoon, as I was on my way from the medical center to the library, a hovercraft came over the mountain peak and landed in the courtyard. Dreena and Calian found me trembling under a desk, too petrified to even move. Ter'ue came over with Dovain in tow. Dreena ordered Calian and Ter'ue to take us to the catacombs. Dovain and Ter'ue hefted me to my feet and practically dragged me to a hidden door Calian opened.

[[The rock will shield us from any scanners. We stay in here until the Elders send word that it's safe,]] Calian explained.

We remained deep in the catacombs for several hours. By the time Dreena came for us, I was sure the worst had happened. "She found us, didn't she?" I croaked.

Dreena took me by the shoulders. "No. It was simply the local peacekeepers doing a routine inquiry about a missing girl."

"Twilight, many peacekeepers are aviary friends. They will accept the word of the Elders. It okay," Ter'ue said in fairly respectable Standard. Since he was Seftan'ue's son, he'd been allowed to sit in on the lessons Dovain and I had been giving the Elders, but I hadn't realized how far he'd progressed with his pronunciation.

I gave him a weak smile and Dovain's hand a squeeze. I hadn't realized I'd been holding it the entire time we'd waited.

[[Ter'ue is correct. Everything is okay,]] Dreena said. [[In fact Twyla, you have a message. I was on my way to tell you when the peacekeepers arrived.]]

•   •   •

I blinked at the screen. "That's it?"

The message was from the Dashia Hunter and read simply: "Message received. Standby for instructions." I was only mildly disappointed that my father hadn't responded. It wasn't like I'd really expected him to, but I had counted on receiving directions to an extraction point from the Hunter.

"It?" Dreena repeated. [[I am confused at the term. Answer please: Is "it" a good or bad thing? We have successfully made contact with the Dashia Hunter. That Hunter is apparently making plans for your rescue. Is that not what you wished?]]

Dovain tried to assure her that this was very welcome news. But I was having none of it. They couldn't ignore the obvious problems. "The message doesn't tell us how soon we might expect help, and there's no location given for a safe place to hide until then. Nothing! We've already been here too long. We can't just wait around hoping the Hunter gets to us before Cassie does!"

Dreena stepped closer. I expected her to try to comfort me. Instead, she spoke in a firm, parental tone, "Twilight, that is exactly what you must do. After all, there is no place safer to hide than one that has already been searched. The peacekeeper conducted their search and reported that you are not here."

Chapter 26

NEARLY A MONTH WENT BY. If aviary life hadn't kept me so busy, I would have gone insane. Between work, school, chores, and the endless string of community events, there wasn't much time left for worrying.

One morning Calian insisted on walking with me to the women's bath after sunrise meditation. Communal bathing was one aspect of the Brassaud life I didn't care for, and I assumed she thought having a friend with me made it less uncomfortable. Then we happened to run into Dovain and Ter'ue lingering about on the trail.

Ter'ue and Calian hurried on, leaving Dovain and me a moment of privacy. We watched the couple lean in against one another as they walked. Her black crown feathers had a slight red highlight to them, while his were reddish-brown. His wings were a bleached gold; hers a rose gold. Otherwise, their silhouettes matched in size and shape. I wondered if the fact that female Sians were the same size as males had led to them being one of the few egalitarian races.

Dovain glanced around. Single young males and females weren't left alone for any length of time until they declared themselves as intendeds. Though Ter'ue and Calian were expected to become intendeds soon, their flirtation was still carefully monitored. Much to my annoyance, Dovain and I were chaperoned just as closely.

Once there was no one in earshot he said, "I was thinking it might be nice to take a walk together tonight. Maybe watch the sunset?"

I pretended not to realize he was asking me out on the Brassaud's version of a date. "Sure. My place or yours?" I said casually, referring to our day-greeting places.

"Twyla ..." He reached out taking my hand. "We'll be getting word back from the Hunter soon. The Fates only know what's going to happen then. I know you have every intention of leaving me behind. While I'm not agreeing to that, the truth is neither of us knows what's going to happen next. I'd just like to spend some time together, just the two of us, before everything goes all crazy again."

I nodded then ran off to catch up with Calian. She stood waiting for me just outside the entrance to the woman's bath. [[Well, did he ask you?]] Her gold-flecked, avian eyes glittered with anticipation.

[[Ask me what?]] I replied, pretending not to know she was referring to the upcoming dance.

Cheering and laughter echoed from the baths. [[We'd better go in before we miss all the good gossip,]] Calian said.

Great! From one awkward situation to the next.

The stone building was constructed around a natural hot spring. Like all exterior walls of the aviary, exquisite life-sized engravings adorned the building. According to Calian, this series of murals depicted the story of Oodan'alka, who had saved her entire aviary from a Katian genocide squad over a thousand years ago.

Once we entered the baths, the reason for all the cheers became obvious. The probationary adults were announcing their dates for the Dance of Passage. Their attention quickly turned to Calian as she made her way toward the water. She bobbed her head with a shy blush. [[Yes, Ter'ue formally invited me to the dance. But we've been planning on attending as a couple for months.]] She removed her tunic and pants and jumped in the bath.

Calian's mother sat in one of the upper grooming stations overlooking the baths, combing the white, wing feathers of her younger daughter. [[It's about time,]] she muttered loud enough for all to hear without taking her eyes off the meticulous task. [[That he waited so long either shows a lack of maturity or that he already takes you for granted.]]

Her mother's criticism did nothing to dampen my roommate's spirits. [[Not at all, mother. Ter'ue had one more test to pass before the Elders removed his probationary status.]] She spotted Dreena among a group of female Elders and level leaders. [[Answer please, Dreena: He passed?]]

[[Was there ever any doubt?]] Deena replied, giving Calian's mother a Sian smile and nod.

The woman renewed her efforts of preening her little girl's wings with undue vigor. The girl, who was about five or six standard years old, jerked her wing away. As two down-like, white feathers drifted to the floor, she squawked in protest.

It occurred to me that I should make some effort to be social. After all, the conversation had taken place in modern, instead of archaic, Ruslo for my sake. [[I don't understand,]] I confessed to

Calian. [[The dance isn't for another month. So what's the big deal?]]

Her mother answered, [[A young lady who is eligible for attachment must be asked at least four weeks in advance if the couple are to become intendeds. Anything less is an insult. It is a declaration that they are not intendeds, even if he does finally ask. It is also very inconsiderate, since she might not find another date for the dance if she keeps waiting for an invitation that is not coming.]]

[[So what if a couple just wants to go to the dance as a date and not intendeds?]]

Calian eyed me. She knew exactly why I was asking; however, she let her mother answer. [[By making or accepting the invitation less than four weeks in advance the two are indicating just that.]] Her voice became firm and reproachful. [[That is why if he wishes to become intendeds, he should ask well in advance of the deadline. Not wait until the last possible moment.]]

Calian shook her head and raised her hands in silent entreaty to the Fates. Once done with her overly dramatic prayer, she splashed at me and motioned for me to join her in the water. I slipped my clothes off as quickly as I could and dipped into the relative concealment of the water.

Once in the hot mineral water, my muscles started to relax. Then one of the females asked if Dovain and I would be attending the dance together. Every eye in the place was now on me.

Calian spoke up before I could come up with an answer. [[Well, after seeing the two of them holding hands this morning, I think they should.]]

The younger women giggled; the older ones raised inquisitive brows. Calian's little sister made gagging gestures complete with sounds effects. Then the girl asked in all seriousness, [[Answer please: a marriage of two outsiders happened before?]]

I opened my mouth to clarify things. We hadn't even gone on a date, and now they were talking marriage. Calian elbowed me. The question had been directed to the Elders, and it was considered the height of disrespect to interrupt them.

Dreena considered the question before answering. [[All the ones I'm aware of took place after the couple had officially become members of the aviary. However, Twilight and Vin have been welcomed into our community. I believe if they were to make the petition, it would be favorably met.]]

Calian became very excited, [[Answer please: would you consider staying? If you left, I would miss you much.]]

I lowered my gaze and mumbled, [[It's kind of up to my father to decide.]]

[[Chaw-Shaw. You are soon to become an adult.]]

I considered clearing up the whole age thing, but Calian's little sister asked, [[Mixed-race marriage? One of those happened before?]]

[[Sergas and Sians marry quite often,]] Dreena said.

[[That's different. They both avian races. I mean other species. Like Twilight and Vin,]] the girl persisted.

Dreena smiled indulgently. [[Such marriages occur outside the aviary all the time. It is not even all that rare. Our sister aviary recently had a wedding between a Flagoan and a Sian member.]]

Her mother quieted the girl before she could ask another question. [[Hush. Dovain and Twilight have conducted themselves honorably. You heard the Elder: they have been welcomed into the aviary. Stop being rude with your questions that risk making Twilight feel like an outsider.]]

The girl seemed stricken at the thought. She rushed to the edge and called down to me. [[Oh Twilight. I sorry. I not mean it that way.]]

If I had chaw-shawed it off, I might have offended her mother, who'd just paid me a great compliment. I glanced at Calian for guidance. She whispered the words for me to repeat, [[Thank you for the apology. No offense taken.]]

•　　•　　•

Though it was Restday, I'd arranged to run through some practice scenarios in preparation for my med-tech aide evaluation next week. Oreewa was in charge of med-tech personnel and training. The Elder Sergan-Sian had taken a personal interest in my education and had voluntarily given up her Restday afternoon to help me prepare. After we finished the last scenario, Oreewa assured me that I'd do fine on the evaluation and excused my pretend patients to go clean-up for supper.

Now there was nothing to keep me from thinking about my walk with Dovain tonight. He obviously wanted to ask me to the dance, and I still hadn't made up my mind what to say. He'd waited until after the deadline, so it would just be a date. No big deal, I told myself. But I wasn't sure how I felt about the guy, and I didn't want to lead him on.

Then Dovain showed up for supper all spruced up. He wore a new outfit that Dreena had made for him as a thank you for all his tutoring. He'd muscled up a lot since our arrival and the suit showed that to advantage. He was still Sian lean: his muscles were just better-toned, and his face wasn't so gaunt anymore. His feathers had been preened until his crown feathers shown blue-black and his golden wings glittered.

I wasn't the only female who noticed. Several single women eyed him, then watched for my response to his fine appearance. They'd never be so crass as to pay undue attention to a "taken" male. If I failed to compliment him, it would mean he was available. Then it would become a race to see which young lady paid him such attention first as a way of signaling her interest. If I did say something, it would confirm our standing as a couple.

I wasn't usually so astute about social subtleties, but this game had been going on all week among the eligible members. Plus Calian had kindly explained it to me. In a way, she'd become as much of a shepherd to me as Ter'ue.

As carefully as I could, I directed my comment to Dreena. [[Elder Dreena, answer please: you sewed Dovain's new clothes yourself?]] When she nodded, I went on, [[You are as fine a tailor as you are a librarian and an Elder.]]

Let them figure that one out, I thought with mischievous satisfaction. The young women around were all a-twitter trying to decide if that constituted a claim or not.

Dovain sat down next to me and asked if I felt ready for my evaluation. I started to list the areas I needed to study more.

Ter'ue quickly grew bored and interrupted, something Brassauds almost never did. [[She is obviously more than ready,]] he said and then changed the subject, clapping his hands excitedly. [[Twilight, Vin has something to ask you.]] He made the announcement so loudly that we now had the attention of everyone around us.

Dovain shifted uncomfortably in his seat. He fluffed his now ruffled feathers, and glared at Ter'ue. [[Actually, it can wait until after supper.]]

Ter'ue slapped him on the back, almost making him spill his soup goblet. [[Chaw-shaaaw, why procrastinate? Just ask the girl.]]

I tried not to laugh at Dovain's bright blue face and devastated expression. He took a deep breath and shrugged his wings, trying once more to get them smoothed. [[Actually, Ter'ue, since you've said so much already, perhaps you'd like to ask for me?]]

Everyone laughed. Dovain took advantage of the distraction to blurt, "Twilight, would you go to the dance with me?"

Like I could refuse in front of all these people. Besides, I loved to dance, and from what I understood, you couldn't attend without a date. Knowing I was about to say yes gave me such a rush, I almost forgot to answer. "Sure ... sounds like fun."

Ter'ue translated our conversation. Cheers and toasts rose throughout the chamber.

Chapter 27

THE MORNING OF THE DANCE, I climbed up to Dreena's office to check in with her like I did every day. She stood at the terrace railing waiting for me. "Twilight, you have a message."

I hoisted myself up the last few rungs of the ladder and nearly catapulted myself onto the terrace. More and more my strength matched that of a Katian. A few days ago, while working at the med-center, I'd scanned myself when no one else was around. Sure enough, it showed that my muscle density was more Katian than Human.

All of that fled my mind as Dreena and I entered her office. Dovain was already there. He stood hovering next to Dreena's husband—the aviary's lead computer tech. The guy sat with his beak almost touching the screen as his talon-like fingers flew over the keyboard. Dovain explained that he was running a scan to make sure none of the security measures had been compromised. I nearly turned blue as the guy worked to make it appear the message was being accessed from a public terminal in Gyfa.

When he was done, Dreena said, [[Twilight and Vin should be the only ones to view this. The fewer who know the plan, the less likely it is that the DeConnetts can obtain the information.]] She tapped her temple, referring to the Kobbi ability to read minds.

He and Dreena moved back and turned away. I was about to ask Dovain to join them, but our gazes locked and I knew he'd be stubborn about it.

"Be in Owoolic City on 7-1-4539, Paraxous Standard Calendar. Delete this message from your files and the servers as soon as received."

I deleted the message as instructed, but also went in and reset the account so it'd show a history of zero messages sent or received. Dovain recognized the name of the city. It was a few hours flight by hover-craft.

Dreena rejoined us. With a great deal of parental concern, she asked, "Answer please: good news?"

"Yes," I answered automatically, though in truth I found myself saddened by the news. My respite was over, and now I'd have to leave Dovain.

As if responding to that thought, Dovain informed Dreena, [[It appears that *we* will be needing that ride to Gyfa within the next few days, honored Elder.]] He looked me in the eyes as if daring me to argue.

"No," Dreena said, surprising us both. Then she explained, [[Gyfa is our nearest city. We cannot risk the DeConnetts tracing you back to us. We will take you to any other city you wish.]]

It made sense. However, she'd used the plural form of [[you]] assuming Dovain was coming with me. I'd already spoken to her about letting Dovain stay. She'd said the aviary would be honored to have him; however, it would probably be easier to keep a pack of hungry memform from their supper than to keep Dovain from my side.

As Dovain and I left the office, my friend looked far from happy. He hung his head and wouldn't look at me. When we were out on the terrace I gave in and asked, "Why so glum?"

"Remember how I said it'd be nice to spend time together before things get crazy?"

"Yeah, what about it?"

"It looks like things are about to get crazy."

I patted his arm in sympathy. We both knew what he wasn't saying. He'd guessed I wasn't going to let him come with me, but neither of us wanted to fight about it on the day of the dance. "Let's just enjoy tonight and worry about everything else tomorrow," I suggested.

He bobbed his head, happy to have a truce for now. Of course, he wouldn't be so happy when he woke in the morning to find I'd already left.

Chapter 28

THE NELSECIAN SUNSTONES surrounding the courtyard bathed the terrace gardens in an almost magical light. Before engaging the 0-grav belt I'd borrowed for the evening, I paused to enjoy the view from the sixth level. The sunstones outlined the courtyard and a large part of the field across the river that had been transformed into a reception area. They also bordered the dance floor, though much of the dancing would take place in the air above.

On the two bridges that connected the courtyard and the reception area, the sunstones were mounted on poles. Their reflections sparkled in the rushing water beneath. Oweena's four moons lit the sky. The big one and its half-sized companion shared center-sky, while the two little ones could be seen just above opposite horizons.

The fact that the dance of passage was held on the quad-lunam was no doubt due in part to the romantic lighting. The moons cast a golden hue that softened the world as if viewing it through the lens used in romantic movies. I hoped Dovain and I would sky-dance. I'd never tried it before, but it looked like fun.

I felt a strange surge of adrenaline at the thought of dancing with Dovain, whether in the air or on the ground. It made me think of how he'd held me and had come closing to kissing me. Would he kiss me tonight?

This would be my first real date. While I'd gone out with my friends almost every weekend back on Earth, my parents hadn't allowed me to date yet. There had been the one time while we were at a movie with Cameron and Nina that Vance had held my hand. But that didn't count. After all, it was Vance, and he was like a brother to me.

The adrenaline turned into a wave of anxiety that struck me hard. Unlike the fear that gripped me every time a hovercraft flew by, this felt strangely good. Holy Makers, I was nervous. Just like any girl about to go on her first date. Maybe I hadn't forgotten how to be normal after all.

I engaged the 0-grav belt and floated down to the courtyard, joining all the other females. Calian spotted me and waved me over to her and the rest of the probationary females. Elder Oreewa shooed all of us into a line.

As the oldest female of the aviary, she served as the Matron at all community functions. She marched down the line inspecting each girl. When she came to me, she eyed the golden gown that Dreena had made for me. It matched the other young women's dresses as closely as possible given the differences in anatomy.

Though there were several other non-avian females, there were no other Humans. And I couldn't help feeling out of place. I had no golden wings to reflect the light of the sunstones. My peach complexion didn't shine in the light of the moons the way their glacial blue skin did. I stood a good head taller than them, but lacked their long slender figures. In fact, my figure had begun to look very Sentagil-like, with a distinctly hourglass shape. Something I'd been trying to hide, but the dress made it all too obvious.

[[You look quite lovely,]] Matron Oreewa announced.

"Thank you," I mumbled. Then repeated, [[Thank you, Elder.]]

By this time, the adult males had lined up on a high ridge across the river, facing us. They all wore white tunics and trousers. In the flickering sunstone light, they seemed like surreal spirit creatures.

The band struck up a marching rhythm. Seftan'ue stood at the head of the line. He launched into the air and came to a graceful landing in front of his wife. The tall, elegant bird-man spread his wings to their full twelve-foot span. She stepped forward, and he wrapped those enormous wings around her.

Everyone cheered and stomped one foot as the couple walked across the bridge together and took their places at the foot of the ridge. The rest of the Elders did the same with their wives. Then it was time for the husbands of the female Elders to take their turns. Dreena's husband went last.

Instead of gliding gently over as the others had done, he zoomed high into the sky. He crossed before each of the four moons, creating a breathtaking silhouette. Then he swooped down. For a moment, I thought he'd crash right into Dreena. She held her ground, hands on hip, chest puffed and beak to the air. He landed and bowed before her. He whispered something. She leaned down to listen.

When he looked up to meet her eyes, there were tears sparkling in them. She gave him a nod, and he rushed to take her in his arms and wings. The aviary members watched with soft coos and bobbing heads. There had been rumors of a marriage-jeopardizing disagreement between them. Judging from the way they clung to each other now, all was forgiven.

The tempo of the music changed, and the procession started again, this time for the rest of the married couples. At least this time the males launched one right after another, so they were done in a few minutes.

Despite my impatience for the dance to start, I couldn't help but notice how much everyone else seemed to enjoy the ceremony. Well, almost everyone. One male launched, buzzed over his wife's head and just kept going. She wiped the markings from her face that indicated she was taken. Then with her beak held high, she walked to the back of the line and took her place with the other eligible females. Everyone craned their necks to see who was at the end of the male line. Presumably he was now her date for the evening. Another time, when a male spread his wings, his wife turned her back on him. They both wiped the married marks from their faces and stormed off in opposite directions.

The music changed to softer, more wistful tune. The first single male launched. He crossed the path of the moons, performing all sorts of aerial acrobatics. He swooped down as Dreena's husband had done, but this time the woman began to run. At first, I thought she was trying to get away, but when he strafed overhead, she reached the launch ramp, spreading, her wings and they flew off in tandem. They banked and curved back around, stroking their powerful wings in unison. As they passed overhead, the crowd went wild. Instead of landing, though, they circled then flew to the aviary.

To my perplexed expression, Calian explained, [[They just got married. We have six couples making the bond tonight.]]

[[They don't even get to stick around for the dance?]] I asked.

Calian looked at me amused. So did those around us who'd heard.

Once the weddings were over, the tempo of the music returned to a marching beat. I couldn't help rolling my eyes when the remaining males marched down the ridge and just stood there across the bridge from us. There had to be a hundred of them. My awe at the spectacle was gone. I wanted to dance!

The first half of the line started walking across the bridge. Ter'ue was in the middle of this group. Calian looked ready to faint as he came across to claim her. Then I spotted Dovain at the end of the line—the same line as those becoming intendeds and not the final group which was for those simply here on a date. All the blood drained from my face, and I became a bit woozy.

Ter'ue practically ran to Calian. He spread his wings and puffed his chest proudly. He took Calian in his arms and wings. I thought they'd kiss or rub necks, he held her so close. The Matron cleared her throat. Arm in arm, the two of them bounded over the bridge like a couple of children.

As they reached the other side and took their places, Dovain approached the bridge. He glanced over at Dreena before heading across. She gave him a conspiratorial wink. We'd come to this dance as friends, but according to Brassaud tradition, we were about to become something more.

I fought the urge to run and planted my feet as he approached. He extended a long elegant hand, taking on the role of a probationary adult, or perhaps he was trying not to scare me off. His eyes pleaded with me not to refuse him.

To my surprise, my hand shook as it took his. I really did like the guy. I hadn't recognized the feeling because it was so different from what I'd felt for Cameron. It was more like the comfortable sense of companionship I felt around Vance, only stronger.

A cacophony of shrills and whistles brought me back to reality. Apparently, we had an aviary full of matchmakers rooting for us. We walked across the bridge, my hand still in his and took our places. The Elders split up. Each one visited with about ten couples or so. Seftan'ue himself came to us.

He stood silently in front of Dovain and me for a full minute before saying, "There was much discussion among the Elders about this." His gaze now rested squarely on me, and his careful use of Standard touched me. "You are so young. And there has been small time for you to complete the tasks; however, in the end it was decided your past experiences, added to the way you have both conducted yourselves, were sufficient to earn you the rights of adulthood."

I'd never been so honored. I found myself squeezing Dovain's hand as Seftan'ue finished his speech, "My one piece of advice would be this: Remember that when recovering from misfortunes and facing an uncertain future, it is better not to be alone."

Dovain thanked Seftan'ue for the honor the Elders had bestowed upon us and his words of wisdom. Seftan'ue gave a nod and moved on to the next couple.

A light, playful tune started. Couples filed into the center of the dance floor. "You tricked me into becoming intendeds?" I asked Dovain with bewildered accusation.

He gave my hand a reassuring squeeze and led me to the dance floor. "Keep your voice down, please. There are some here who understand Standard."

"I know. I helped teach them. Now explain how we're intendeds when you didn't ask until there was less than a month before the dance. Calian explained it all to me. I thought I understood the rules. You were two days too late."

He worked hard to keep his tone from sounding too triumphant. But there was a sparkle in his eyes. "By the Paraxous Standard Calendar, yes. Not by the Oweenian calendar."

He pulled me against him—probably to keep me from hitting him. We swayed gently to the music pretending to dance. Ter'ue and Calian worked their way to us. After heartfelt congratulations on our match, Ter'ue teased, [[Come on, Twilight. For someone who claimed to love to dance, you're hardly moving. You don't wish to smite the Fates on your first dance of passage as betrothed, do you?]]

Dovain purposely spun me around to hide my reaction from our friends. "Did he just say betrothed?" I choked into Dovain's ear.

"What did you think 'intended' meant?" he replied with a touch of humor in his voice.

My temper flared. He might have understood this culture, but I didn't. The term "intendeds" in most cultures in the Cluster was based on a Katian word that meant a couple merely intended to spend time together in order to test their compatibility. Like declaring someone your boyfriend—not a fiancé!

"You tricked me. It's totally not fair."

His gaze remained steady as he cocked his head and peered at me. "Perhaps. But neither was your plan to take off tomorrow without me."

I was about to ask him how he knew, but there was only one way. I glared at Dreena. She'd seemed unhappy when I'd requested she arrange to have me transported out of the aviary in the morning without telling Dovain. She'd said it was my responsibility to tell him. I hadn't realized that meant if I didn't, she would.

Dovain pulled me close so my head rested on his shoulder. "I'm sorry I deceived you. However, becoming intendeds only means you'll give me a chance. It implies no more of a commitment than that. It does mean, however, that you can't go ditching me without the courtesy of at least saying good-bye."

I settled myself into the dance, unsure what else to do. "You can't hold me to this nonsense. I'm just sixteen. So I'm not even old enough to be a probationary adult by Sian standards."

Now Dovain dared a wide, open beak grin. "Ah, but you heard Seftan'ue. The Elders have granted you adult status." The grin suddenly fell, and he jerked his head down to look at me. "Wait. Sixteen? You had a birthday without telling me?"

I stopped dancing and put one hand on my hip. "I wasn't aware I needed your permission to have a birthday."

Dovain guided me gently back into the dance. In a crestfallen voice he said, "No. Of course not. I just would have liked to have gotten you something, or done something special, for you. That's all."

I wished I could go back and recapture the lost moment. Then it occurred to me: "Actually, since it was just yesterday, I kind of figured this was my belated birthday."

The idea pleased him so much his smile returned even larger than before. It revealed dimples that I'd never noticed. He really did remind me a lot of Vance.

The song ended and Dreena approached. "I do not wish to interrupt."

"You are invited," I said automatically.

She ducked her head and asked hesitantly, "Answer please: everything is all right?"

I smiled, forgetting how mad I'd been. With a deep sigh, I surrendered to the inevitable. "Yes. Everything is fine. It seems that Dovain will be leaving with me tomorrow, after all."

She clapped her hands together and nodded in approval. "Excellent. While we will miss you both, it is good for you to remain together. I am happy for the two of you."

She and her husband sashayed away to the music. Dovain leaned down and whispered in my ear. "Thank you. I promise to support you in whatever may come and remain at your side for as long as you'll let me."

So many had died trying to help me. Having Dovain care so much for me scared me witless. I wanted to run away with him to some place safe. There had to be somewhere in this universe Cassie couldn't find us.

I realized Dovain was waiting for a response from me. "Ah heck, Dovain. I don't know what I'm supposed to say."

"Just don't say no," he said, staring into my eyes.

I was so caught up in the moment I didn't notice the prickling of my senses until it escalated into the sharp pain of Cassie's empathic invasion. "Oh shit! No!" I screamed, startling everyone around us. [[Take flight! Get away!]] I yelled. [[Hurry or you'll all die.]] To Dovain I said, "We need to get out of here fast."

Chapter 29

D OVAIN LOOKED AROUND FRANTICALLY. He knew what my terror meant. The Elders didn't waste time asking questions. They started shouting orders at the crowd to evacuate the area. Several hidden passages suddenly opened in the architecture of the courtyard. Those on the ground either ran for the passages or the nearest launch ramp and took into the air. Those who'd been sky-dancing flew straight for the aviary.

Dovain tried to pull me into a nearby passage as hover-cars and crafts moved in, surrounding the reception area. I could feel how pissed Cassie was. She'd tear the aviary apart looking for me. Innocent people would die.

I turned to Ter'ue and Calian, who had run up to us and were motioning for us to follow them to the nearest passage. [[My mother already knows I'm here,]] I shouted over the sound of the crafts preparing to land. [[You have to hide Dovain—Vin. Save him. Please!]]

Not waiting for their answer, I ran in the direction of the first of the three hovercrafts to land. I glanced back to see Calian, Ter'ue and two other Sians dragging my loyal friend into the passage. He struggled and called out to me, but more Brassaud joined the effort to get him into the passage before the doors shut.

Once they were out of sight, I approached the ramp to the craft Cassie was on. As I did, a warning shot pierced the night sky. Everyone left in the air swooped into the aviary. Everyone on the ground froze. There were at least three dozen Brassaud who hadn't managed to escape. I waved my arms frantically, hoping Cassie would be satisfied with my surrender and not kill anyone.

I tried to imitate a kick-ass movie heroine and called out, "I'm right here, m'other. You don't need to be so dramatic."

Armed guards, Prigtas and enforcer droids piled out of the craft and down the ramp. I did my best to ignore them and waited for Cassie to appear. The bemfornte struck a conqueror's pose in the doorway.

"You hardly need four squads to catch one teenage girl," I called up to her, wishing like hell I'd been allowed to keep that pistol so I could have shot her. But the best I could hope for was to minimize the damage.

She eyed me suspiciously. Holy Maker, I'd surrendered too quickly. I'd done it to save Dovain and the Brassaud, but now she knew how important they were to me. With a cruel smile, she asked, "Where is Dovain?"

She didn't wait for an answer. She nodded to the Katian guard next to her. He fired into the crowd.

The shot hit Dreena's husband. He'd been trying to hold her back and keep her from approaching. She let out such a cry that the sergans nested in the nearby cliffs took flight.

Suddenly a spaceship streaked through the air. It fired at the three hovercrafts on the ground before the hovercars above could return fire. The triangular transport/cargo ship was small for a spacecraft, but it dwarfed the hovercrafts and made the hovercars look like angry insects. The hovercrafts' shields absorbed the spaceships strikes. Unfortunately, Cassie and her minions on the ramp were all within the its protective shielding.

The panicked crowd scrambled for any safety they could find. The passages were all sealed now. It was impossible to even tell where they'd been. So those close to launching points ran for them and took flight. Some got away before those hovercars opened fire, killing at least two. A few dove into the river.

The triangular ship came around for another pass. I neither knew, nor cared who it was attacking Cassie. Though in the back of my mind I hoped it was the Hunter. At that moment, the only thing that mattered was that Dovain had somehow managed to free himself from Ter'ue and the others. He reached me just as the ship opened fire again. Using the distraction, he wrapped me in his arms and wings and hauled me to the river's bank before Cassie yelled for him to stop.

"Don't kill him!" I shouted with everything I had. "I give up! I give up. Just don't kill him!" Dovain refused to let me go. We reached the river's edge. Our eyes met just before he shoved me away. As I fell backwards into the water, I watched helplessly as a shot hit Dovain and he collapsed.

Hoping to draw Cassie and her henchmen away from Dovain and the Brassaud, I swam along the bottom until reaching the river's deep center then followed the current. I held my breath for a lot longer than humanly possible and refused to surface until well past the bend. When I did finally come up for air, a shot hit me in the shoulder. My arm went limp.

I dove back under, kicking with all my might. The shot was a stun-bolt. Maybe Dovain was only stunned. I clung to that hope as the rapids battered my body against the rocks. At the very least, the battle would be moved away from the aviary.

After a while, I resurfaced, and the crashing sound of the waterfall ahead was deafening. I'd gone a lot farther than I'd realized. The "lesser fall" might have been only half the height of the one next to the aviary, but that was still plenty high enough to be deadly. The place I'd chosen for my day-greeting place was about to kill me.

I struggled against the frigid torrent, trying to reach shore. But it was too strong and my one arm wouldn't work. I went over the waterfall expecting to die. I smacked into the lake below, then drifted in an eddy that held me under. Eventually, I hit the bottom. My legs pushed against the rocks beneath, propelling me to the surface. I came up gasping and coughing out lungs full of water.

As Cassie's hover-craft passed overhead, I saw the little pier not too far away and swam for it. If I evaded capture long enough, maybe the attacking ship would be able to take her out. Halfway to the pier, a long, squishy tentacle wrapped itself around my foot. I opened my mouth to scream as it dragged me under.

Ter'ue had warned me about the plebgee that inhabited this lake when I'd chosen it as my day-greeting place. He'd described the creature like a freshwater octopus. But this thing was like no octopus I'd ever seen. Its entire head split open to reveal a gaping maw filled with jagged teeth. The Brassaud wore safety bracelets that produced a signal which kept the creature away whenever they swam in the lake. Of course, I wasn't wearing one. As it drew my foot toward its mouth, I reached out with my good arm and punched it in the eyeball.

It released me.

I fought my way back to the surface. Cassie and a few of her thugs stood on the pier watching me. I searched the sky above hoping to see that ship again. Nothing. Even if the attacker had been the Dashia Hunter like I hoped, there'd be no rescue for me today. But maybe Dovain had gotten away.

While I floated there trying to decide what to do, multiple tentacles wound themselves around my legs. The plebgee tugged hard, trying to pull me back under. "Something's got me!" I called out to Cassie, barely managing to keep my head above water.

My not-so-dear mother flashed to me telepathically, *Why should I bother saving you? You've been nothing but trouble. I'll enjoy watching you drown.*

She expected me to beg for help. Just how many times would she demand cooperation in exchange for mercy? Well, I was done playing her game. I broke the empathic link between us, gave her the gesture she hated so much, and let the plebgee drag me under.

Just then a different mental voice called to me. *Twigh, where are you?* It wasn't Cassie, but it didn't feel like Dovain either. There was something familiar about it that I couldn't place at first. *Twigh, where are you?* it repeated. The thought was in English, and I sensed the deep concern that went with it.

It was Vance! Somehow my best friend from Earth was aboard that ship. And he was with the Dashia Hunter. I freaked out. No longer content to die, I brought one of the plebgee's tentacles to my mouth and bit down even as it bit into my leg. I gnawed, like a dog with a bone, until I'd chewed through the rubbery skin, and my teeth sank into warm gooey flesh beneath. The plebgee let me go and streaked away.

I'm here, I flashed to Vance then realized how incredibly unhelpful such a message would be. I could almost feel him rolling his eyes and asking where "here" was. I drifted to the surface. After a big gulp of air, I thought to him, *In the lake beneath the smaller of the two waterfalls near the aviary.*

I couldn't tell if Vance received my telepathic message or not. The contact had been extremely weak. In fact, I couldn't be sure it hadn't been a product of my cyanotic imagination. I sensed nothing of my friend now. As I reached out, I accidentally touched Cassie's empathic senses.

She stabbed into my head, ruthlessly gripping my mind. *Get yourself over here, right now, or Dovain dies … Don't make me come get you.*

I sensed she was lying. She didn't have Dovain. Hoping she couldn't tell I knew she'd lied, I decided to stall. Maybe if I took long enough, the Hunter would show up again. Slowly, oh so slowly, I swam to the pier pretending to be totally defeated. No one moved to help me, so I grabbed onto one of the pillars and just clung to it.

"If you want to save Dovain, you'd better hurry up," Cassie said impatiently.

I started pulling myself onto the wood-planked deck, making a show of how hard it was with only one arm and a body that had been beaten by rocks and half-drowned. As I lay partway out of the water, one of Cassie's henchmen shouted, "It's heading straight for us!"

I pushed myself backwards and fell back into the water. As Cassie had done to me so many times, I sent out a telepathic jab and then concentrated on closing her airway. She dropped to one knee. Now the guards were too busy saving Madam Cassiopeia to worry about catching me. They ushered her up the ramp, half carrying her into the hovercraft.

One of the henchmen turned back to come after me, but shots from above made him change his mind. He barely made it into the craft before those shots lit up the craft's shields. I watched the same triangular ship that had attacked Cassie at the aviary roar by and disappear. Right on its heels, the two hovercrafts followed, firing an almost constant barrage at Cassie's attacker.

A hovercar approached the lake from the direction of the aviary. It was much older than the ones that Cassie's goon squad had used. I hoped beyond reason that it was Dovain.

Cassie's craft took off after ejecting two guards who were obviously left behind to capture me. Unfortunately for them, the ship did an about-face, strafed the ground, blasting them to pieces. This time I was positive I felt Vance. The emotions contained a mix of revulsion at the hunter killing the guards, and a determination to rescue me. Fearing the hovercar coming my way would be mistaken for an enemy target, I thought as loudly as I could while picturing the old vehicle, "Friend! Friend! Friend!"

The Hunter's ship broke off its ground attack and fired a barrage that disabled one of the crafts pursuing it. The battle went by at such velocity, they all become nothing more than shooting stars against the dark sky in just a couple blinks. Except for the damaged one. It limped in for an emergency landing somewhere on the other side of the mountains. I kept an eye on it as the older hover-car pulled up to the pier. Then I shifted my attention to my potential rescue. The hovercar had a beautifully rendered sunset painted on the side. From the artistry, there was no doubt in my mind the thing belonged to the Brassaud.

Ter'ue and Calian bailed out of the hover-car, calling frantically for me. I coughed and sputtered, but my lungs were too waterlogged to call back. Fortunately, they heard me splashing around. Without hesitating, Ter'ue dived in and pulled me to the pier. Calian helped me out of the water, but as Ter'ue hoisted himself onto the deck, he squawked in surprise, [[Something has my leg!]]

I reached under his arms and pulled him up despite the plebgee's added weight. I told Calian to hang on to Ter'ue so the thing couldn't drag him back into the water. Then in a rage like I'd never experienced before, I pounded on the offending creature in the eye until it released my friend.

When I didn't stop hitting the thing once he was free, Ter'ue reached out, grabbing me by the shoulder. [[Twilight, come on. We've got to go!]]

We piled into the hovercar. Dovain's unconscious body sat limply strapped into a seat. I stared at him until he took a breath. I shrieked in delight and hugged his limp form. [[Do not celebrate our victory yet,]] Ter'ue cautioned. [[The DeConnett's hovercars might not be too far behind us.]]

[[Oh Makers, the aviary! How bad is it? Are Cassie's people still there?]] I asked in a panic.

[[Three or four dead,]] Calian said. [[Many hurt. It was awful.]] Her hollow voice quavered and her expression was completely blank. She opened her beak to say more but only a chirp came out.

[[The good news is,]] Ter'ue went on when she couldn't, [[the invaders were too concerned with going after the ship that attacked them, and recapturing you, to stay around and inflict any more harm.]]

"I guess that's something," I muttered more to myself than to them. I thought back to all the choices that had led to this. *We shouldn't have stayed. We certainly shouldn't have stayed for so long*, I berated myself.

It had also been a mistake to surrender the gun. It was the last time I'd go without some way of defending myself and those around me. As soon as possible I'd find a weapon and learn how to use it, I swore to myself.

"Where we go?" Ter'ue asked, reminding me that before I started making any sort of plans, we actually needed to escape. The worst possible scenario would be Cassie finding Dovain and me when we were still with Ter'ue and Calian.

I checked Dovain's pulse. Strong and steady. [[I think he's just stunned. He should be fine, so we don't need any medical aide. But we need to ditch this craft before the DeConnetts track it down.]]

Chapter 30

DOVAIN CAME TO once we were about halfway to Gyfa. I'd refused to tell Ter'ue where we were to meet the Hunter. Not because I didn't trust him and Calian, but because I figured the less they knew, the safer they'd be. So the plan was to drop them off in the city where they had friends and relatives they could contact for a ride back home; Dovain and I would borrow the hovercar and continue on to the rendezvous since we hadn't come up with a safe way to acquire a new mode of transportation.

Ter'ue filled Dovain in on the plan while I thought about all the things that could go wrong. Though still a bit groggy, Dovain thanked Ter'ue for letting us borrow the hovercar and asked how we could make sure the Brassaud got it back. Ter'ue actually laughed after he chaw-shawed. [[My very good friend, the value of this transport is of no consequence compared to making sure the two of you are safe.]]

[[I wish we could take you to the Dashia Hunter,]] Calian said. [[However, I understand the need for caution.]]

[[Are you sure you two will be okay?]] I asked feeling guilty about dumping our friends at the first public landing pad we came to.

[[Chaw-shaw.]] Ter'ue gave a dismissive wave. [[We'll be fine. And as we discussed, we don't want this hovercar being tracked to whoever we go to for aid.]] Seeing my worried expression, he added, [[Be assured, there are no public landing sites that are not within flying range of a Brassaud ally.]]

Gyfa came into view, lighting up the dark horizon. As we came closer, the city appeared to be a smaller version of the area around Cassie's fetshouse. Several of the mega-buildings were surrounded by thousands of structures that, though smaller than the fetshouses, dwarfed anything on Earth. The view held zero interest for me. I just wanted the hell off this planet and away from Cassie without anyone else getting hurt.

Ter'ue landed the hovercar at a public lot on the top of one of the lesser buildings. He and Calian hesitated before getting out. They both said they'd miss us and wished us the best. "May the Fates be with you," Ter'ue blessed us with all sincerity.

"Thank you," Dovain replied. "And with you. Please convey our gratitude to the rest of the aviary."

"And please tell Dreena how sorry I am about her husband," I added.

He gave a grave nod. Any sign of the happy-go-lucky guy we'd met just over two months ago was gone. Gone thanks to Cassie. Calian finally started to sob. We hugged and held onto each other as if we could choose to never let go. After a couple minutes, Ter'ue said softly, [[Please forgive me, but we really must leave.]]

We exchanged good-byes, and they hopped out of the hovercar. They waved then ran off the roof at a launch deck and joined the few avians flying between the buildings. "I can't believe we may never see them again," Dovain commented as they disappeared into the distance.

"I know. It makes me sad too," I said. Another hovercar came in for a landing, and I couldn't help but be scared. "But right now, we need to get going. Are you okay to drive?"

He took a few deep breaths and gave a nod just as grave as Ter'ue's had been. "Yeah. I think I'm okay now." He climbed into the cockpit, and I moved to the co-pilot seat. After a moment we were cleared to take off. Dovain merged into the low-flying traffic gliding just over the lesser buildings, but funneled around the humongous fetshouses.

"Okay. We need a plan," I said as we came to cruising speed and altitude.

Dovain cocked his head and looked at me quizzically. "I thought we had a plan. Drive straight to Owoolic City and hide until the rendezvous in a couple days."

"Too easy for Cassie to track us. It's not like there'd be many hovercars coming from the aviary. And this one's pretty obvious with all the artwork. Besides, we don't know if the Hunter will change the plan after having to engage the DeConnetts. We need a terminal to check for messages."

"Why don't you just use the one in here?"

I'd assumed this thing was way too out of date to connect with any network. I was wrong, and in a few minutes I had my answer. A new message alert flashed. I opened it after running a scan to make sure it held no unwanted extras. It was written in Standard but seemed like gibberish at first. Then I realized that it was in code. The Hunter wasn't taking any chances.

"How are we supposed to interpret it?" Dovain asked.

"I sensed a friend of mine from Earth on the ship with the Hunter when it attacked. So this is probably one of our old codes," I said, thinking out loud.

"A friend from Earth? Really? How do you know?"

"I *sensed* him," I repeated, while staring at the gibberish. My mind focused on figuring out which of our codes that were meant to disguise our messages in English would work in Standard. "Head out of the city toward Owoolic while I try to translate this," I ordered, halting any questions he might have about how I could have sensed someone at that kind of distance. Now was no time for discussing my telepathic abilities and how instinctual they seemed to be.

Only one code worked to translate the code in a way that made sense. It said, "Be in Safanalue's central landing pad at 28:00 on 7-12-4539 Oweena Standard Time. This time be sure to do what you're told."

"So we go to Safanalue?" Dovain asked, as he entered the city into the nav computer and waited for it to supply the coordinates. "Um. Twyla, that's really far away. It'll take forever in a hovercar."

I smiled. "Yes, it would, wouldn't it? But remember that comment about doing what I'm told?"

He nodded. "Yeah. I thought that was kind of an odd and unnecessary admonishment."

"That was my friend's way of telling me to do the opposite of what the message says. Our code's not anything Cassie's people couldn't crack. I'm guessing they're assuming the site's been compromised, and they're expecting the message to be intercepted. So they're using it to send her in the wrong direction."

"So hopefully Cassie and her goons will be searching on the wrong side of the planet from where we're actually headed."

Dovain nodded in approval. His pale, drawn face regained a bit of color. His eyes narrowed in thought. "That's a lot of guess work. Are you sure?"

"Absolutely. Trust me. Vance loves this cloak and dagger stuff."

He looked at me, mystified. "What does a cloak and a dagger have to do with this?"

I slapped my forehead. "It's an Earth phrase. Never mind. What's important is that we figure out what's the opposite of the location given."

After a little figuring, Dovain got the coordinates to the exact opposite point on the planet to Safanalue's central landing pads. It wasn't more than a few hours' flight south of us. "I hope you're right," Dovain said. "But that still leaves us the issue of whether to just fly this thing directly there or try to find another means of transportation."

"We could always just steal another peacekeeper's hovercraft," I suggested flippantly.

He gave me a sidelong glance. "Somehow I doubt that would help us avoid attracting any more unwanted attention." Then a thought occurred to him. "If we're supposed to do the opposite of what the message says, what about the date and time? Do we go by what the message says or ... what would the opposite be?"

Before I'd been kidnapped, Vance and I were so close I could almost read his mind even without my telepathic abilities. I willed myself to think like my friend. "Well, the date given is tomorrow so the opposite of that would be today. So that's easy: we check today and if not, we go again tomorrow and the next day. No harm done as long as we don't get caught." But the time thing wasn't so simple. There was no A.M. or P.M. in Oweena Standard time. And it couldn't be at minus 2800.

I shook my head in frustration. I understood the need for caution if the Hunter believed our method of contact had been compromised. But how the hell was I supposed to know if the time was different or not? *First things first*, I decided. *Lead Cassie away from Gyfa.* "For now let's head to the coordinates as given, in case Cassie's goons track down this vehicle."

He reset the navigation for Safanalue. We came up with several ideas for getting transportation back to our real destination after we ditched the hovercar, but discarded all of them as either too dangerous for us or the person we used to obtain it. After a while Dovain said, "Okay, so we just change directions in some big city and hope no one notices. At least, according to Ter'ue this craft doesn't have a tracking device. What about the other thing? The time?"

"Let's hope it's the right time. I can't come up with anything for ..." A lightning bolt struck my brain. "Oh shit! Oweena Standard Time!"

"What about it?" Dovain asked.

"The message said 28:00 Oweena Standard Time. So the opposite of that would be—"

"Local time!" Dovain cheered. "All right. So now we know."

I pecked at the computer to check the time zone at the real rendezvous location. My heart fell into my stomach when I saw the display. "Oh no. No. No. Twenty eight hundred local time is only two hours from now. How far are we?"

Dovain pulled into traffic in the city we'd come to and had the computer recalculate. "ETA to DeZartone is two hours and thirty-two minutes," the automated voice announced cheerfully, oblivious to the fact that those thirty-two minutes could cost us our chance of rescue.

Chapter 31

DeZartone came into view at 28:11 local time. If we hadn't been eleven minutes late for our rendezvous with the Dashia Hunter, I might have been awed by all the lights in the sky. Unlike Gyfa, DeZartone bore no resemblance to any city I'd ever seen. While it didn't float in the clouds, it didn't sit on the ground either. Instead, buildings rested on stilts above the trees, leaving the forest below pretty much undisturbed. As we approached the outskirts of the city, I could make out the 0-grav drives mounted beneath the buildings.

Dovain slowed our craft, and we joined the hovercar and craft traffic flowing into DeZartone. I glanced at him and then the display set to local time. He bobbed his head in understanding of my unspoken message, but then explained, "Speed limits will be enforced within the city. I'd hate to get us pulled over."

I forced my frustration down. Dovain was right. The last thing we needed was a repeat of what happened after we'd escaped. We'd gotten lucky once. We weren't likely to run into another sympathetic security officer. "Yeah, let's avoid drawing any attention to ourselves."

"We'll just have to hope they stick around for a little while," he said as much to himself as to me.

"They'll be there," I said with confidence. Dovain looked over at me, cocked his head and regarded me with a quizzical expression. Though I was so tired my bones ached—and I probably looked like a dead woman walking—I wasn't nearly as worried about being left behind as he expected me to be. "My friend Vance is with the Hunter," I told him. "Trust me. There's no way he'll let them leave without us."

He refrained from commenting and set the autopilot to find the nearest landing pad to the coordinates Vance had given us. We arrived just a few minutes later to find the pad empty. We circled a couple times hoping for some sign of the Hunter. We watched a few spaceships descend into the city. Each time they failed to resolve into the Hunter's house-sized, triangular ship, I felt a sharp pang of disappointment.

Dovain landed our craft, still not saying a word. Neither of us wanted to admit that after everything we'd been through, we'd missed our chance at escape by a matter of minutes. For a while, I sat there completely stupefied, just blinking as if that might make the ship magically appear. It didn't.

Dovain stared intently at the view screen, fluffing and unfluffing his feathers. "Recheck the message site. Maybe your friend sent new instructions," he suggested.

I nodded eagerly and typed away at the computer console with shaking hands. Nothing. Now my throat tightened and tears welled in my eyes. Fear took root in my gut. The fact that Vance wasn't here meant something bad must have happened. A herd of angry memforms couldn't have kept him away.

"Um, Twyla," Dovain said softly. I looked up. He pointed up at the top right corner of the view screen where a tiny dot was zooming toward us. It grew larger by the nanosecond. It wasn't the Hunter's ship. This was a basic shuttle craft meant for ferrying people and cargo to ships or stations in orbit. "Ours or theirs?" he asked, glancing nervously at the shuttle. It was now clearly coming in for a landing next to us.

"I have no idea?"

"Can't you sense it?" Dovain asked.

"It doesn't work like that. I'd have to reach out with my mind to scan them. And like I told you, that could tip off Cassie. I haven't gotten a handle on all this empathic crap, yet." Then I added, "And I don't intend to." What I didn't tell him was that I already had the nagging feeling she was trying to locate me through our telepathic link.

"So what do we do?" he asked, his hand hovering over the controls in case we needed to make a quick departure.

The shuttlecraft circled the landing pad a couple of times before heading for the space next to us. We held our breath as we watched it touch down, waiting for some sign of whether it was friend or foe. Just as likely, it might not have anything to do with us.

"It's not powering down," I finally observed, breaking the silence and remembering to breathe again. "Let's hope it's our ride."

The bay-door in the back of the shuttle lowered into a loading ramp. In the holo-vids Vance would have been standing there to greet me, and we would have rushed into each other's arms, glad to be reunited. But this wasn't some sappy movie. No one was there, and no one got out of the shuttle to come get us.

Just because I didn't sense anything didn't mean this wasn't a trap. Then again, after tangling with Cassie's people, maybe the Dashia Hunter couldn't risk showing up in the same ship. It made sense to send someone else to pick us up.

"Let's go," I said, even as I made up my mind to take the chance. It wasn't like we had a lot of options.

Dovain and I stepped slowly out of the hovercar and headed over toward the shuttle. The shielding over the cockpit window peeled back. I telescoped my vision to get a better look at the Katian female at the controls. She stuck a clawed finger at us then pointed to the open bay-door. We trotted around to the back and went part way up the ramp, but hesitated, reluctant to enter the empty passenger/cargo compartment.

The barrier between the cockpit and compartment retracted. The tan coated Katian swung her chair around to face us. [[Well, do you intend to just stand there darkening my doorway all day? Get in!]]

I wanted to ask where Vance was, but thought better of it. No reason to give anything away. "Who are you?" I asked instead.

"Your ride to the Hunter. Now let's go," she replied in heavily accented Standard.

We wanted to obey, but were too wary to trust her so quickly. "How do we know you weren't sent by the DeConnetts?" I asked.

She hissed. Not a Katian sigh of frustration, but an honest to goodness cat-in-a-fight, hair raising hiss. Her ears went flat, and she snarled as she spoke. "I'll let the insult slide this once, since he warned me you'd suspect as much. But never make such an accusation again."

"Who warned you?" I asked, hoping I knew the answer.

"Your friend and a pain in my ass. That's who." She rolled her eyes when I didn't respond. "Vance Volkner, of course."

Dovain let out an involuntary squawk of surprise. He looked from her to me, renewed hope making his eyes sparkle.

I forced back my own surge of hope. Trying to sound calm and in control, I demanded, "Let me talk to him." I stared right into her eyes, not caring if she took it as a challenge.

"Here!" She hurled a datapad at me. "He sent you a message. Listen. Then hurry your asses aboard."

I hit play and Vance's voice came from the speaker. It wasn't his Human avatar's voice, but that of his true body. I'd only heard it that one time when we were in the safe house back on Earth, but it was indelibly engraved into my brain.

"Twigh, it's me. This is a friend. Trust her. She'll bring you to me."

To Dovain I admitted, "I guess they could have faked the message but—"

"He said you'd say that, too," the Katian called, cutting me off. Her tawny mane stood on end, and she bared a fang of impatience. "Play the next message."

"Twigh, it's really me. Little Miss and everyone else from back home is safe. Sorry I couldn't be there in person. But I was on that ship. It's now wanted in connection with an attack on a Brassaud reservation, so we can't approach the planet. But I'll see you when we rendezvous."

My senses suddenly began to tingle. I could feel Cassie whittling away at my telepathic shields. If she broke through, it wouldn't take her long to track me down. I reinforced my shields, blocking her efforts for the time being. I rushed up the ramp and motioned for Dovain to do the same.

"All right," I called to the Katian. "Let's go."

"About vreking time," she muttered to herself. "Strap yourselves in," she ordered, then closed the barrier between cockpit and bay.

We'd barely gotten our restraints buckled before she launched, slamming us against our seats. I wondered if the little shuttle's inertia dampeners were malfunctioning or if she preferred flying with them at minimum. Most likely the irritated Katian just wanted to mess with us. Dovain turned three shades of grey before we cleared the planet's gravity and the g-force from the thrusters abruptly released their grip.

"ETA to rendezvous fifteen minutes," the Katian's voice came over the speaker. "Use the time to study your new identities."

"Not very friendly, is she?" Dovain commented, trying to put some humor into his voice.

"As long as she's getting us the hell away from Cassie, she can be as rude as she wants. I don't really care." Then something dawned on me. Or rather the lack of something dawned on me. The pressure from Cassie's telepathic search had vanished. I was out of her range. We were free.

There were so many things I wanted to say but couldn't put into words. The same realization seemed to strike Dovain. He started to speak several times but stopped each time. Maybe we were both too afraid to jinx ourselves or maybe we were in shock. For whatever reason, we couldn't speak for the longest time. We both began eagerly reading through the information on the datapad.

Dovain's siblings, along with his aunt and uncle, had been safely relocated on another planet under assumed names. Vance and his family also had new identities, and his parents were willing to take me in.

"So you're going to go live with this Vance guy, huh?" Dovain asked. "Just how close are you two? Should I be worried?"

I wasn't sure if he was joking or not, but I couldn't help it. I laughed right in the poor guy's face. "Oh Holy Makers. We just escaped one of the most dangerous criminal families in the entire Paraxous Cluster, and you're worried about Vance?"

He ducked his head like a baby bird afraid of having it bit off. It was the exact gesture he'd made the day we'd first met and I'd yelled at him. He fluffed his feathers then let them settle. He looked into my eyes with a piercing gaze that held me. This time when he spoke there was a firmness and confidence the old Dovain had completely lacked. "Twyla, of course I'm worried. You're my intended. And I'd hate to lose you to some past love."

I laughed again, this time a nervous giggle like the girl in some damn chick flick. "Vance and I are more like brother and sister. If we'd grown up in the Paraxous, we'd be considered co-siblings. There's nothing for you to be jealous of."

He perked up and his eyes sparkled again. "Good."

Dovain leaned in and was about to kiss me, but the Katian opened the partition right then. We drew back, but apparently not before she noticed. "Am I interrupting something?" She didn't wait for an answer. "I thought you would be interested in the latest report. The DeConnett plot against Sovereign Zartous was uncovered. Thanks to the information you sent us, many arrests are being made, including several members of the Sovereign's own cabinet. And ..." She paused for dramatic effect. "... a military taskforce has been mobilized to take down the DeConnett holdings on Oweena. They have orders to capture, or if necessary, kill all DeConnetts."

With that, she shut the barrier again, leaving me and Dovain alone to absorb the news. "We did it," I said in disbelief. "We really did it." Even if Cassie managed to escape the taskforce, they'd keep her busy for a while.

"We did, didn't we," Dovain agreed, bobbing his head. Then he leaned in once more. "Now where were we?"

Our eyes locked, and I felt myself blush. I struggled to think of something to say to break the spell of the moment. But I couldn't hold a single thought in my head except to wonder what it'd be like to kiss a guy with a beak.

I tensed at the shock of my first kiss, but then found myself melting into it. We reached out to hold each other. Without Cassie's influence, I was free to love without fear of turning into a Dashia. And while Dovain and I had no idea what this new life would bring, at least we would face it together.

Seftan'ue had been right: it is better not to be alone.

AUTHOR'S NOTE

The industry has changed a great deal since I wrote my first draft of this novel at 15 years old. These days, books die on the vine if they don't get enough reviews. Please consider supporting this author by posting an honest review on-line on whichever platform you prefer.

Thanks!
Rebecca Inch-Partridge

ABOUT THE AUTHOR

By day, Rebecca Inch-Partridge works as a mild-mannered freelance editor. At night, she's the ruler of Paraxous Star Cluster. After years of sharing stories from the Paraxous, she's excited to share the tale of Twyla Splendor with you.

An avid science fiction fan since childhood, Rebecca graduated from Sierra Community College after convincing her creative writing professor that science fiction could qualify as literary fiction. She received her Bachelor's Degree from William Jessup University in Management and Ethics—which she swears is not an oxymoron. She's held many jobs, but found writing was the only career that allowed her imagination to remain untamed.

Rebecca lives in Auburn, California with her husband, their dog McKraken, two cats, four chickens, and one turkey.

COMING SOON

HUNTING THE DASHIA
THE PARAXOUS STAR CLUSTER: BOOK TWO

by Rebecca Inch-Partridge

ARRIVING SPRING 2026

YOU MIGHT ALSO ENJOY

THE ABDUCTION OF JOSHUA BLOOM

Michael Thal

Abducted by aliens, a high school track star explores strange worlds is thrust into extraterrestrial politics that could decide the fate of Earth.

SMASH THE WORLD'S SHELL

Michael Thal

Abducted by aliens, a high school track star explores strange worlds is thrust into extraterrestrial politics that could decide the fate of Earth.

A WRECK OF DRAGONS

Michael Thal

Abducted by aliens, a high school track star explores strange worlds is thrust into extraterrestrial politics that could decide the fate of Earth.